RESURRECTIONS

BILL KENNEY

Copyright © 2024 Bill Kenney
All rights reserved
First Edition

NEWMAN SPRINGS PUBLISHING
320 Broad Street
Red Bank, NJ 07701

First originally published by Newman Springs Publishing 2024

ISBN 979-8-89061-776-7 (Paperback)
ISBN 979-8-89061-777-4 (Digital)

Printed in the United States of America

PROLOGUE

The shooter was placing his British-made AW50, specially tuned, .50-caliber rifle on its bipod, the barrel of the weapon just peeking over the windowsill in the two-inch-high space below the sash and six inches above the floor. He was training its telescopic sight on the restaurant door across the street. His spotter/communications link partner was quiet, not wanting to interrupt the shooter's all-encompassing mental focus. They had been doing this kind of thing together for years now and knew each other's quirks intimately. They had been tracking a guy for over a week, a guy who had betrayed seven other US agents, leading to their capture, torture, and slow deaths. They were setting up on the second floor of one of the many derelict apartments in this bumfuck Serbian town, the name of which they could never pronounce. The restaurant was the only decent one operating in the town. The target was in the restaurant, eating his last fancy lunch, his location pinpointed by a local source, but to be confirmed visually.

The apartment smelled of piss. The shooter lay down on the linoleum floor, mindless of the smell and the dirt on the floor. He settled in to wait, not moving, breathing slowly.

The spotter's radio earbud chirped with an incoming message. After listening for a moment, he cursed and grabbed the shooter's arm. "This is bad—as bad as it gets. There's no easy way to say it. Your wife was killed in a car accident the day before yesterday."

The shooter was stunned but kept going on with his set up as if in another world. He said one word, "Shit," but said it quietly.

His spotter went on, "Your daughter is home from college. We need to get you on a plane home today."

The shooter looked out the window for a moment. On this bright afternoon, with little traffic on the intervening street and only a football field distant from the door, the chances of the mission failing approached zero.

He said, "If we don't get this bastard today, we may never get another chance. Another hour ain't gonna make any difference. Let's get it done."

The spotter gawked but was not really surprised. While he pondered the situation, the restaurant door opened. A man stuck his head out, looked up and down the street, turned back, and said something. He then stepped out onto the sidewalk and waved. A black SUV parked about two hundred yards down the street started up and rolled slowly toward him. In those moments, the shooter had settled into position, chambered a single bullet, and focused the sight. The target stepped through the restaurant door. The spotter said, "That's him," and ducked away from the window. The shooter squeezed off the shot and blew the target's head apart. While he was at it, he shot the bodyguard too.

They were out of the apartment by the back stairs in two minutes, brass cleaned up, the rifle disassembled, no words needed or spoken—all a well-practiced routine. In another minute, they were in a waiting car, driven by a local CIA operative. As they sped toward the military airfield in Germany, a drive of several hours, the spotter reported in. The shooter sighed deeply, beginning his return to the real world.

As it turned out, even those few minutes did make a difference. The shooter missed the last military plane leaving Europe for home that day.

Chapter One

The opening bars of Beethoven's Fifth blasted Liam Martin from a peaceful sleep in his hotel room in San Francisco. *Who the hell is calling at six o'clock in the morning?* he thought. *Only two people have this number.*

The caller ID on the smartphone was blocked, but curiosity overcame him, and he answered.

A distorted voice said, "Good morning, Liam. How are you today?"

"There's no Liam here. You have the wrong number."

"Oh, come now, Liam. I know you call yourself Jerry Sweeney these days, but the people I represent have a need for the guy we knew as Liam Martin. His special skills are required once more to save this country from a disaster."

Jerry was struck dumb. It had been over a decade since he had heard that sort of bullshit. Since then, he'd had four names, no real home, no need for any job, and no interest in any. He was doing all the things he had foregone while obeying orders from guys like the one on the phone, making up for all those sacrifices he made while using his "special skills" to help his country. He still had many things on his bucket list, and his time seemed to be slipping away faster than he liked. He ended the call.

He barely had time to get out of bed before the phone rang again, as he figured it would.

He sighed and answered it.

The voice said, "Come on, Liam. You know the drill. We're not going away. We know where you are and even what seat you have at the 49ers game this afternoon. We'll contact you there. This phone call is just an alert so that nothing bizarre happens when we tap you on the shoulder. Have a nice run, but wear a couple of layers. It's a bit chilly this morning."

Liam sighed. He had chosen this modest hotel as part of his ingrained attempt to live his fiercely independent life several levels below the radar. It was far from the stadium and the tourist areas downtown. His room was at the corner of the building with windows fronting on both the main street and a smaller-side street. He looked out both windows and saw what he expected: a guy reading a newspaper on a bench in the small park on the other side of the main street and a man walking a dog on the side street. *Getting a dog in the act was different*, he thought. It was just after dawn, and these guys stood out like a neon sign. The message was clear. We have you covered.

Well, he would go for his run, as he did every day, regardless of the weather. Running and the time spent in gyms, wherever he happened to be, kept his five-foot-seven body at its historic 155 pounds despite approaching his sixty-fifth birthday. In fact, the amount of weight he lifted at those gyms generally attracted the attention of the personal trainers cruising for clients at the bigger places. When he tarried in a town for even a week, he rotated through several gyms to preserve anonymity.

He liked running in San Francisco. The hills were a challenge. He kept track of his times from visit to visit to be sure he wasn't losing anything. It was just a little game to add some spice to what was a totally self-centered life. The chilly temperatures this mid-November morning were a boost for his energy, and he beat the time from his visit four months earlier on the same route.

As usual, Liam went to the stadium early, dressed in jeans, a leather jacket, and a knit cap covering his thinning gray hair. He liked to select his lunch from the sophisticated food offerings that were unique to this ballpark. A hot dog and a beer were fine at some places, but here, there were fancier options. A plate of sushi and a glass of pinot grigio served as starters, which he topped off with a cup of lobster bisque before going to his seat.

His habit was to sit at the end of a row filled with people rooting for the visiting team. At this game, both men and women came in Raiders regalia, some in simulated helmets and some in various ugly masks as well.

The game started without incident, and the Raiders scored a touchdown on their first possession. Liam didn't root for either team; he just appreciated the violence these superb athletes visited on each other and the skill and speed with which the small guys—those who weighed only two hundred pounds—avoided disaster.

He got a forceful tap on the shoulder as halftime approached. He turned to see a big guy in a skeleton face mask jerking his thumb toward the concession area. *Might as well get this over with*, he thought and got up.

The guy wore a Raider jersey and a navy-blue knit cap with the team logo. He was big enough to play linebacker for them and went up the stairs two at a time without looking back.

He led Liam to the table farthest from the field in the food service area that featured sushi. Liam took the seat, which let him see the rest of the area. Everybody in the stadium went through a metal detector on entering, so he was confident no one had a gun, but you could never be sure. Still, he was sure he could handle one attacker even if he had a gun. Still, his heart rate was revving up.

"Before I sit down, do you want a beer?" the big guy asked.

"I'd prefer a glass of pinot grigio."

The guy laughed. "Why not?" he said and strode off.

After a few minutes, he returned with two glasses of wine. He sat down opposite Liam and raised his glass in a brief salute.

"All right, let's get to the point," said Liam.

"Of course, Liam. We—"

Liam interrupted, "Nobody here answers to the name Liam."

"Or to any of the other three names you've used since your… retirement. Suppose you stop fussing about names and hear me out."

"I guess that makes sense. I don't want to miss too much of the game." His eyes searched the man from head to foot.

"I'm just the messenger," the guy said, "but it's a very private message. Please put your phone on the table."

That didn't surprise Liam. The guy didn't want his message recorded. He did as asked but made the guy reach across the table to grab it.

The guy slid it over in front of him and then removed a metallic-looking cloth from an inside pocket and spread it over the phone. It looked like the chain mail knights of old wore to battle but was probably more sophisticated. The guy then searched Liam with his eyes.

"Nice ring you have there. May I see it?" he asked.

The ring was heavy antique brass, with an emerald on top and shamrocks inscribed on the sides. He slid it off his right ring finger and pushed it across the table. "There's no recorder in it."

"Can't be too careful." The guy inspected it, poked at the stone a bit, shrugged, and slid it under the cloth with the phone. "All right. Let's get to it. There are several wise, powerful, and patriotic people who are convinced that the country is headed for disaster. They want to hire you to prevent that."

"How many people?"

"What difference does that make?"

"Humor me."

The guy stared at Jerry for a long moment, then said, "Eight at the moment."

"Who are they?" asked Jerry/Liam.

"You're kidding, of course."

"Okay, go on."

"These people are convinced that the president-elect is a racist, narcissist, woman-abusing bully, a shameless liar, and living in La-La land. His trade war with China will ruin our farmers, and his promise to sell war equipment to Taiwan will drag the country back into the Dark Ages. Russia and Iran are exerting power over the Middle East and conquering parts of Ukraine. What does he do? He kisses Putin's ass. And then there's the wall. He'll bankrupt the country building it and isolate us from one of our nearest neighbors. He's insane. Our solution is to never let him take office and rely on his vice president to be rational. If the Electoral College certifies his election next month, they want him dead before the inauguration."

Liam laughed. "So murdering the man elected president by the people is now thought to be patriotic? That's a new twist."

"We're told it's nothing you haven't done before in the name of the good old US of A, and the fee is astronomical."

"How astronomical?

"Five million dollars."

That stunned Liam. These guys were more than serious. They either had more money than they knew what to do with or stood to lose much more if the meathead just elected got his hands on the controls of power.

After a moment, Liam said, "These guys must be nuts. Nobody in his right mind would get involved with them. Can I have my phone and ring back?"

The guy held up his hand. He had been prepared for that initial response. He said, "We know you don't need the dough, but think about what your daughter's charity could do with the money. How many mosquito nets, AIDS pills, and clean water systems would that money buy in Africa? And she could probably leverage it two or three times with her current donors. Wouldn't that make up for some of the shit you've done to earn your current pleasant life and, by the way, help mend some of the hate your daughter has for you?"

Liam snorted. "Do your 'wise men' really think that their money can buy my daughter's affection? They don't know a damn thing about either me or her." He was starting to see red, and hints of fear were starting to gnaw at his calm.

The man said, "Relax, please. We're not done yet." His voice was edged in steel. "We're experiencing the emasculation of America. On top of that, top-secret material appears regularly on the front page of the *New York Times*. If some of the noble things you did for our country became public, you might find yourself branded a criminal. It would be a shame to spend your last years being hunted rather than crossing off the things on your bucket list."

Liam studied him in detail. He was white, with a deep voice that harbored no identifiable accent. There were no tattoos, no rings, no scars. What you could see of his hair outside the knit cap was brown with no strands of gray. His clothes were typical for a football fan, except maybe for his shoes. They were leather—black and shined. His fingernails were clean; his hands strong; his bearing confident. Except for his size, he was the kind of guy who could disappear in a crowd. Liam felt he needed to know more about this guy.

The guy went on. "You're probably right in that your daughter will never forgive you for not getting home after your wife's accident and death, but aside from the personal satisfaction you might get for making a major contribution to a noble cause, there might be another consideration. Your daughter travels to a lot of dangerous places in her charity work. Sometimes, in her zeal for her causes, she goes where the security situation is less than ideal. The world would be a sadder place if she were to suffer an accident and be unable to continue her crusade."

"Is that a threat?"

"No, just an observation."

Liam sat there for a full minute in silence. Then he locked eyes on his antagonist and said in a quiet voice, much like that of a teacher explaining the playground rules to students, "Well, this is a threat. If anyone touches my daughter, even causes her to be worried, the real Liam Martin will materialize out of the dark, cut your balls off, and stuff them down your throat. That done, he will find the 'wise men' and do the same to them. Am I clear?"

"Easy, Liam. It doesn't have to be this way. It's a win-win proposition. She gets a wad of money, the country avoids a big mistake, and your past secrets remain secret."

"How long did it take you to find me?"

"You can't run away from this, Liam. If we can't find you in time, we do know where your daughter is every day."

Liam was quiet for another minute. He breathed deeply, fighting the urge to drive his fingers into the throat of the masked hulk sitting across the small table from him. Gradually, the workings of his ever-active mind overcame his anger. He looked the big guy in the eye and said, "There are still some futile attempts to change the result of the election. I hear people are trying to get the Electoral College delegates to change their votes. If that doesn't work, there are rumors that his opponents are trying to cook up some legal BS to prevent him from taking office. With all the demonstrations in the streets turning to riots, he may never get to the inauguration anyway."

The guy did not look away. He said, "We aren't going to take that risk. You have a well-paying job, whether you want it or not, and even bigger incentives to get it done."

"Yeah, yeah. So it seems. And you have two clowns following me around. Don't let me see them anymore. It might be bad for their health."

"If I were you, I wouldn't waste any time," the big guy said. "Considering the idiots protesting in the streets, the Secret Service will be all over him. It will take some planning to get the job done."

Liam laughed. "Thanks for the advice. I'll take my phone and ring back now."

"Of course," said the man in the skeleton mask. He removed the covering cloth and pushed both across the table with the tip of his finger, one at a time.

"You can go now," said Liam, through clinched teeth.

"Of course," the man said again. He picked up the wine glasses as he stood. "Wouldn't want to be a mess maker, you know."

Or leave his finger prints, thought Jerry, as he rose to see what the guy did with the glasses. He did not return them to the bar but rather tossed them into a large trash bin. Jerry heard them shatter as they landed. He looked to be sure the messenger was gone, grabbed a couple of paper plates off an empty table, and opened the top of the bin. Its plastic bag liner was almost empty. After a look around at the fans crowding to the concession stand at halftime, he took the liner out of the bin and rolled it up into a football-sized package. Carefully, he took it back to his seat to watch the rest of the game. His "little guys" had a big day, and the visitors won, which suited Liam because the 49ers quarterback was such a jerk.

Chapter Two

Two days later, a CIA operative named Sean Doyle got a phone call. He didn't even bother to look at the caller ID. Almost all the calls he got were from anonymous sources. He said, "Doyle."

"Top of the mornin' to ya, Sean," said the voice on the other end of the line.

"Oh shit, Liam or Jerry or whatever you're calling yourself these days. Are you going to fook up my Thanksgiving?"

"Of course, not. Just a little data gathering with no apparent collateral complications."

"I've heard that song before. I'm an analyst now, remember?"

"That's what I need, wisdom. It's been a two-way street for us."

"Yeah, I know, Liam. What wisdom do you need?"

Liam said, "Why don't we go for a little picnic?"

"It's freezin' out."

"A little brisk fresh air is good for the appetite. If your desk job has softened you up so fast, we can eat inside after we talk."

Sean sighed. "The usual?"

"Any reason to change?"

"No. See you there."

There was a small park along the Potomac River, which was a very pleasant place most of the year, but today, a harsh wind blew off the river, making it uncomfortable even in a winter coat. Still, the two men who met by a water fountain did not stand out. Liam wore a tan woolen coat and tweed cap straight from Dublin. Sean, who was seven inches taller than Liam, was more formal in a black overcoat and fedora. A clutch of white curls showed below the brim of the fedora, and there were still a few freckles sprinkled on the broad cheeks below his green eyes. They greeted each other warmly and started walking south along the river path.

"Is all well with you and yours, Sean?"

"Yeah. Have both the kids in college now—different colleges, of course—and Liz and I are making up for all the together time we missed while I was in the field. How about you?"

"I had been enjoying myself immensely until I ran into this spot of trouble."

"Can you talk about it?"

"Hopefully, you don't need to know."

"Christ, Liam. You're sixty-five years old. What have you been doing to get involved in that kind of shit?"

"I've been an angel, invisible even, but some supposedly wise men have tracked me down to do one last patriotic chore."

"What kind of help do you need?"

"Right now, just a little research. I have some pieces of broken wine glasses with fingerprints. Some are mine. Some are from a man I want to know more about. He is a big guy who looks military. The second thing is some info on an elite and secret society of some sort. Eight people, big into patriotism. Lots of money to spend."

"Sounds easy enough. There may be several societies of that sort, though."

"There's one thing more. I think the guy is tracking me through my smartphone. I've programmed it to roll over to a new one, and I'm looking for someone to keep them guessing about my whereabouts by carrying my old one around. He never has to answer it. Just let it roll over. The arrangement can't be public knowledge, though. Any ideas about who I can get to do that for me?"

"I thought there weren't going to be any collateral complications."

"I could probably hire a messenger or someone like that, but he might decide to steal the phone and find himself with a visit from some nasty people."

"Your concern for the common man is admirable," scoffed Sean. "How long do you think this will go on?"

"That will depend on how long it takes me to track down the source of this bit of bother. It will surely be over by January 20."

"What sets the end date?"

"Think about it."

They walked another hundred yards before Sean said, "What the fook are you into?"

"I see your operative instincts have not all gone dormant since you've become an analyst, but all I need is a little bit of research. Have you got any good ideas about moving the phone around?"

"If I carried it to work every day, anybody who was tracking it would soon know something fishy was going on. You need some random destinations to look as if you were doing things, going places. You could mail it to various PO boxes, but then you'd have to show up periodically to claim it. There might be a problem keeping it charged if you did that. What if you just took it apart until you were ready to talk to whomever?"

"No. The only way I can get any insight into what they are up to is to have them call me."

After a moment, Sean tugged at his cap. "What about your daughter?"

That idea stopped Liam cold. He hadn't even talked to Cathryn since last Christmas, much less see her face-to-face. Some of that was because she was running around the world, but mostly, it was because of the hostility she bore him. She never really understood what he did for a living, why he was gone for long periods, and would never talk about where he went. He suspected that she imagined the worst. Sometimes, he woke up before dawn, wondering what he might have done differently then. It had taken only a short while for those mornings to catalyze his leaving the service he now considered ungrateful for his loyalty.

"You know, Sean, that's a hell of an idea, a hell of a challenge, but a hell of an idea. If they think I'm with her, they won't get near her."

"The guy threatened her?"

"You know the drill. Not-so-subtle hints have been dropped. Your brain is still perking, Seany boy. Get me that info as soon as you can. I'm off to find my daughter. Can I count on you to serve as an emergency contact?"

"Of course. What about lunch?"

"Another time. You'd spend the whole meal trying to interrogate me. I've already said too much. Thanks, Old Son. Thanks."

As he walked away, Liam's mind flashed back ten years to that terrible day when he faced his daughter after missing his wife's funeral and was excommunicated from her life. That meeting had ended with her berating him in a profane tirade about how he loved whatever dirty work he did for "the fuckin' government" more than he did his wife. With that, she literally shoved his numbed body out of their house. That day had led him to realize that his life was a shambles: his twenty-year-old daughter hated him; he had been used by the agency to the point where he had no conscience left—no moral compass. The "special ops" people were special to the agency but not special enough to make a plane for home to wait for him even though he was finishing a mission.

The assassinations were not the worst of his assignments. At least those guys were well-documented killers. But there had been some kidnappings followed by watching interrogations in offshore hellholes by a team of truly evil agents of his government, who seemed to enjoy inflicting pain, both physical and psychological. He had justified all this out of loyalty to his country, which he finally realized was naivete or maybe some of his own dark side. Feeling totally alone, he retired from the agency but still felt the tug of its spider's web. He started this life of hiding from everyone except Sean, his partner, in what he now considered a crime.

He used some of the tools acquired while working in the agency to support his new hermit-style life: an offshore bank account, false names and IDs, and an all-cash approach. He made some progress in checking off many of the items on his bucket list while moving under everybody's radar. The plan and techniques worked fine for years until this one. Now he had to restore his version of order and would need help.

Chapter Three

Cathryn Martin was comfortably ensconced in a first-class chair on the Acela Express from Boston headed toward Manhattan. She much preferred the train over the crowded shuttle flights and door to door; the plane didn't save any time on this kind of trip.

She dozed a little, only to be awakened by the Bruce Springsteen bellowing from her cell phone. She looked at the caller ID. Her father! *What the hell did he want?* She thought she was shed of him. But she answered the phone.

"Hello, Cathryn," he said. "I'm glad I caught you."

"I shouldn't have answered, but at least you didn't hide behind one of those 'private number' IDs."

"I could say that I just wanted to wish you Happy Thanksgiving, but you wouldn't believe that."

"You're damn right about that," she interrupted.

"I need to talk to you for a few minutes. It's important."

"We're talking now."

"It's more complicated than that. We need to meet. Where are you now?"

"None of your business."

"Come on, Cathryn. I assure you that I can find you if you make me. Let's do this the easy way."

There was that steely sound of command in his voice, the same one she found herself using from time to time. It made her shrivel a little inside when she thought of those things of him that she saw in herself. And she knew he was right: He would find her. She doubted that he'd lost any of the skills he used when he did whatever he did for the government.

"All right, I'm on a train to Manhattan."

"What hotel are you staying at?"

"The Empire."

Liam tried a little laugh. "Not the Mark or the Ritz?"

"I don't piss my foundation's money away on lavish living. The Empire costs a fraction of what those two rip-offs charge, and it's close to Penn Station."

"I'm glad to hear that the foundation has low overheads. I assume you have plans for Thursday. What about Friday?"

"I have a lunch meeting."

"Suppose I show up at ten. Shouldn't take more than half an hour."

She sighed. "If you must, but don't expect a welcoming hug."

"It's much more important than that."

She hung up. *The old bastard still has no idea how important hugs are.*

*****

Liam didn't bother to bring flowers or any other stress reliever to the Empire on Friday morning. That would just have been a waste of time and money. He had flown into Newark the night before amid the mob of Thanksgiving travelers, camped at the airport hotel, and taken the train to NY Penn Station in the morning. He had the front desk call up to announce his arrival. No surprises either.

She opened the door promptly, scowling. She had just finished a run and was dressed in a blue jog suit. If he could get her to agree to his plan, he was going for a celebratory run in Central Park. He, too, was dressed in a blue jog suit. *Sometimes God provides*, he thought.

The old bastard still looks fit, she thought.

She had her mother's brown hair and hazel eyes, and her brows were kitted into a frown, just as her mother's often were when he announced he would be leaving on another assignment. She was now about the same age as when Liam had first met the woman he married, and the resemblance always shocked him.

She grabbed her water bottle and sat on the side of the bed. There was a TV console, a nightstand, and little else in the room. It smelled a little musty, like a southern motel in summer.

He sat in the only chair.

"Okay," she said. "What's this all about?"

"What does your itinerary look like for the next two months?"

"Why do you care?"

He took a deep breath, pondering how to proceed. He found that he had no wonderfully creative idea, so he took his usual full-speed-ahead approach.

"There has been a credible threat against NGOs operating in Africa. Obviously, yours could be a prime target."

"Why would anybody want to do that? Where did you get this story?"

"I still have sources. A friend knows about your foundation and passed the word along. The wackos don't need a reason to tear things up."

"So what did your friend say I should do about the rumor? Stay home? I don't go anywhere alone in Africa. I have security."

"Sorry, Cathryn, but those wimps you travel with couldn't fend off a pussy cat and would probably be oblivious to all but the most obvious trouble. That's just not their role in life. Now I'm not saying you should hire an army, but if I know where you are, I can keep connected to the source. If anything specific comes up, I can give you a heads-up."

"Big Daddy comes to the rescue? No thanks. You haven't even sent me a birthday card in the years since that day. Why are you on your high horse now?"

"That day" was two days after his wife's funeral when he had finally got back to the small house in Fairfax, Virginia, that they used to call home. He had found his twenty-year-old daughter throwing his clothes, books, and even the paintings from the bedroom walls out of the house onto the small porch. She had been shouting profanities as she threw each item and turned them all directly onto him the moment he showed his face. Cathryn would not even let him into the house. All his explanations and arguments had proved futile, and he had slunk away like a defeated black sheep. The memory stopped him for a moment.

Then he said, "I'm not going to be able to help from thousands of miles away, but forewarned, you could change your plans or hire that army."

"My image in Africa—in the world, really—is that of a Good Samaritan. I'm not connected to the government or to any political ideology. Bill Gates is my friend and role model. We are viewed as innocents."

"Yeah, but you both are building independence among poor, subservient people. Look at your project to farm souped-up sweet potatoes to cut malnutrition. There are warlords and such who want those people to remain weak. They don't care how many of them die from malaria or bad water. They just want them as slaves."

"You seem to know more about what I do than I ever did about your projects. What did you do for the government?"

"Whatever they asked me to," he said. "Look, you're doing good stuff. You just need to be careful."

"You're preaching to the choir. We're not going to stop."

"I'm not trying to get you to stop. There are two simple things I'm asking you to do. One, give me as detailed itinerary as you can and keep me up-to-date. That way, I can get the daily terrorist forecast and put you in touch with the experts if necessary. Two, I'd like you to carry my cell phone. Don't answer it. It will roll over automatically to a second one in my pocket if anyone calls. It also has a one-button connection to possible help in case there is an emergency. That's not hard, is it?"

"This is all very mysterious. I suspect you're not giving me the whole story."

"I've given you the essence of it. All you have to do is keep my phone charged with you and turned on. The details of who is involved and how it all will work will just distract you from your main purpose, probably for no reason. Trust me on this." He stretched out his arms in a sort of welcoming gesture.

She was quiet for a full minute. His intensity was palpable. Until this moment, she didn't think he gave a damn about her safety, but something had his motor revving now. She had hated this man for so long she didn't know what to believe. To give her some time, she said, "Trust you? Why the hell should I do that?"

"Okay, I guess I deserved that. I need your help, and you get some extra insurance on your safety. My price is pretty low."

She looked him in the eyes. It was as if their brains connected as they once did the summer he taught her how to swim. *Whatever he was up to was important.*

She said, "I assume you have the phone with you."

Liam reached into the back pocket of his jog suit and pulled out two of the smaller smartphones. He handed her the one with the yellow dot in the corner of the screen.

"You have my number. Call it from your phone." He was relieved to see that she had his number on her speed dial, although she had never called it.

She did, and the yellow-dot phone buzzed once; a second later, the other phone rang with the opening bars of Beethoven's Fifth. He answered it with, "See, it works."

"That's not surprising, I guess."

"If you get concerned about anything, call me or press the yellow dot. It will ring the cell phone of my friend at the agency 24-7. He'll advise you and call me with an assessment of the situation."

She sighed, got up, and opened the soft briefcase lying on the bed. She handed him two pages of computer printout. "Here's my planned itinerary through year-end. I expect to be back home for Christmas and remain through the first couple of weeks of January. Plans could change."

Liam smiled, looked at the papers, and found she was leaving next week. "Perfect," he said. "What are you doing in New York?"

"Raising money. I have lunch with two of the president-elect's people today. They're not sure how to separate his business from the Oval Office. Maybe they'll be ripe for a big donation and some good press for a change. I need to get dressed."

"Sure. Hopefully, none of this will be needed. Be safe."

They stood and nodded at each other, and he left.

Chapter Four

As Liam exited the elevator in the lobby, he saw a guy staring at him from a chair opposite the door. He looked like a typical businessman in a navy suit, clutching a copy of the *Wall Street Journal*, except for his shoes; they were white Nike running shoes. Liam noticed but thought nothing of it until he got two blocks away. *Maybe the guy just wore comfortable shoes on the way to the office. Not too many office types working on the day after Thanksgiving. Or maybe he wore running shoes to be able to tail a jogger.*

He stopped and reversed his path double time.

Back in the lobby, he took a seat from which he could see the man but was out of the line of sight between the elevator and the front door. Five minutes later, Cathryn came down dressed for business, already moving fast. The guy put his paper down and headed for the door. Liam got there first and blocked his path.

The guy said, "Excuse me," and tried to brush past Liam. Liam moved to continue blocking his path. He then pressed the muzzle of the SIG Sauer he always carried in his ankle holster into the man's ribs. The guy's eyes popped open.

"What the hell is this?" he said. "A robbery here? Hotel security will be here in seconds."

Liam said, "Are you sure you want to call them? She'll be out of sight in a minute, and I'll testify you were following her. Stalking is a crime. The hotel won't like the publicity of harboring such folks in their lobby. You and I are just going to have a nice little talk."

Liam's victim looked over his shoulder and saw Cathryn was already out of sight. He shrugged.

"What do we have to talk about?"

"Who sent you to follow my daughter? Let's go into the bar."

They sat at a small table in a corner. Liam held his gun under the table. "Who sent you and why?" he pressed.

"A confidential client. I'm a private detective."

Liam shoved the muzzle of the gun into the man's crotch. "Nothing is confidential from me," he said, "unless you like the thought of becoming a eunuch."

"Are you crazy? A security guy is standing by the elevators."

"I've been called that at times. How is their catching me going to help you, lying on the floor with your balls blown off? Give it up, bro, and walk out of here to stalk another day."

"I'm not sure he gave me his real name. I don't have a contract or nuthin'. He said his name was Harry, Harry Bennet."

"What did he look like?"

"He was a little bigger than me, but not a linebacker type. Blond hair: eyes never stopped moving. He paid me for a week up front."

"What did he pay you to do?"

"Just watch your daughter, write down her routine, where she went, who she saw. Like that. I was told not even to talk to her. He calls every night to get a report."

"You don't have a number for him or a meeting place?"

"No."

"Well, when he calls tonight, tell him you've got a better gig."

"What's better than gettin' paid two hundred a day to follow a woman with a nice ass?"

"Going home to one every night with whatever kind of ass she has. Don't let me see you within a mile of this place ever again. Come on. I'll walk you to the subway."

They got up and walked the few blocks to Penn Station, and Liam watched him get on a downtown train.

Later that day, Sean called.

Liam answered, "You're working on a holiday? I'm impressed."

"Whatever my country—or a friend—needs demands my attention. You will be surprised to learn that the fingerprints on the glass belong to one James Carson, a special agent at the FBI. He lives in Georgetown."

"What?"

"Yeah. He's a very special agent, reports directly to the director emeritus, and roams the country at his behest."

"Who the hell is the director emeritus?"

"About a year ago, Obama forced Angus Nixon out as director when he got to be seventy years old. Claimed new blood was needed. Nixon didn't go quietly. He negotiated a special slot focused on finding treason. He has a small staff, Carson being number one, and carte blanche to investigate one and all for some indeterminate period, in total secrecy, of course."

"Wow," said Liam, immediately lost in thought.

After a full minute of silence, Sean said, "You still there, old horse?"

"Yeah, yeah, Sean. Just thinking. This is very strange news."

"Yes, it is. I'm still working on the secret society thing. I'll get back to you next week."

"Thanks, Sean. I did get Cathryn to carry my cell phone to Africa. She's leaving next week. We had a little chat. A guy named Harry Bennet hired him to follow her and chart her activities. That was all he was supposed to do. I think I ran him off. Hopefully, that's the end of it unless any specific threats show up on your radar. I really appreciate your help."

"Just remember, you owe me lunch."

"Have no fear. Talk to you next week."

Chapter Five

The one place on the planet that could masquerade as a home for Liam Martin was Washington, DC. He owns a house under the name Jerry O'Hara in a modest neighborhood in the northeast area of the district near the junction of Quincy and thirteenth streets. The house is a few blocks east of Catholic University and the National Shrine Cathedral. He also owns a six-unit apartment house in College Park, next to the University of Maryland, an easy trip on a state route. He rents five of those to students and keeps one as a safe house.

When he arrived back from New York, he found an extensive file on James Carson on his computer. Aside from the ability to speak both Arabic and Spanish, the résumé was just average: two years in college in computer science; five years in the army, retiring as a technical sergeant; and two tours in Iraq. He must have had something special that was not listed to even get accepted in the FBI, much less advance to a freelance assignment after only six years in the organization. *There's more to this guy than meets the eye. Maybe Nixon discovered some special talent suited to his search for traitors and super-patriots and is using them to work a private agenda, or maybe they're using him.*

His house sat on a thirty-five-foot-wide lot in the shadow of an elevated through street. There were traffic noises and exhaust fumes most hours of the day, but most of the inhabitants of the almost-identical homes on the street didn't seem to mind. The adults would sit out on the front stoops on nice evenings, watching their kids play stick ball in the street and socialize. Liam wasn't part of that, and sometimes he felt left out. Each house had a narrow driveway leading to a garage in a small backyard. Liam kept his ten-year-old Honda there when he traveled. It didn't have a lot of miles on it but was starting to have things fail. Some neighbors had a serious garden back there. Liam had most of his covered with concrete. He had furnished the house sparingly but comfortably and modernized the kitchen and bathroom. Though he did not plan to spend much time there, he saw no reason to suffer while doing so.

One thing Liam did get a little warmth from when he slept at his house was breakfast at the diner around the corner. He could, of course, cook his own breakfast in two minutes by pulling a Jimmy Dean biscuit out of the freezer and popping it into the microwave. Yet after his years of flying below anyone's radar, there was something a lot nicer about sitting at the counter and having a chat while he downed his coffee.

The place was situated on a lot that amounted to an island enclosed by city streets. Its front wall was a series of tall windows that abutted a wide sidewalk that led to a metro station on the next corner. Inside the windows was a row of booths and tables spaced about six feet from a marble counter with eleven stools. The kitchen was behind a wall that supported a narrow shelf that held coffee cups and other supplies. At the end of the counter was a hall that led to the restrooms and the back door that opened onto a small parking lot squeezed between the building and another street. The place opened at 7:00 a.m. six days a week to serve the breakfast crowd that came mostly on foot. It did not open until noon on Sunday to serve brunch to churchgoers and a meat and potato dinner to the neighborhood.

The diner had a comfortable buzz and was redolent of coffee and frying bacon. Liam found it fun to eavesdrop on the guys in suits as they shared their opinions about the Redskins, the team's name controversy, the election, and their vision of the future. That broke up his self-centered life and let him believe he still had an interest in other people.

One caution that entered his mind was the fact that he had gone there for breakfast the last four times he had slept at his house. Developing a regular behavior habit was antithetical to his security rules, but what the hell; those four visits were spread over the course of a couple of months. His worry stemmed from having been tracked down by the "patriots" he'd just encountered. The chances of the diner visits contributing to that seemed insignificant to him this morning.

He had broken another of his life rules this morning: He'd slept until nine o'clock and foregone his run. *Am I getting soft in my old age?*

The chats came with Mary Flynn, the cheerful and nosy counter waitress. She was Irish, one of those Irish whose hair got cumulus-cloud white rather than gray as maturity set in. She wore it short, just covering her ears, and seemed quite comfortable with not only her hair color but also herself. She was clearly only a few years younger than Liam, and her trim body was full of energy. She had a smile that lit up her face and made her blue eyes sparkle. She had gotten him to admit his name was Jerry but not much else. That was one rule he hadn't broken. Their first chat had occurred when he was the only customer left in the place after the breakfast rush cleared out, and she took the opportunity to sit on a stool after a hectic four hours behind the counter.

Mary opened the conversation with, "So ya don't have a job to go to? Lucky man."

"No. I'm retired. Worked hard while I was at it, though." *That was dumb*, he thought. *Will just invite another question.*

It did. "What did you do?"

"Worked for Uncle Sam."

"In the service?"

"Not really."

"I didn't mean to pry. I serve a hundred or more men every week in this job. Many guys come in every day. I know what they will order. They tell me about their jobs, their families, and sometimes their problems. You're different, don't ya know? You pop in occasionally, sit on the same stool, order the same breakfast, and are reluctant to even tell me your name. You strike me as a very private person."

"Is that a bad thing? Does it offend you?"

"No, but it fires up my curiosity. There's a little of the Irish bartender in me, I guess."

Liam laughed. "I know a few of those, but they don't know much about me either."

"I'll try to loosen you up by telling you a little about me. I work at this job because I need to be around people. My husband was an army engineer. He and most of his squad were killed while installing a temporary bridge over one of those rivers in Iraq during the second war there. Our only child, a daughter, is off at graduate school in New England. She is almost thirty and still going to school. She's working on finishing her PhD in English lit. Wants to teach in college one day. Leaves me quite alone these days. Now what about you?"

Liam thought, *This is one wacky lady*, but he said, "I have a daughter too, about the same age. She's doing charity work in Africa. You send them off to college, and there's no telling what they'll choose to do."

"And your wife?"

Wacky and nosy. "Like your husband, she died prematurely."

"I'm sorry to hear that. Is that what put you in your shell?"

"No."

Mary was quiet for a long moment, her eyes fixed on his. Then she smiled that beautiful smile. "Okay, I see that's as far as it goes today, and I probably scared you out of ever coming back."

Liam's brain was scrambling for an excuse to leave. *This is getting too damn personal.*

She looked ready to ask another question. But thought the better of it. "I need to go," she said. "I want to get to the noon Mass at Catholic U. A bit of a walk, but it's good for my body as well as my soul. It's been nice talkin' to ya, Jerry. Hope you'll pop in again soon." She offered her hand.

Liam stood and took her hand. "Say a prayer for me. It's been a while."

He had no idea why he said that, but she smiled that beautiful smile again.

"I'll do that," she said and strode briskly out the door.

This is interesting. It is not at all part of any plan and scary. Will I come back? He would, but would not let this thing, whatever it was, interfere with his priority.

CHAPTER SIX

The next morning, Liam packed up a bag of disguises and headed for Carson's house in Georgetown.

He parked on the opposite side of the street, a little past the three-story brownstone building, and settled down to get a feel for the place. A couple came out, kissed cheeks, and walked in opposite directions. *So the building is multifamily.*

Liam saw the postman working his way down the street. He went to the bag in the trunk and drew out a pair of thick glasses that made his blue eyes look brown, a Boston Red Sox ball cap, and a quilted jacket that made him look obese. He walked across the street, arriving at the building just as the postman opened the outer door.

"Hey," he said. "You saved me having to go through the ring the bell/intercom thing."

"Who are you?" asked the postman.

"Jerry Sweeney. I'm Mr. Carson's accountant."

"Well, I doubt he's here. Look at his mailbox. It's stuffed full. He hasn't emptied it in days." He pointed to box 3A, which was indeed overflowing.

"Well, I'm going up to at least leave a card on his door. If you want, I'll carry some of that mail up and stick it in the door as well."

The postman laughed. "Thanks, but no can do. Privacy, you know."

"Sure," Liam said and thought, *You can't win them all.* He headed for the stairs.

The postman called after him, "There's an elevator in the back."

Liam turned and said, "I know, but I need every bit of exercise I can get." He smiled and started up the stairs.

There were two apartments on each floor. Carson's was on the right, with the door in the middle of the hall directly opposite the door to 3B. The hall was rather elegant, with nice carpet and moldings along the ceiling. *Not exactly the low-rent district.*

Liam listened at the door, heard nothing, and then went across the hall to listen at the other door. There were no sounds there either. He decided it was safe to have a look inside Carson's home. There was a deadbolt, but his nimble fingers defeated that in less than a minute with his lock-picking tools.

Not surprisingly, the guy was anal. There was no thread across the door jam or other gimmick drawn from some TV thriller, but everything was meticulously in its place. He would have to be very careful if he chose to touch anything. He donned his latex gloves and started to poke around.

There was no computer—nothing in the waste baskets. The bedroom closet held three suits, a sports jacket, and a half-dozen shirts on hangers covered in plastic from the cleaner. After studying the arrangement of the shoes, he chose to move them, looking for a hidey-hole in the floor. No luck. He carefully replaced the shoes and backed up a step to check his work.

The bathroom was more of the same. The granite countertop was empty except for the charging station for a toothbrush and a heavy-duty plastic drinking glass that looked like crystal. There were no spots on the stainless-steel faucet. The medicine cabinet contained a big bottle of Canoe aftershave, some extra-strength Tylenol, toothpaste, and a prescription for Tylenol with codeine. *Does the guy have migraines?* A towel was neatly folded on a bar next to the shower; the waste basket here was also empty, and Carson was one of those guys who chose to put the free end of the toilet paper next to the wall.

Liam turned on the TV to see what channel was last viewed. Fox News came up. Liam concluded that all this neatness was not the doing of a cleaning lady. An oak rolltop desk, the top closed and locked, stood against the wall opposite the TV. It was an invitation he could not refuse. Unfortunately, the interior of the desk was as sterile as the rest of the place. He had trouble getting the top to relock but finally succeeded. *So far, a lot of work for nothing.*

He took a last look around to be sure he left no trace of his visit, peeked into the hall to be sure he was alone, slipped out, and relocked the door. Liam went to his car and settled down to wait and ponder the situation.

Carson came home just after dark, dragging a wheeled carry-on bag behind him. He struggled to get all his mail out of the box, tucked it under his arm without even a cursory look, and walked past the stairs to the back of the building and the elevator. The third-floor lights came on, and Liam settled to see what came next.

The answer was nothing. Carson never came out, and the lights went out before ten o'clock. Liam was glad. He had an urgent need to take a leak.

Liam was back on the job at dawn the next day, dressed in jeans and a gray New York Giants hoodie. A taxi pulled up in front of the building at seven. Carson got in the car, carrying only a slim nylon briefcase. Liam followed him to Reagan Airport. He quickly dumped his car in the daily lot and hustled into the terminal to see what Carson was up to. The answer was the eight-thirty shuttle to Boston.

Liam scrolled through his contacts until he came to the name of Detective Tim Sullivan of the Boston Police. He called the precinct office. The sergeant who answered the call said, "Timmy is out of the office right now. Can I take a message?"

"You can give me his cell phone number. This is urgent," Liam replied.

"What is this about? Who are you?"

"This is his uncle, General Jerome Sweeney. I understand your reluctance to give out his cell number, but the matter really is urgent. Suppose you call his cell and tell him who's asking and get his permission. I'll hold on."

There was a long moment of silence on the other end of the line. Liam could almost hear the working of the sergeant's mind. *Who the hell is this arrogant bastard?* Then he said. "Hold on."

Jerry listened to him talk to Tim. "I got some wacko on the house phone who wants your cell number. He says he's a general and your uncle. You want me to blow him off?"

There was a moment of silence, and then the sergeant came back on the line. "He says okay. The number is 606-5532."

"Thanks, Sergeant."

Tim was laughing when he answered the phone. "It's been a long time, Liam, or whatever name you're using now. I almost forgot about the general/uncle code you pounded into my head when you were my training officer at the 'company.' It's been what? Fifteen years?"

"Yeah, Timmy. I was a failure at training you. You quit."

"You couldn't be more wrong about that, Liam. You got me to realize that my idea of a CIA career was a delusion. I quit because I couldn't tolerate the thought of becoming like you: totally dedicated to doing without question what some fucking amoral bastard demanded. I got out, got a job with the Boston PD at half the salary, and put my wife to work, and now we have a house and two kids, and we're living the 'happily ever after' fairy tale. I'm grateful to you for that. Why did you call?"

"I've been pretty successful flying under the radar, but some bastard has smoked me out, and I need to find out where he's getting his juice from. He's on the 9:30 shuttle from Reagan."

"Ha," snorted Tim. "Nothing like planning ahead. What is it you want me to try to do? I'm not up for any monkey business."

"If there's any animal in my request, it's a bird dog. I just want to know where he goes, who he sees. He's a kind of roving FBI agent."

"You've the FBI on your tail?"

"I don't think so. This guy seems to be a messenger of sorts. I don't believe the people he's connected to have anything to do with the government."

"So you want me to tail the guy and report on his appointment calendar? That could take days. I know I owe you, but I do have a full-time job and a hot case right now."

"All he has with him is a small nylon briefcase. It's probably just an in and out."

"All right, Liam. I'll call as soon as he heads back to the airport. If it gets to be more than that, we're going to have to renegotiate."

"Thanks, Tim. I knew I could count on you."

As the sun was coming down in Boston, Tim called Liam. "Your man went straight to a nice lunch in Southi with Mickey O'Loughlin. No stop at the local FBI office to check in."

"Hmmm," said Liam. "Who the hell is Mickey O'Loughlin?"

"He's a distant relative of Whitey Bulger. Remember him?"

"Yeah, you just caught him in California after chasing him for a decade."

"More than a decade, sixteen years. The murderous bastard goes on trial here next year. The vestiges of his mob still function. O'Loughlin runs it, and it's more civilized now than when Whitey was in charge. Once in a while, we even get some cooperation on other bad guys."

"So why would an itinerant FBI agent have lunch with him?"

"That's for you to figure out. I can tell you that his little nylon briefcase looked to be about twice as full when he left compared to when he arrived. Okay, he just boarded the four forty-five for Reagan."

"Great, Tim. Thanks. If you guys have a brief on what this O'Loughlin has been up to recently, I'd appreciate seeing it."

"I'll try to get you the executive summary. The file fills about ten boxes."

"Thank you, Timmy boy. Say hello to Marie and the kids for me."

"No point in filling her mind with anxiety. She doesn't even need to know that you popped back into my life for even a couple of hours. I hope you can work things out without any further help from me."

"Should be no call for you to get involved in any messiness on this one. Have faith."

"Okay, Liam. Good luck with it."

Liam was waiting at Reagan when Carson got off the shuttle flight from Boston. The man went to the FBI office, left the briefcase, spent an hour, and went home, where he stayed.

Chapter Seven

In the next few days, the man the secret group wanted killed got certified as the president-elect by the Electoral College, Carson went to the office daily like a typical bureaucrat, and Liam got bored to tears. There was nothing from Sean on any secret societies.

Then he got a phone call. The voice was electronically distorted. The message was simple: *The man was confirmed as president-elect. We want a progress report on your plans for the project. Call 999-666-1235 for a secure conversation.* He chose not to call.

While he contemplated his next move the following day, his phone rang again. It was Sean. He answered immediately.

In a wary voice, Sean said, "Your daughter pushed the yellow button. Two guys have been following her group for a couple of days with no attempt to be discreet. They made her nervous enough to call."

"Any other info about them?"

"No."

"I assume you're not able to talk."

"Right."

"That's fine. I suspect the two guys are a message for me. I appreciate your help."

He understood why his stubborn daughter would rather call a government agency than rely on her father for help. Still, she must have been worried more than a little to have done anything at all. He thought about grabbing the first plane to Kinshasa, but it would take a couple of days to get there, and she might not appreciate his arrival. On top of that, he needed to stay close to Carson, his only contact with the "wise patriots," in case he fled. He needed to find a way to keep a closer watch on that guy.

He connected his computer to the dark web using Tor so that his message could not be traced and sent an email marked "very urgent" to Carson. It read,

> *Okay, Mr. Messenger Man, I know who you are, where you live, and where you work. Your super-secret society has sent two clowns to follow my daughter, I assume, as a message to me. I have a message for you. I meant every word I said about cutting off your balls and those of your friends if my daughter is even threatened in this escapade. Have your principles send the two guys someplace else immediately, or you will have a visit from Liam. That won't be pretty.*

That done, he called Sean back.

"What the hell do you want now?"

"Just a little more research. How about a beer at your favorite pub on your way home tonight?"

"I've got a family, Liam. I need to get home for dinner."

"This won't take even half an hour, I promise. You won't have time to finish your beer before we're done."

"Make it a martini. Mahoney's?"

"Sold."

Mahoney's was a neighborhood bar a few blocks from where Doyle lived in Oakton, Virginia, where they had met often in the past and were very unlikely to be seen together by anybody affiliated with his job. Liam got there early and was sipping his martini at a booth in the back when Sean arrived, scowling. The sight of a martini in a frosted glass awaiting him calmed him a bit.

After a sip of the ice-cold drink, he said, "You told me you wouldn't get me involved in whatever you're up to. What do you want?"

"Have you made any progress on the list of secret societies yet?"

"The first pass at the list is very long. I was having some friends try to narrow it down to a few, but that had to stop. The FBI went to my boss and raised hell about the CIA going through files on domestic organizations. He came to me and cut off my water. My friends are in various places and have remained anonymous, but I'm not ready to retire. My pension won't come near covering the tuition bills from my daughters' colleges."

"That's bad, but this is about Carson. He's involved in something strange. He went up to have lunch with the head of what's left of the Irish mob in Boston the other day. I have no idea what that's about unless Nixon is working a sting. On top of that, those two not-very-skilled guys are following my daughter's group in Africa. I don't see how those things are connected, but I need a way to stay closer to Carson and find out what he's up to. Have you got any connections that might help me do that?"

They each took a sip of their martini and felt the warmth slide down into their core. Sean remained quiet. Liam let him think.

"I know the director's assistant, Maggie. Both she and the boss are not at all happy with Nixon's not going to pasture quietly. Moreover, Nixon is doing some stuff he keeps secret from the director. She can't do more than clue you in on Carson's whereabouts and maybe who he meets with in the office, but that might help."

"Come on, Sean. You're a better spook than that. What else can you give me?"

After another sip and a long moment, Sean said, "Have you got any money for this?"

"For whom?"

"There's this kid named Matt we sometimes use as a contractor. He can hack into anything."

"Better than your in-house guys?"

"No, but much more private."

"You think he could hack into Carson and Nixon's electronic communications even if they're encrypted?"

"Not sure, but he's done that kind of stuff for us, all very hush-hush."

"There's the Sean Doyle I know. How do I contact this boy wonder?"

Sean took a gulp of his martini, sighed, reached into his pocket to retrieve a business card, and wrote on the back of it. He covered the card with his hand. "Liam, you rescued me from those fanatics in Iraq who were going to cut my throat and lied like hell about how they caught me to save my career, so I owe you big time, but my suspicions about what you're involved in are making me nervous as hell. On top of that, if the bastards are getting your daughter involved, it's really ugly."

"I'm sorry about getting you in a tight spot, Sean. I thought I was all done with this kind of shit, but it seems I can't escape my past just yet. I'm running on all cylinders right now. It can't be long to the end of it, and there's no connection to you. I really appreciate your help."

Sean finished his martini and slid the card across the table. "You'll need that code to get him to cooperate. Call him tonight. I'm going to change the code tomorrow." He stood.

Liam looked at the card, studied it a moment, and handed it back to Sean. "Thanks, ole buddy. You're grand."

Sean tore the card to bits. He patted Liam on the shoulder and left, with the bits in his coat pocket.

Liam went to the bar for another martini, returned to the booth, and contemplated his situation. Finally, he decided to call Matt. After a lot of what he thought was electronic nonsense, he got connected to Matt and got quite an interrogation.

"Where did you get this code?"

"From a long-time friend."

"How long time?"

"We worked together for the government for more than a decade."

"Doing what?"

"Why is that important?"

"Because you're probably going to ask me to do something illegal, and I need to know the answers to what I think is important before even asking what you want me to do."

Liam paused for a long moment before going on. "You know who gave me your code, don't you?"

"Yeah, but you could have twisted his arm somehow."

"You could check with him. He's home by now."

"I'd rather know who I'm dealing with. How did you and he work together?"

Liam took a deep breath. "We worked in a special ops unit. As a team, we were tasked with secret projects. It was all very stressful, and there were prices to pay."

"I gather you're no longer working for the government."

"Retired almost ten years ago."

"Doing work for your private account?"

"No. Trying to sail below the radar, but somebody is trying to force me out of retirement for one last project."

"Who?"

"I don't know. That's the help I need."

"Whose life do you want me to pry into?"

"A couple of guys at the FBI."

"That gets expensive. Who are they?"

"Angus Nixon and his right-hand man, Carson. They claim to be connected to some 'wise patriots' who have decided that I should kill a prominent citizen. They will pay big time but aren't giving me any choice in the matter. They've threatened my daughter if I fail."

Liam felt relieved to have gotten the whole story off his chest, even to this mysterious stranger over an insecure telephone. He took a deep breath and got his game face on again. There was silence on the other end of the line for a long moment.

"What is it you want to know about these guys?"

"I need to know who they're talking to. Who they're meeting with. Are there any secret groups of rich men they're in contact with? Is Nixon involved, or is Carson freelancing? What's their connection to the Irish mob in Boston? What are they trying to hide? I need knowledge and leverage."

"That's quite a plateful. Who is the target they want you to kill?"

"I can't get into that. Let's just say his assassination would be a major headline and have a monumental impact on our country. I need to cancel the plan somehow."

"This sounds like a major crime. Why not go to the cops?"

"Because right now, it's my word against an unknown, but more importantly, they've threatened my daughter."

"Do you think it's a hoax?"

"Not likely, and I can't take any chances."

"Okay, this is what I can do. It may take a day or so, depending on how encrypted they are, but I'll set up a site on the deep web to collect everything I gather. Do you know what that is?"

"Yeah. I can get on Tor sites."

"Okay, give me your normal email address. I'll send you the URL for a Tor site and will send an alert to your normal email every time something new is added to it. You will have no way to contact me. I will send you an invoice at the Tor site along with delivery instructions for the payment. Is that okay with you?"

"Any idea how big a blank check I'm signing here?"

"Does it really matter?"

Liam laughed. This had been one lousy negotiation on his part. He said, "How old are you?"

That got a laugh on the other end of the line. "Physically, not very, but there are lots of chevrons on my soul. I doubt I'll break your bank. Your email address, please."

Liam gave it to him.

Matt said, "Good luck," and ended the call.

Chapter Eight

At five o'clock, two mornings later, Beethoven's Fifth once more jolted Liam awake. It was Cathryn!

"What the hell did you do?" she shouted.

Dumbfounded, it was a long moment before he was able to croak out, "About what, when?"

"About those two guys I called your friend about."

"All I did was contact the guy I thought might be responsible for them being there to say that I didn't like anybody following you around."

"Well, now they're dead. Shot in the head in their hotel room. We didn't see them around yesterday, and when we got back to the hotel, the place was crawling with cops carrying machine guns They questioned us all until dawn. Some of my group wanted to split and run. We argued all morning and lost a day on the project. In the end, I convinced the group I had a backup plan and that we'd be safe. My backup plan is to get you to stop fuckin' around. Will you do that? This was scary as hell."

Liam jumped off the bed so rapidly that he dropped the phone. He scrambled to pick it up while his daughter shouted, "Did you hear me?"

"Yes. I had nothing to do with that. I am totally amazed. The people who sent them must have wanted to be sure that no one ever found out who they were. If they're tracking my phone, they think I'm there and would likely be interrogating them sooner or later."

"Who are those people?"

"That's what I'm trying to find out. So far, I only know their messenger boy. Did the local cops arrest any of your people?"

"No. They just disappeared. I hadn't seen them since I called Sean. Seems like things are being manipulated from over there. Will you stay the hell out of my business? Obviously, there is a lot more to this than the bullshit you gave me before I left."

"Yeah, but none of it involves anything you're doing. The bastards are trying to force me to do something I want no part of, and vague hints at messing with you are part of their sales pitch."

"What do they want you to do so badly?"

"That's way above your pay grade, Cathryn. Trust me. I'll work it out. You just need to be alert. When are you getting back here for Christmas?"

"Next Thursday. I'm going to spend some time—"

"Whoa! Save the details for when I catch up with you."

The interruption shut her up for a moment. Then she said, "And I'll want details too."

"We'll work that out when we get together again. Stay alert, and good luck."

After a moment, she ended the call.

Liam was astounded by the news. Either Carson scared his principles, or they were brutally demanding privacy. In which case, either Carson or Nixon, or maybe both, was in danger, depending on who knew what about the guys behind the plot.

Later, Liam saw Carson go to the office and stay there. Liam's phone signaled the arrival of an email a little after three. It read:

URGENT: Go to I'mbeingscrewed.Tor for critical message.

The message sender's address was a random sequence of letters, numbers, and signs.

Liam figured it had to be from Matt and cranked up his big laptop to access the deep web.

There was a single item on the page: Carson has rented a Hertz car at Reagan for 9:00 a.m. tomorrow under a phony ID.

Perhaps his failure to return that phone call had triggered more than one response. Whatever was going down, there would be a break in the boredom for one day at least.

Liam watched Carson get into a cab with his thin nylon briefcase the next morning and then drove to the Hertz rental car lot at Reagan airport. There, he waited for Carson to get off the shuttle bus from the terminal, pick out car, and start out of the lot. He followed Carson onto I95 south. Three hours later, Carson pulled into an elegant residential community called Fords Colony in Williamsburg after turning onto 64 at Richmond. The entrance road, which was divided by an island planted with crepe myrtle trees, was open ahead, but Carson turned left to stop at a brick guard building. Liam continued straight and swung a U-turn at a break in the island. He pulled to the side of the road and waited for Carson to leave the guard building.

Carson reentered the entrance road, drove past Liam, and turned right onto a road blocked by a traffic barrier arm. He put some token into the machine, the arm lifted, and he drove past the green of one of the holes on the golf course to turn left at the second side street. Part of this community was being kept private from the rest.

Liam drove up the entrance road to what looked like the pro shop for members of the golf course that surrounded the area ahead. It turned out to be the clubhouse for a large recreation complex, complete with a pool, restaurants, card rooms, and all the other amenities of an elite country club.

Liam cornered the golf pro and asked to rent a golf cart for an hour or so. He said, "I'm looking for a retirement homesite, and a friend thought Ford's Colony might be a fit. I'd like to tour the golf course and some of the homesites. I see that at least some areas are private."

The pro replied, "That's Nathan Hale Village. It's only a small part of the complex but has a Revolutionary War character about it. There are all sorts of rules about what kind of house you can build, what materials you can use, what colors you can paint your house, et cetera. A lot of retired military folks live there. I can lend you a token if you'd rather drive your car through the neighborhood."

"I'd rather use the golf cart to get a close look at the course as well as look at all of the neighborhoods if that can be arranged."

"Okay, sure. Let me get you a map of the course and of the housing sites. The eighteenth green is right here, the first tee on the other side of the building. Pick a cart while I get the map."

Liam expressed his thanks, got his laptop out of the car, and climbed into a nearby cart. Map in hand, he drove onto the cart path and started around the course in reverse order. While there was no one playing on this chilly December day, the course looked in great shape, and the flags were still out on the greens.

The cart path crossed the road with the barrier in it to give access to the sixteenth tee. Liam took the road, slipped around the barrier, and headed toward the street he had seen Carson turn into. The sign identified it as Holinswell Road. The houses were impressive. They were not huge but were magnificent in design and construction. There was a lot of natural stonework in the facades and in monuments marking the entrances to driveways, which were short and led directly to front doors covered by porticoes supported by carved columns. There were no three-car garages like in the usual suburban McMansions but rather functional one- or two-car versions, some of which appeared to have apartments above. *Servants' quarters?* he wondered.

He found Carson's car in front of number 134 about halfway down a short street that ended in a patch of woods. The mailbox said "Townsend" in elegant calligraphy. He drove down to the end of the street and stopped. He turned on his computer and connected to the local telephone directory. He found that General and Miles Townsend lived at 134 Holinswell.

The wife was a general and still bragging about it? He got on the horn to Sean Doyle.

"What now?" came the growled greeting. "I told you I'm cut off."

"Good afternoon to you as well. I just need to test your memory a little. I'm sitting in Williamsburg looking at the house of the Townsend family. She was apparently a general and is still in charge."

"Well, at least that's an easy question. Eleanor Townsend was the first female general the army ever made. She ended up a three-star, even though she never had a combat command. She ran logistics and supply and was not afraid to step on toes to get what she needed. Her husband was a big real estate baron but always supported her career."

"Would she, by any chance, be involved in any of those secret societies I asked you about?"

Liam heard some papers shuffling on Sean's desk.

"Funny you should ask that," he said. "The Linonian Society came up in our first list. Nathan Hale and his brother were in a society by that name at Yale back in the day. It was a discussion group that liked to talk about the future, science, slavery, and the inevitability of war with England. General Townsend was listed as president of a local reincarnation of the group last year in a local newspaper article, praising them for collecting winter coats for underprivileged kids in the area. They sounded harmless enough."

"Do you have the names of any other members of the group?"

"I'll email what I have to you. There were several retired military men listed as members."

"All bossed around by a woman. Man, she must be something."

"Can you add them to what Matt's doing for me? I'm down here because of a tip he gave me about Carson renting car."

"Matt's good. I'll whisper in his ear."

"Thanks."

Liam watched as three other men entered the general's house. *Another sub-rosa lunch for Carson?*

Two hours later, the party broke up. Five men and Carson said their goodbyes and left. Liam was left to decide whether to rush around and try to follow Carson but realized he could never retrieve his car in time. *Not too bright,* he thought. Carson drove off, but the rest of the group walked. One of them lived only two houses away, one turned right at the cross street, and the others went left back to the main road and then right to the first side street. All local homeboys.

Liam contemplated his options. After a few moments, he decided on the direct approach he often followed. He took his laptop, walked down to 134, and used the big antique bronze door knocker to announce his visit.

Chapter Nine

Mr. Townsend answered the door, his eyes wide at seeing a stranger.

Liam smiled and introduced himself. "I'm Jerry Sweeney, a freelance writer. I'd like to interview you folks for a story I'm working on to follow up on the very supportive piece that appeared in the Williamsburg Press last year about the winter coat drive the Linonian Society sponsored then. Do you and your wife have a few minutes?"

Townsend looked around and then asked, "How did you get into the Village?"

"A pie, Mr. Townsend. At my age, it pays to keep all the body parts moving. May I come in?"

Townsend turned to call toward the back of the house. "Eleanor, there's a reporter here who wants to talk about last year's coat drive. Okay?"

The general came marching to the front door, drying her hands on a striped kitchen towel.

She was short and lean, and her hair was jet-black. *She must have colored it to preserve her command image*, Liam thought.

The general looked Liam up and down and then asked, "Why are you interested in that?"

"The Linonian Society got some nice press last year. I thought a follow-up story might be mutually beneficial."

She scowled. "You mean you could make a few bucks selling it to the local rag."

"And the Society might get a few more kudos for its current good deeds."

The Townsends looked at each other for a moment. "I guess we have a few minutes," she said and stepped aside to gesture him in. They sat opposite each other on upholstered couches, the ends of which abutted a granite-framed fireplace with a carved wood mantel. The room was painted in light gray and sported wide moldings on both floor and ceiling. Several paintings, including a portrait of the general in uniform, adorned the walls. The rugs looked like authentic Afghan handmade to him. Liam saw no family photographs anywhere. There was a lingering aroma of baked fish.

Liam started with, "Please, tell me more about the current role of the Linonian Society. All I really know is that Nathan Hale was a member during his days at Yale way back then."

Mr. Townsend answered, "The Linonian has always been a small group of people who thought about developments in science, society, and government. Members organized groups demanding that the US never get into World War II. Once Pearl Harbor happened, they all went to volunteer for service."

"That's very interesting. It doesn't sound like a group likely to be sponsoring a coat drive, though. How did that come about?"

The general took up the narrative. "One of our members wanted to undertake a major charitable event before he died. He motivated us to sponsor the coat drive. The timing seemed preordained. He died about six months ago."

"How many members does your chapter of the society have?"

The general answered, "Right now, eight. We are looking for candidates to fill one open spot."

"So there are strict limits on the size of the membership and criteria for membership?" asked Liam.

Mr. Townsend started to fidget, but the general thrust her chin forward and replied, "We place a premium on thoughtful discussion. We can't have that with too many people involved or if members have nothing meaningful to say."

"I can relate to that," said Liam. "Is that what you were doing today, interviewing a candidate?"

"Today was just a Christmas lunch," said Townsend, perhaps a bit too quickly.

"What are the major topics for the society these days?"

"The country's security, our economic problems, the divisions in our society, and the lack of political leadership," replied the general.

"Wow," said Liam. "That's a very heavy set of topics. Do you ever reach an agreement on any of them?"

Mr. Townsend said, "Sometimes we reach a consensus."

"And then what do you do about it?"

The general stood. "The society is private, Mr. Sweeney. We don't want our thoughts made public, nor will we advertise anything we do. I think this conversation is over."

"How about a hypothetical question? What would your group do if you reached the consensus that the incoming president of the United States was going to drag the country into a stupid war or worse?"

"This conversation is over," repeated the general.

"That might be unfortunate. You won't learn something that I know about the guest at your Christmas lunch."

The general was quiet. Her husband asked, "What does that mean?"

"Tell me why he was invited first."

The general was back in the conversation. "We sometimes invite nonmembers to provide information not readily available to us from other sources."

"What did this man say his name and occupation were?"

"That's private."

Liam pressed hard. "I know the man's real name and who he works for. I know he drove down here from DC this morning. I'm interested in what bullshit story he told you folks."

"It's time for you to leave, Mr. Sweeney," ordered the general.

"Very well, but that leaves me with the troubling question of why a special agent from the FBI was invited to a luncheon with an intellectual debating society. Perhaps you folks ought to seek an answer to that question as well."

There was a long moment of dead silence as the Townsend couple looked at each other in surprise, and then Mr. Townsend said, "I doubt you have all your marbles, Sweeney. Get out."

Liam put a business card on the end table. "If you change your mind about talking further, you can reach me here." Then he got up and left.

Liam got only halfway to Richmond on his drive home when his phone went off. The general sounded businesslike and determined when she said, "Your card said you were a consultant. What field do you consult in?"

"Mostly I try to enjoy my retirement, but sometimes I try to help people solve problems."

"What kind of problems?"

"As you say, that's private."

There was a prolonged silence on the general's end of the line. Liam could almost hear the wheels grinding in her head. He suspected she was used to having many moves planned out in advance and was having a bit of trouble making decisions on the fly.

"What makes you think the man who visited us today is connected to the FBI?" she asked.

"Aside from following him to the office, I have documentation."

"Can you prove that?"

"Give me a minute to pull off the road so we can talk safely." That done, he asked, "Would a copy of the mug shot on his agency dossier convince you?"

Again, there was some thinking time, then, "Yes."

"I haven't gotten very far up the road. Suppose I turn around, you alert the gatehouse to give me a pass, and we discuss this face-to-face."

"All right."

"I should be there in about half an hour."

Before pulling back on the highway, Liam opened his laptop and pulled up Carson's FBI dossier. He made a copy of the top half of the first page, which showed his mug shot, and saved it in a separate file. *That ought to be convincing*, he thought and closed the computer.

He arrived back at the general's house twenty-eight minutes later. It took only a few seconds for the thick oak door to open after he stroked the bronze knocker. The general gestured toward the living room without a word.

As before, they sat on the couches adjacent to the fireplace, which was now warming the room with a crackling blaze. "Some tea?" asked Mr. Townsend, gesturing toward a silver service on an end table. Apparently, this was going to be a civilized conversation.

"No, thanks. Let's get right to business." Liam opened his computer and scrolled to the file with Carson's mug shot. "Unless I'm going blind, this is the man who came to lunch here today."

The general and her husband both studied the image on the computer screen. She said, "Very well, Mr. Sweeney. We do have a lot to talk about. Please call me Eleanor, and this is Miles."

"Thank you, Eleanor. I'm Jerry. What name did Carson use today, and what was the nominal purpose of his visit?"

Eleanor said, "The Society has been applying for status as a nonprofit organization for several years. The IRS has been giving us the runaround. After some serious research on the Internet, we found a Mr. Arthur Kinkaid, who claimed to have expertise in unraveling such log jams. We asked him to share his wisdom with some of our members at lunch today."

"And did he have a good story?"

"He seemed quite businesslike. He reviewed our application and other correspondence, suggested a few improvements in our filing, and offered to carry the revised version to a contact he thought could help."

"How much would he charge for this service?"

"Nothing. He claimed his organization's role was to correct such bureaucratic overreach."

"Well, at least he wasn't piling greed on top of mendacity. Do you have any idea why the FBI is secretly investigating you and or the Society?"

"None whatsoever," replied Miles and Eleanor almost simultaneously.

Liam said, "Let's go back to one of my earlier questions. What does the Society do with the conclusions from its discussions? What actions does it take?"

Eleanor took a sip of her tea. Miles got up and put his cup down on the silver tray. Still standing, he said, "I've had a very successful career in real estate here in Virginia. During that, I made some connections with politicians, some of whom have grown to have influence at the national level. The senior senator from Virginia, Jesse Richardson, is one of these. Sometimes, we discuss the Society's ideas and concerns with him, but there is no pressure."

"That's it? No political action? No contributions?"

"Not in the Society's name. Eleanor and I are sort of tea party people privately, but we never use our reputations to try to influence local elections, nor do we lend our names to state or national campaigns."

"How about other members of the Society?"

Eleanor said, "None of them is active politically, to my knowledge. Most would rather study and discuss things than take to the trenches."

"Did the Society reach a consensus on the results of the election?"

"We reached the conclusion that America deserved a better choice of candidates. It was a lose-lose situation."

"So the Society is not going to take to the trenches as you call it. You're just going to wait four years and hope for better."

Miles shrugged. "What else can anybody do?"

"Was Jesse Richardson upset about the election result?"

"He was not at all pleased but felt the system would keep things under control. He had campaigned for her in Virginia, of course, but that didn't take much. She was a shoo-in here. He has four years left on his term, so he is pretty comfortable."

Liam said, "All the protests in the street are a little unusual. Have any of your contacts hinted that something more violent might be in the wind?"

The general said, "Like what? Some flaming liberals might file some legal action or try to inflame the usual thugs with some profane TV show, but I can't picture anything seriously violent. Nobody is that afraid."

Liam said, "Back to square one. Why is the FBI sniffing around?"

Miles said, "Maybe they're investigating the IRS."

The general laughed. "That would be fun to see, but I won't hold my breath."

Liam stood up. "I'm going to dig into what this Carson character is up to. I have a few contacts who might know something. I'll pass on anything that seems pertinent. In the meantime, I would suggest that the Linonian Society keep its ear to the ground."

The general frowned. "That's not going to cut it, Mr. Sweeney. I want to know everything you find out. I don't like being scammed. I don't like the smell of this, and the Society's reputation is important to us."

"I understand that, Eleanor. I promise to do my best to get to the bottom of what's going on. Call me anytime. I'll tell you what I know."

Chapter Ten

Liam pondered the situation during the drive home. The General seemed like a true patriot. Was Nixon really concerned about the Linonian Society? Who was this Senator Richardson, really? Was the society an indirect way for Nixon to approach the senator? Christmas was in three days, and Cathryn was coming home tonight. Time was running out. It was getting to be "damn the torpedoes" time.

He booted up his laptop when he got home and found an email from Matt. Shifting to his Tor site, he learned that Angus Nixon had been holding offsite secret meetings with members of congress and others. More to the point he was hosting one this very night at a restaurant in a less-desirable neighborhood of the District. Liam knew the place. It was not far from his house. He grabbed his camera and headed out.

The restaurant was on a one-way street at the corner of a block of row houses. It was a brightly lit oasis among drab buildings. He found a parking spot just around the corner where he would have a good angle to capture the faces of those who entered the place with his long lens.

Nixon was the first to arrive in his government car. He was an average-sized guy dressed formally in a dark suit, white shirt, and the kind of blue tie you see congressmen wear on TV. His driver took the car off to some unknown parking place. Others arrived by taxi. Liam wondered how they were going to leave. There would be no cruising taxis in this neighborhood. A total of seven others showed up, some of whom Liam recognized. There was Senator Solomon from California, who had cried on TV a few days earlier as he criticized the president-elect's nomination for Attorney General; Senator Frank from the Midwest; Congressman Murray from Manhattan; outgoing cabinet member Kerr; and the flaming liberal congresswoman from San Francisco, whose name was Hahn, and had a reputation as a big-time fund raiser. He got good photos of the others. A little more research for Sean.

The meeting lasted over two hours. He took a couple of photos of the group of seven as it assembled on the sidewalk outside the front door. In a matter of minutes, a van showed up and collected the group, except for Nixon. He stepped out a few minutes later with a companion that Liam had not photographed. Hurriedly, he got the camera back into action and captured the pair getting into Nixon's car. The guy must have been waiting for Nixon inside the restaurant before anyone arrived. Liam waited fifteen minutes after Nixon left to see whether any other unknowns would emerge. None did.

Back at his house, Liam loaded the photos of the unknowns onto his computer and emailed them to Sean with a plea for a quick response on the identities of the subjects.

Early the next morning, Liam got a call from an unknown number. He answered it. The distorted voice said, "We see that your daughter is back in New York. It's much easier to have access to her there. What progress have you made on the project?"

Liam responded, "If you wanted to piss me off, you've succeeded. You know the consequences of bothering her. Mr. Carson will be first in line. Let's talk about how I'll get paid for this project."

"The money will be transferred to your account after the job is done."

"Do you think I'm a fuckin' idiot? I want half now. A Christmas present, call it. There will be a new account at the bank in the islands. I'll email you the details."

The voice on the other end of the line repeated Liam's question. "Do you think I'm a fuckin' idiot?" His anger sounded comical through the electronics. "We will set up the account at a bank of our choosing and text you the information. Meantime, we'll see what kind of down payment is appropriate."

"Half up front," rejoined Liam, but then he realized he was talking to a dead phone.

If it wasn't Carson who made the call, Carson now had a target on his back, Liam thought. *I had better play Santa in a hurry, or there may be only a dead body to visit.*

Liam looked at his watch. Without any new messages from Matt, Liam concluded Carson would be at the office by now. As safe as he could be, Liam decided to get some breakfast at the diner.

"Well," said Mary as he took his usual stool, "I thought I'd scared you off."

"I'm hard to scare. Just had some urgent business to take care of."

"I thought you were retired."

"So did I."

Mary laughed. "None of my business, eh?"

He had to smile. "I thought I was being more diplomatic than that."

"Maybe I'm just being sensitive to the vibe you're giving off. The usual?"

"Yeah." *Maybe there would be no chat today.*

When she brought his pancakes, she asked, "Tell me, Jerry, are you Catholic?"

Okay. I am wrong about chat, but this seems harmless. "Mary, did you ever know an Irish lad who was not brought up Catholic?"

"But you don't go to Mass now. Why?"

"That's a long story, Mary. Let's just say that life got in the way."

"Another thing that's none of my business? I just wanted to tell you that I did say a prayer for you the other day as I said I would."

"Thank you. I appreciate that."

She was silent, just sitting there, looking him in the eye. He knew that silence was a wonderful interrogation technique, especially if the subject was a little nervous. *Am I nervous, or do I just want the conversation to continue? Where the hell had my trade craft gone?*

"Mary, a lot of people fall away as they grow up. The rules and the fears they were indoctrinated with as kids just don't seem pertinent anymore. Didn't you feel some of that when your husband was killed, at least?"

"No. I found I needed the faith more than ever."

Liam was quiet for a moment and then said, "I guess you got more than the rules and the fear when you were a kid."

She asked, "Are you going to Mass on Christmas?"

"Haven't given that a moment's thought."

"It's a real celebration over at the U. If you're willing, I'll take you with me."

He was struck dumb and choked on a mouthful of coffee. *What the hell is going on here?* When he could talk again, he said, "I don't know. I have this business to take care of."

"On Christmas?"

"Believe me, these guys don't care about any holiday. Are you trying to save my soul?"

Again came those long moments of silence, her eyes boring into his. "Not really. That's up to you, but all Christians are supposed to help their neighbors to find their feet, as we say. To be honest, my daughter is spending the week on St. John with her roommate and that family, and I really don't want to go to Mass on Christmas alone. Something told me you might be able to appreciate a little companionship."

There she goes again, psychoanalyzing me. He shrugged. "Well, you got me there. My daughter got home from Africa yesterday. She's probably somewhere in New York, but I don't even know where she'll be on Christmas. She's pretty much put me out of her life since her mother died, and I have just let that happen."

"That's sad. Even more reason to come with me."

Liam laughed. "If I do go, the church might be struck by lightning."

"That's how St. Paul got turned around. I'll meet you outside this place at nine o'clock. It's about half an hour's walk."

Unable to think of a single word to say, he gulped the last mouthful of coffee and got up, his eyes locked on hers. He grunted, "Okay." They shook hands, and he left.

He walked home, wondering what the hell he was doing. The sight of his front door put him back into focus: Carson!

Chapter Eleven

Liam put some tools in a battered sample case, donned his "obese" disguise, and went to await Carson's return from the office. The street was busier this afternoon, with people coming home early from work and from last-minute shopping. He had a little trouble finding a parking place from which he could intercept Carson before he got to the door of the brownstone. He settled on one and hunkered down to wait.

Carson came down the street from behind Liam just as dark was falling. Liam stepped out of his car about fifteen feet before Carson got even with it. He said, "Mr. Carson, we have to talk."

Carson said, "Who the hell are you?" and started to push past him. He stopped when he felt the nozzle of Liam's Glock 19 in his ribs. He backed up a step and studied Liam, then he said, "Shit."

Liam said, "Right, Mr. Messenger Man. This is really an opportunity for a win-win conversation. It might even save your life."

"You can't shoot me right here on the street with all these people around."

There were still a few people still hurrying down the street, but Liam answered, "In my experience, the safest place to kill somebody is in the street. All the possible witnesses will just scream and run for their lives. They never see the guy who pulled the trigger. Let's just go up to your apartment and talk."

Carson grunted something and then shrugged. They walked to the front door of his apartment house and entered. Two men in dark coats were sitting on the chairs in the foyer. One smiled and said, "Jim, glad you got home a little early today. Good to see you."

Carson froze. "Harry, what are you doing here? Haven't seen you in years."

"Just came to discuss a possible opportunity, but I see you're busy."

Carson looked at Liam, who said, "Yes, we have some urgent business. Mr. Carson has some problems with the IRS. I'm his accountant." He gestured with the sample case as if that explained everything."

After looking at his partner, Harry said, "Okay, Jim, we'll check back with you later. Wouldn't want to put off your getting square with those bastards." The two buttoned their coats and went out.

They took the elevator up to Carson's apartment. The big man was pale and hardly breathed on the trip. Once inside, Liam asked, "Who's Harry?"

"A guy I met in Iraq five years ago. Harry Bennet. He worked for Blackwater then, guarding big shots. I'm told he's freelancing now."

A light went off in Liam's head. *Harry Bennet was the guy who hired the PI in New York to follow Cathryn.*

Liam asked, "Did you call me earlier today?"

"No, why?"

"Whoever called now knows that I know who their messenger man is. I suspect that Harry is here to prevent you from telling me who that might be."

Carson got even paler and said, "I need a drink." He went to the bar, ignoring Liam.

Liam looked out the window to see Harry and his partner talking on the sidewalk opposite the building. After a moment, the partner walked back across the street and disappeared from Liam's view. Harry went to sit in a blue Ford about twenty feet up the street from the house.

Carson took a big slug of his whiskey and shouted at Liam. "I should just tear your head off right now."

Liam replied in a businesslike voice, "That would be a dumb thing to try."

Carson threw the glass at Liam and charged. Despite still being encumbered by his fluffy jacket, Liam took a quick step to his left, slipped his left arm under Carson's right armpit, and pivoted, using Carson's own momentum to trip him and toss him across the room. Before Carson could recover, Liam was on him, cranking his right arm up behind his back until his hand touched his shoulder blade. Carson screamed with pain and tried to toss Liam off his back, but the twisting and bucking only exacerbated the pain. As the man lay still, moaning, Liam said, "I can help save your life if you give me what I need to know."

"I don't know anything, I swear," croaked Carson.

"Bullshit. Now I'm going to let you up, you're going to sit in a chair, and we're going to talk." With that, he jumped up and backed away.

Carson slowly straightened his arm, used his left one to push himself to his knees, and glared at Liam. After a moment, Liam took a light armchair from the wall and slid it over to the humiliated big man, who used the back of the chair to pull himself to his feet.

"Just sit right there, and don't try anything else stupid." Liam slipped out of the oversized coat and reclaimed his sample case. "One of the things I did in my past life was interrogate hostile prisoners. Some of the techniques we used are no longer legal in this country, but I still have the appropriate tools." He gestured toward the sample case. "We can do this the easy way or otherwise, but you are going to tell me everything you know or suspect about these 'patriotic men' who want the incoming president killed."

Carson hugged his right arm to his side and looked bug-eyed at the case. He said, "Look, I just do what Nixon tells me to do. I don't know more than that."

"Why did Nixon have you go to talk to the Irish mob leader in Boston?"

"He was told that they could help us bring down a growing Russian mob in Boston. To him, every crook is a terrorist."

"Did they help?"

"Not really. To them, it was just a turf war. They felt they could take care of it, but I talked him into letting the FBI take over. Two days later, we bagged the top Rusky and his bodyguard."

"And the trip to Williamsburg. What was that about?"

"Damned if I know."

"Have you been poking around into Nixon's private meetings with congressmen and others?" asked Liam.

That stopped Carson cold. "What do you know about those?"

"Never mind what I know. Have you?"

"The current director has been on my case to find out what Nixon was doing that he wasn't telling the director about. He said an FBI agent ought to be able to find out something if he was capable."

"So what did you find out?"

"What do I get out of this if I tell you that?"

"As I said, I might be able to save your life. If you know as much as I think you do, you might even turn out to be a hero. But those two hoods are waiting for you outside. If I leave, they'll come to see you. If they know the whole story, they'll leave me alone. If they don't, they may try to eliminate a witness to your kidnapping or murder. That would be a big mistake on their part, but it would only postpone your problem. If we leave together, I don't know what they might do, and no doubt backup is on the way. That's too big a risk to take. I have an idea about how to get you out of here to a safe place, but you have to earn that opportunity."

Carson contemplated the situation for a moment. Then he said, "Nixon has been meeting secretly with a number of people ever since the election. He initiated those meetings, but I don't know if they were his idea or if he was following someone else's orders. He would have his driver get him to the place early and then leave so he wouldn't see who came after. I bribed the driver to find out where the meetings were, but that's all he knew. There were six meetings in all."

"How many before he sent you to visit me?"

"Two."

"They met before the election?"

"Once."

That tasty tidbit caused Liam to pause. *This whole plot is somebody's plan B.*

"Were you the guy who tracked me down?"

"No. Nixon must have had other people tracking you. Two days before the game, he called me into the office, gave me all the information about you and your daughter, and handed me a plane ticket to San Francisco. He told me that you would be hostile but would know someone would be contacting you at the game. I was just a messenger, like I said. I don't know where he got all the information about who you were and what you were doing."

"Do you think Nixon is the mastermind of this thing?"

"I don't know. He fiercely protects everything American. He didn't want to give up his job as director because of the danger he saw for the country, but I never heard him say anything about who was running for president."

"Let's go back to the meetings. During this period, do you know if any of the following people met with Nixon? Senators Solomon and Frank, Congresswoman Hahn, and outgoing Secretary Kerr."

Carson said, "I've never seen any of them at the office, but then I've been out a lot."

"Do you think Nixon is shipping you out on a bunch of wild goose chases to keep things secret?"

"Maybe. I don't know. He does seem a little more circumspect these days, but he's always kept things close to his vest."

"Do you know anything more about these meetings or anything else Nixon is up to?"

"No. There seem to be more frequent meetings in the last two weeks, though."

"Do you know where he lives? His email address? His phone number? The names of any friends, clubs, that sort of shit?"

"No. Never had any contact with him outside the office. Look, I've told you all I know. You said you'd get me out of here."

Liam took a minute to digest all that he had learned and contemplate how it fit in with what he already knew. Then he said, "Okay. You're a witness to the fact that Nixon authorized you to demand that I kill the president-elect before he is sworn in. We need to keep you safe so you can testify. Tell me about this building."

"There's one other exit at the back. It's one of those fire exit–only doors with a crash bar and alarm."

"There's no way anybody can get into the building that way?"

"Right."

"There's got to be a fire alarm. Does it ring at the fire station?"

"No. You have to call 911."

"What happens if there's a power failure?"

"There's no backup generator or anything. Everything just shuts down except the emergency lighting at the exit and stairs."

"How about a hidey-hole in the basement or attic or under the stairs?"

"None that I know of."

"You need to find a safer place to live. Let's do a little reconnaissance. Take off your coat and drape it over the back of the chair."

They found nothing helpful. Liam asked, "How's your heart?"

"Yeah. Perfect physical only a month ago."

Liam gestured toward his sample case. "One of the tricks we used to play on prisoners was to inject them with a chemical that caused their hearts to beat frantically. We told them we'd give them the antidote if they talked before their heart burst. In reality, the chemical gets metabolized in about an hour, and their heart rate returns to normal all by itself. I could give you a shot of that stuff, call 911 to get the EMTs to ambulance you to the hospital, and sneak you out the back door to a safe house in about an hour. How does that sit with you?"

Carson stood with his mouth open. "Who are you? How can you get a safe house?"

"I still have some connections. How do you think I found you? It won't be the Ritz, and there will be a lot of guys asking you questions. It won't be fun. I'd be happy to listen to any better ideas."

Carson got up and went to the window. He shuddered when he saw a man in a black SUV talking through the passenger-side window to the man in the blue Ford Harry had gotten into.

The guy then drove down the block and found a place to park the big SUV.

Carson said, "We could just wait for a while and see if they fall asleep. Stakeout is boring."

"We could try that. Of course, they could get impatient and just bust in here to get you. I assume you have your service weapon. How about a vest?"

"It's at the office."

"Well, it's just a question of how many of them come after you. I don't like the odds."

There was a long moment of silence, and then Carson said, "Okay, I'll try your chemical."

Liam prepared his needle and injected the chemical into a vein just as a heroin addict might. Then he took Carson's wrist and monitored his pulse. Soon, it began to speed up. Liam dialed 911 and shouted for an ambulance.

Chapter Twelve

An ambulance from the Georgetown University Hospital arrived in less than ten minutes. Liam met them at the front door and led them upstairs, where they found Carson sweating profusely with his heart racing. The EMTs bundled him onto a gurney and rushed him into the back of the ambulance. Liam slipped out of the building while all this was going on.

Liam arrived at the emergency entrance of the hospital about twenty minutes after he left the apartment. To his surprise, no one at the place had heard of James Carson. Everyone seemed overwhelmed by the talk of an accident.

After a few minutes of eavesdropping and probing, he learned what he never expected and did not want to hear: the ambulance carrying Carson had been T-boned by an SUV, both EMTs had been injured, and Carson was nowhere to be found. Liam was shell-shocked.

He raced to the site of the accident on foot. The ambulance was up on the sidewalk at the corner of Wisconsin Avenue and P. Street jammed against a utility pole, its back door standing open. The nose of a black SUV was embedded in the passenger-side door, steam still rising from the engine hood. One of the original EMTs walked unsteadily toward a second ambulance. Two women carried the other strapped to a backboard. Yellow tape surrounded the whole intersection.

A few bystanders gawked at the scene.

Liam worked his way over to one of the uniformed policemen guarding the scene. "I'm a friend of the guy who was in the ambulance. I'm told he has just disappeared. Is that right?"

"Who are you?" asked the cop.

"My name is Sweeney. I was at his apartment when he had the attack, and they got him into the ambulance. How could he just disappear?"

"You got me, Buddy. Nobody saw nothin'. Let's talk to the detective over there." He led Liam over to a frazzled-looking, gray-haired man with a notebook, who looked as if he would rather be anywhere else than at the scene of a crazy accident a day before Christmas that was bound to screw up his holiday.

"Who are you?" asked the detective.

"My name is Sweeney. The guy in the ambulance was James Carson. We were working together at his apartment when his heart started racing, and I called 911. There's no trace of him?"

"Slow down, Sweeney. You were working on what?"

"Carson is FBI."

The detective looked as if he were going to scream. "Oh, that's great news, just fuckin' great. What were you working on?"

"You know I can't talk about that."

"Why were you involved with an FBI guy?"

"Sometimes I provide information that helps Carson."

"You're his snitch?"

"I prefer to call myself a consultant, a friend even. Where is he? Is he dead?"

"I have no idea. All I know is that there was nobody in the ambulance except the EMTs when a uniform got here. The one in the back with the patient was knocked out in the crash, and when he woke up, the gurney was there, but the guy was gone. Do you have any idea who this Carson was working with at the FBI?"

"Hell no."

Just then, a uniform showed up with an older lady in tow. "She saw something from her window," said the cop.

Liam listened in. "There were two SUVs," she said. "The second one came right after the first. Three guys got out. One helped the driver of the first SUV, and the other two dragged the patient out of the ambulance kicking and screaming and forced him into the back of the second SUV."

"We need to talk some more," the detective said to Liam. "Just hang out over there for a few minutes while I finish up here."

Liam slipped back under the tape and studied the scene in more detail. Carson had been carried off bodily by Harry or one of his buddies. *To an early grave or to be set up as a scapegoat?* Liam slipped away from the site like a ghost, wondering where the hell to look for James Carson…or his body. He felt guilt and a fear that he was losing it. There was no way he would have let Carson go off in that ambulance alone when he was at the top of his game. *Is that what I thought this was—a game?* He felt totally detached from the world about to celebrate Christmas. He was exhausted. He went home, hoping to sleep.

*****

Sean Doyle called at 7:00 a.m. on Christmas Eve. "I see you fucked up with Carson last night."

"What do you mean?"

"The kidnapping from the ambulance is the number one headline this morning. You had to be involved somehow."

"There were two mercenaries waiting at his apartment when we got there last night. I was trying to help him escape."

"Yeah, and your monumental ego got in the way again. I can guess what you did, and it's clear you totally underestimated the opposition. Why didn't you call for help?"

"I promised you I wouldn't get you involved in any messy stuff."

"Right, but here I am. Did you get anything out of Carson?"

"Yeah."

"I'm going to lunch with my family at noon today. I'll pick you up in front of Mahoney's in an hour. We'll see if we can figure out a way to shovel out of this shit heap you've got us into." Then he hung up.

*****

It was one forty-five before Sean picked Liam up. "Now give me the whole damn story."

Liam sighed. He had debated this with himself as he tossed and turned last night. He had to admit he needed help, especially if Nixon, or whoever decided to involve Cathryn. "You know that Carson was the messenger demanding that I murder a prominent citizen. That citizen was the president-elect."

"I guessed that. Any particular reason given?"

"Just who he is. Carson can testify that Nixon assigned him to deliver the message. Beyond that, he knows that Nixon has had a half-dozen secret meetings with congresspeople and others but doesn't know what they were about or who was there. Thanks to your Matt, I saw the group at one of the meetings and recognized several. You were going to find the names of the others for me."

"I did that. The guy who left with Nixon that night was the chief agitator for Greenpeace, Jacob Keller. He's organized things like harassing Japanese whaling ships in the Pacific and shutting down a unit at the DuPont chemical plant in New Jersey with human shields. One of the other two was a lawyer from the ACLU and then Senator Richardson from Virginia. Do you have any info on what they talked about?"

"No, but General Townsend knows Richardson. Maybe she can find out something. Meantime, I'm concerned that the Carson thing may mean they start to hassle Cathryn."

Sean said, "Yeah, I've been thinking about that. Perhaps it's best we provide Cathryn with some Irish lads for local bodyguards."

"Irish lads?"

"Call them what you will. I have a connection with a group of Irish tough guys from Breezy Point in Queens, some of whom may have overstayed their visas. Their leader owes me big time. They will do as I ask."

After a moment's thought, Liam said, "She doesn't have to know but needs to be able to tell the good guys from the bad ones."

"Tell her anybody wearing an Irish tweed cap is a friend."

"They won't be able to arrest anybody."

"No, but they can discourage any unfriendly actions."

"Sounds like a plan. I'll make sure she understands. I'm going to have to create a legend about my activities anyway. She's had it with being kept in the dark."

Sean changed the subject. "Now we need a plan for Carson and Nixon. Got any ideas?"

"I'd love to get Nixon in a private room. Do you know where he lives?"

"Yeah, I'm sure you'd like that, but Nixon is not urgent. He's not going anywhere. You and Matt can keep an eye on him. What was the name of the merc who came to see Carson?"

"Carson called him Harry, Harry Bennet. He met the guy in Iraq. Harry was working for Blackwater at the time. Now he may be freelancing."

"He definitely sounds like an international threat, don't you think?"

"And therefore a subject for the CIA to investigate, I assume."

Sean drove around a corner, and low and behold, they were in front of Mahoney's again. He said, "Get hold of Cathryn and tell your lies. And no more fuckin' heroics, understand? I'll call you tomorrow sometime."

"Yeah, Sean. I got the message. I'm sorry you got dragged into this."

"I'll bet. Say Merry Christmas to Cathryn."

Chapter Thirteen

Liam got to the diner about nine ten on Christmas morning.

Mary was waiting. She greeted him with, "I was beginning to think you chickened out on me."

"There was at least one time in my life when I should have done that, but not today."

"Good. Let's go. It will take about half an hour, and I don't want to miss the carols before Mass." With that, she strode off at a pace Liam struggled to keep up with without jogging.

Well, I'll get some exercise today anyway, he thought.

They reached the "chapel" at Catholic U. at nine forty as a large choir was serenading the arriving crowd with "Silent Night" on the steps of what looked like a major cathedral.

"This is the chapel?" he asked.

"It is the Catholic University of the US of A." She said, "Let's go in and get a seat before it fills up."

There must be a lot more Catholics around than I ever thought.

Inside, the pews in the cavernous nave were already more than half full, with a crowd full of Christmas sweaters, laughing kids, and a few women in fur coats and fancy hats.

When Mass started, Liam found he remembered when to stand, sit, and kneel and the words to a couple of the Christmas hymns but didn't do more than whisper as the congregation blasted out the lyrics with enthusiasm. As they stood for the Our Father, Mary took his hand. He almost flinched, but then he saw most of the other people doing the same and relaxed…a little.

A personal crisis came just after the Our Father when the priest invited everybody to share a sign of peace. Amid a lot of handshaking, hugging, and kissing, Mary whispered in his ear, "May God give you peace, Jerry," and kissed his cheek. Liam almost crapped his pants. He couldn't wait to get out of there but had to wait for the crowd to go to Communion and sit through several more hymns before that was possible.

Outside, he asked, "What is all that 'sign of peace' stuff? I never heard of that."

"It has been a long while since you've been to Mass. It's a little ritual aimed at building community among Catholics. We do it all over the world these days."

Liam said, "I was surprised at how much I remembered, but some of it was all new."

"You seem to have survived okay. And there was no lightning."

"Yeah. Let's go get something to eat."

"I'll cook breakfast."

"Er, no. You've worked hard enough for today."

"You've had enough of me for today, have ya?" she asked.

There she goes again. "No. I just thought it would be nice if you got served some food instead of the other way around."

"Okay. There's a MacDonald's in the next block."

"Cut it out."

They found a fancy-looking diner a few blocks away with a large sign in the window advertising a family Christmas dinner, but it was early enough, so they were well ahead of any crowd and could get breakfast.

While they waited for their food, he asked, "Have you heard from your daughter?"

"She called this morning. They were on a beautiful beach by the Caribbean Sea. I doubt she went to Mass this morning. Her roommate is not Catholic, Christian, but not Catholic. I hope they went to some kind of service."

"Well, at least you heard from her. Mine is either out running or sitting in a hotel room someplace."

"Have you called her?"

"Not yet. I will right after we finish."

The food came, and they finished the meal talking about the Washington Redskins and the new president. They parted outside with a handshake and a smile, and Liam turned to the business of the day.

Liam called Cathryn's cell phone at about noon. "Merry Christmas," he said, hoping for a civil reply.

"What do you want? It's Christmas. I'm going to a friend's house for dinner tonight."

"We need to talk. How about tomorrow morning?"

"Where are you?"

"DC."

"Why?"

"Working on the problem I need to talk to you about. Ten o'clock at the hotel, okay?"

After a long moment, he got a one-word reply in a voice that screamed of reluctance. "Okay." There was nothing further to say for either of them.

Sean called while Liam was driving to Manhattan more to check in on what he was doing than any other reason. He did give Liam Nixon's home address and said that the Irish boys would arrive at the hotel tomorrow and mount a twenty-four-hour watch.

Liam said, "I'll introduce myself if I see one."

"You'll see one. When will you be back in DC?"

"Tomorrow evening."

"Then I won't have to worry about you undertaking any heroics until then. That's my Christmas present."

Liam ended the call with, "You're welcome."

*****

The traffic going back into New York City was horrendous on Christmas night. Liam had enough at Exit 14 on the NJ Turnpike. He turned off, drove into Newark airport, and took a room at the Marriott Airport Hotel. He could take the train to Penn Station in Manhattan in the morning and walk to Cathryn's hotel.

Before going to see Cathryn the next morning, he called the general. He was greeted enthusiastically. "Ah, Mr. Sweeney, you saved me a call. I wanted you to know that your characterization of the Linonian Society as a toothless gaggle of gossiping old women provoked a very angry response. This was particularly true for a retired Marine Corps colonel who had spent two tours in Vietnam and was wounded. The group decided that the first thing they would do would be to find out who Jerry Sweeney really was."

"Have you had any luck?"

"Not a lot. You seem to be like a shell corporation: a name but no substance. We are, however, working our connections very energetically."

"Well, a group of rich, supposedly patriotic men has managed to find out who I am and are trying to force me to do something that smells rotten. I'm trying to root out the key player in the group and end the plot."

"What kind of plot are we talking about?"

"As they say in the spy movies, if I told you, I'd have to kill you. But you may be able to help me unravel the puzzle if you want a project."

"Mr. Sweeney, we're not likely to commit to helping a mystery man with some mystery project."

Liam contemplated the situation a moment and then decided he really could use their help. "Let me save you some effort by filling you in on some of my background. As you have discovered, Jerry Sweeney is the name I'm currently using in my attempt to live what's left of my life under the radar. I am a retired CIA operative, a very special operative. If some of the things our group did reach the public domain these days, there would be hell to pay. I'm sure your marine colonel has a few secrets as well."

"That's quite a folktale."

"Yes, but you can verify the essence of it by calling a man named Sean Doyle at Langley."

"Another Irishman. Is he a cousin or something?"

"I understand your being skeptical. Sean is much more than a cousin. He and I were teammates for ten years in what passed for the trenches in the spook business. He's doing what he can to help me on this."

"And what exactly is this?"

"These 'patriotic' men want me to assassinate a prominent citizen this month. They are threatening my daughter if I refuse."

The general was quiet for a long moment and then said, "And your friend Sean will verify all this?"

"First, he'll have a heart attack that you know all that. If he survives that, he'll confirm my story."

"What is it you think we can do to help you?"

"Your friend Senator Richardson has participated in at least one secret meeting organized by Angus Nixon. The group included some other congresspersons and a couple of outsiders. There were at least six such meetings, but I know the attendees of only one. I need to know what that meeting was about. Can you probe that for me?"

"Tell you what, Mr. Sweeney, or whatever your name is, if your story checks out with Doyle, Miles and I will have a meal with Jesse and see what he's willing to say."

"Soon, General, soon."

"You've got balls, Sweeney. I like that. Talk to you soon."

*****

Liam checked his emails before getting on the train. There was an alert from Matt. Nixon was having another secret meeting tonight back in DC. He'd have to get back for that.

He knocked on Cathryn's door just before ten. She was again dressed in her jog suit when she opened the door and got right down to business. "All right, what's so important?"

Liam slipped out of his coat and sat in the desk chair without being invited. "This will take a few minutes, so you better sit down too."

She frowned but sat on the edge of the bed in her "low overhead" hotel room.

"We might as well jump right into the details. My career with the government involved special operations for the CIA. Not all the things I did would have been legal if our government hadn't ordered them. What details do you want to know?"

She thought about that for a long moment. "I want to know why you didn't come home for your wife's funeral. It was bad enough she died in a terrible accident, but to have to bury her alone was more than I could bear."

"I've thought about that a lot since then. It didn't take long to realize that I had sold my soul to some guys who had none. I realized I had to retire."

"What exactly were you involved in when Mom died?"

"It was the critical moment of a month-long project."

"The critical moment to do what?"

Liam took a very deep breath and then said, "Assassinate the man who had caused the death of seven of our field agents."

Cathryn's mouth dropped open. She gasped. "You assassinated him?"

"Yes."

It became so quiet in the room that Liam could hear himself breathe. Cathryn stood, hands on hips. Then she asked, "How many people have you killed?"

"I had no reason to keep count."

"You are an evil monster!"

"No. I was a naive fool who bought the line of shit they gave me that I was doing my patriotic duty. My father was a soldier. It was in my genes, I guess."

She ran to the door and jerked it open. "I hate you. Get out."

Liam got up, clamped his hand on her arm, shoved the door closed, and dragged her back to the bed. "Sorry, Cathryn, you don't get off that easy. You are in danger because of me and need to take serious precautions. Some deluded assholes are trying to force me out of retirement to murder a prominent citizen. They have threatened your life if I fail at the job. I will find them and end the plot, but in the meantime, you will have bodyguards and can go nowhere without them. Think of yourself as the first lady."

"There is no fuckin' way I'm going to submit to that. If I get killed, it will serve you right. Both of your women died because of you."

Liam had to smile. "That's what I might say in the same situation. I guess some of my genes are in there. Get this straight, Lady. The alternative is for me to have some guys snatch you up and take you off to a safe house until I catch these bastards."

"You can't do that!"

Liam just laughed. "The bodyguards won't look like the Secret Service. Get real, take a deep breath, and we'll go downstairs and meet them."

She tossed her head and stood, hands on her hips again. She said, "I guess I don't have much choice with a murderer giving me orders."

"I can see you planning to escape them already. You won't be able to, so forget it."

They went down to the lobby, where Liam greeted a young man dressed in a beige turtleneck sweater, jeans, and tweed jacket and cap. He introduced the man to Cathryn. "This is Brian. He and his team will wear this uniform. They are Irishmen through and through, loyal, stubborn, and dedicated to the task. Kinda handsome, too, don't you think?"

Brian doffed his cap and did a little bow. "My lads will be with you any time you're not in your room and be available in the hall outside when you are. We'll need to know your schedule a day ahead in case we need to make different arrangements. We can clean up pretty well for special occasions." He smiled a smile that would charm any lady into taking his arm, but all he got was a scowl from Cathryn.

Still smiling, he said, "Aye, and if you want to fight us, I'll just have to put more lads on the job. We'll do our best to interfere with your life as little as possible."

"Where are the rest of your lads?"

"They're around. Look for the caps."

She did and saw two in the coffee shop and another smoking a cigarette outside. She huffed. "You've got the whole IRA here."

She turned and strode toward the elevators. Liam saluted Brian and followed her.

Back in her room, the conversation was brief. Cathryn stormed into the bathroom and slammed the door. Liam immediately opened her purse, grabbed her wallet, and slipped a disc about the size of a quarter behind one of her credit cards. He was startled when he heard her shout, "What the hell are you doing with my purse?"

"Err, I was looking for my phone."

"It's over on the top of the TV. I forgot to charge it on the trip home."

"That's probably the smartest thing you could have done," said Liam. "I think they've been tracking the phone, thinking I have it. I don't want them tracking you now that you're here."

"The big, bad boogeymen man story again."

"Cathryn, the guys who are doing this are ugly bastards. They've already kidnapped my only witness, and he worked for the FBI. Do this by the numbers. I should have this over in a week."

"Are you going to kill them too?"

"If I need to." He turned and left.

Chapter Fourteen

He got back to the Marriott at about one o'clock. He collected his bag, and as he was leaving the room, alarm bells went off in the back of his brain. A man was approaching from his left and another from the right. They looked casual but moved purposefully. Liam left his bag in the path of the man from the right. The man on the left, who was closer and reaching behind his back, said, "Ah, Mr. Martin. I'm glad we caught up with you before you left."

Liam took a quick step toward the man and drove his right foot into the man's groin, dropping him to his knees. Then he whirled and smashed his elbow into the face of the other man, catching him just under his nose and stunning him. A left hook put him on the floor and caused him to drop the gun in his hand. The first guy was struggling to his feet. Liam pivoted on his left leg, swinging his right leg in a whirling kick to the man's head. Liam picked up the gun and slammed the butt into the second man's head. Both attackers were down for the count. *Yeah. I still have it.*

Liam searched them but found nothing except a bunch of plastic restraints. *Should not have been so fast to put them out,* he thought. *If I didn't have to sprint back to DC to see who shows up at Nixon's meeting, I would stay until they wake up, but Nixon must be my priority.* He bound their hands and feet, dragged them into his room, and put the "do not disturb" sign on the door. He went down the stairs to the lobby and saw no one watching the elevator or the car valet kiosk. He pressed a twenty into the valet kid's hand and said, "Give me my key and point me to the general area where you put the car. No point in your going out in this freezing rain if you don't need to." The kid was delighted to take the deal.

Liam thought about the developments as he tailed an eighteen-wheeler down the turnpike. His two attackers were happy to catch up with him. They could only have found him at the hotel because someone was tracking his credit cards, which he seldom used. They had to have a warrant to do that, or maybe the FBI could do it sub rosa. Whoever it was had to be federal. Nixon?

These thoughts led him to consider what he needed to do with his original cell phone now that it was back in the states. That was the only number his tormentors had to reach him, but he didn't want them to know where he was any more now than he did a month ago, nor did he want them to know where he lived. He needed to plug it in and leave it somewhere that would tell them nothing or, better yet, lead them astray. Food for thought on the long ride back to DC.

Liam got to the restaurant where Nixon's secret meeting was to take place half an hour before it was scheduled to start. It was in a marginal neighborhood well away from the usual water holes frequented by government folks. Still, many of the houses on the side streets were festooned with Christmas lights, giving a cheery look to the area.

Nixon arrived soon after Liam. He was without a hat, and his bald skull shone in the lights of the neon sign in the restaurant's window. As before, his driver left before the others started arriving by cab. Senator Richardson was one of the six men and one woman who showed up.

All were members of Congress whom Liam recognized, but he took their pictures anyway.

After an hour, Richardson came out alone. He stood at the door as if waiting for a car to pick him up, but none came. After ten minutes, he was pacing the sidewalk. No one joined him.

Liam got out of his car, rooted in his trunk for his Red Sox cap, and went to talk to Richardson. In his leather jacket, he might have looked like a denizen of the neighborhood. "Hey, mister, do you need some help?"

The scowl on Richardson's face faded a little as he saw Liam. "Are you the Uber driver? What took you so long?"

Liam was tempted to say yes, but he wanted to see how long the meeting would last. He said, "No. I'm a member of the neighborhood watch committee. It's not really a good idea to be standing alone at night around here, especially dressed up like you are."

Richardson looked up and down the street and saw no one and no car coming. "Yeah, Uber might not be too enthusiastic about coming here either. Is there a local cab company?"

Liam said, "Sorry about that. If you want, I'll hang here with you until your car comes."

"How do I know you're not a mugger?"

"If I were, it would be over with by now. What brought you down here this late anyway?"

Without thinking, Richardson said, "A meeting. The guy who organizes them likes to pick out-of-the-way places. I think he's a little paranoid." Then his brain kicked in. "It's no big deal. Uber should be here in a minute." He looked at his phone, got no encouragement, and cursed.

"Are there a bunch of other rich-looking dudes in there still?"

"I suppose they're rich-looking on the outside, but I think they're pretty poor in the brain department."

"Sounds like there was a disagreement."

Richardson looked at him, now fully focused. "It was nothing."

Liam knew the end of an interrogation when he saw it. "Did you have a nice Christmas?" he asked.

"Ha," scoffed Richardson. "With all the panic in the press and protest in the streets about our new president, it's lucky we even noticed Christmas."

Liam probed again. "Obviously, you come from that part of town where people worry about that shit. Up here, we just try to live the best we can." He gestured toward the houses with the Christmas lights.

"That's a blessing. Hold those thoughts. Ah, here comes a car."

Shit, thought Liam. "Let's just make sure it's Uber." He went to the driver's window and checked him out. He gave Richardson a thumbs up, who returned a little salute and got into the car. Liam went back to his car. *Something went on in there that Richardson wanted no part of.*

It was over an hour before the rest of the group came out, still talking and waving their hands around. Nixon admonished the group to tone it down. The van came again to carry the group away. A minute or so later, Nixon's car arrived but was not empty. There was a well-dressed Asian man in it who stepped out of the passenger seat to greet Nixon. They got into the back seat together.

*****

Liam slept in his house that night. He left his original cell phone turned off but plugged it in to charge. He got up early the next morning and called the general.

"Merry Christmas," he said when the general answered the phone.

She answered with, "Ah, Mr. Martin, you saved me a call."

"I see you've talked with Sean. It must have gone well if you know my name."

"Yes, and he gave us a few hints about what you're involved with. It doesn't take much imagination to figure out the worst-case scenario. If that's right, what is it you think we can do to help you?"

"Let me bring you up-to-date on a couple of things. First, Carson has been kidnapped. I fear for his life. I already told you about the secret meetings his boss, Angus Nixon, has been holding. He had another last night. Senator Richardson stomped out the meeting an hour before it was over, fuming. I think Nixon and those meetings are the key to the plot. We need to find out what was discussed and what drove Jesse Richardson out of the last one. Can you do that?"

"Jesse is coming back here today. We will sit down with him as soon as we can do so civilly."

"Great," said Liam. "Meantime, I'm going to glue myself to Nixon. I'm available 24-7."

Nixon lived not far from Maryland University. Liam decided to drop his phone at the apartment in the complex he rented to students. That would give him a chance to see how badly the place was torn up, though he usually had pretty good luck with the tenants he picked.

Nixon's house was a two-story colonial with a stone front and meticulously kept yard in a neighborhood peopled by professors. His car was parked in the driveway, motor running. It was late to go to the office. Something else must be on the agenda.

In a little while, Nixon came out, wrapped in a black overcoat and wearing a matching fedora. He got into the car, and it headed back toward the city. His driver let him off at a coffee shop about two blocks from the Chinese Embassy and drove off. Liam found a place to park on the opposite side of the street, a few doors short of the shop. Five minutes later, the well-dressed Asian man from the night before joined Nixon at a small table near the window. There were only two other customers in the shop at this midmorning hour.

They were served steaming cups and sat back to chat, but soon, the Asian man got agitated. He started gesticulating. Nixon held his finger to his lips in the universal sign for quiet.

The man leaned forward, putting his head very close to Nixon's ear. They talked that way for six minutes by Liam's watch, and then the man emptied his cup, jumped up, and stormed out of the shop. Another piece of research for Sean. Nixon hit a button on his phone and savored what was left in his cup while he waited for his driver. They went to the FBI office.

Liam emailed Sean the photo of the Chinese guy and settled down to see what Nixon did.

The answer was to work until 7:00 p.m. in the office and be driven home. It was interesting that Nixon would be working overtime during a week when lots of FBI agents were on vacation.

He got another call that came through his original cell phone while he sat. Once more, it was an electronically distorted voice that said, "The account is opened at the Bank of the Cayman Islands, account number 137596-1. The first password is *graybeard*. That will let you see the amount in the account, but you will need a second password to take out the money. That will come after the job is done, along with the rest of the money."

Liam snapped, "This is a farce. You can take back the money anytime. You have put up nothing. Go back and think again. I want half up front. I'll be sticking my neck out while you hide behind your voice box." He hung up before the voice had a chance to respond.

He did check to see that the account existed. It did and had a million dollars in it. He called Sean to pass on the information."

The general called the next morning. "We had a drink with Jesse last evening. He's quite concerned about what's being talked about at the meetings but feels it's classified. He was reluctant to talk to us until I described your situation. That helped fit some pieces together in his mind, and he realized we had to share all."

"What were the meetings about?"

"The things discussed escalated over time. The early meetings talked about raising money to litigate the validity of the election. Congresswoman Hahn has a benefactor who was willing to put up a million if others would match. After the litigation failed, Greenpeace offered to lead a consortium that would provide paid rabble-rousers to foment riots. Some of the money went for that. The topic that drove Jesse out of the last meeting was a proposal to set off some flash bangs in Times Square at midnight on New Year's Eve. There was a hint that others would use the chaos as a cover for even more violent action. Your story filled in that gap."

"Did he hear what decision was reached?"

"Nixon gave quite an animated exhortation pleading for the group to prevent the destruction of America's future by stopping the inauguration of this guy at all costs. All the group tolerated the idea of violence. There is no telling what that group may do."

Liam added, "Nixon met with a Chinese guy after the meeting and again off campus yesterday. One thing that happened after that was someone opened an account in my name at a bank in the Cayman Islands with a down payment for the murder."

"Good God," said the general. "This is insane."

"Sean is trying to track down the source of the funds but is not optimistic."

"We'll pass this on to Jesse. He was going to talk with the director of the FBI anyway. This ought to make that happen right away and get scrutiny on Nixon. Has there been any word on Carson?"

"Not yet."

"Keep in touch on any detail. If I were running this, we'd all sit down to make sure we were all on the same page. I'm in this up to my eyeballs. This is treason, and it ain't gonna happen." She slammed down the phone.

Liam could see how she got to be a three-star. He looked at his watch and decided it was time to call Sean.

"Good morning, Sean. Have you got something for me?"

"Yeah. Drop your crusade immediately. The Chinese guy is a staffer at the embassy. The big boys are now all over this like flies on roadkill."

"Great. I'm sure that they'll jump through hoops to prevent bombs in Times Square, but I don't think they'll move too swiftly to protect me and my daughter. Remember the bank account in my name."

"You still have a couple of weeks before it's crisis time. You gotta give them a chance. If you want to come along, I can provide a little distraction tonight."

"What's that?"

"We and the FBI found Harry Bennet and believe Carson is with him."

"Whoa," said Liam. "How did you do that?"

"Fundamentally, Bennet used Carson's credit card at an ATM in Reston. The FBI was looking for him, and locals found the blue Ford in the parking lot at a pretty nice hotel nearby. We're mounting a team to go pick them up. You want to tag along? You should have a chance to get some answers."

"Count me in. Where are you meeting?"

"Be here by four o'clock."

*****

The team was huge, complete with a SWAT squad and observers from both the Reston Police Department and the official FBI. It arrived at the hotel just after dark. The room next to the one Bennet was in had a connecting door to his. The FBI guy slipped a tiny camera under that door to check out the situation. Bennet was sitting in a chair, facing the TV, watching the Duke-UVA college basketball game. Carson seemed to be sleeping on one of the two double beds. Bennet's gun was on the desk in the far corner of the room.

Sean whispered, "All right, let's do this as quietly as we can." He lined up his forces in the hall outside Bennet's door: first, the lead FBI agent, then two SWAT guys, then himself, and last Liam. They slipped the electronic key into the slot and saw the green light come on, and the first four men charged into the room. Harry Bennet was standing next to his chair, his hands in the air. Carson still slept on the bed.

Bennet said nothing and looked perfectly calm. Liam went to check on Carson and found him totally out of it in what looked like a drug-induced coma. There were needle tracks in his arm and paraphernalia on the desk next to Bennet's gun. Sean called the backup medical team in from the parking lot.

After a thorough search, Bennet was handcuffed to a chair. Sean waited until the medical team checked out Carson and pronounced him okay, but clearly zonked out on drugs. There was no chance he was going to sober up anytime soon. They put him in their ambulance and started for the medical center at Langley. The FBI conceded Carson was likely a victim of an international plot.

Sean ushered everyone out of the room, ordering two SWAT guys to guard the door. He and Liam sat down to talk with Bennet. The lead FBI agent stayed as a witness.

Sean said, "Well, Mr. Bennet, we've got you for kidnapping and assault. You're looking at a lot of time unless you help us."

"I've done a lot of work for the government: the FBI, Homeland Security, and others. They'll tell you that this was just part of one of their covert operations. I'm clean."

"Really," said Sean. "Tell us about who you're working for on this case."

"You should know. Don't you guys do your homework?"

"We're not the FBI, Bennet. We're the CIA. Somehow, you're mixed up in a Chinese plot."

That took some of the bravado out of Bennet's face. He said, "I've been doing freelance security for the last several years after I got back from Iraq. For the last three months, I've been on a retainer with the FBI. This was just another of those projects as far as I was concerned."

"Who is your contact in the FBI?" asked Sean.

"I'm not sure. I get instructions over the phone. The money appears in my bank via wire."

"Is the voice on the phone always the same? Would you recognize it?"

"It's the same, but it's garbled with one of those electronic things."

"What made you think that the caller was from the FBI?"

"He said he was—sort of—and he gave me the usual 'secret, in the national interest BS' that they always do. I'm used to dealing with clients over the phone. The test is whether the money shows up."

Sean looked at the FBI guy, who shrugged and turned his hands palms up. Then he said, "So you really don't give a damn who you work for as long as you get paid?" snapped Sean.

"Look, nobody wants to be too public in these operations. I assumed I was working for the FBI. I didn't know who."

"And what exactly did this mysterious voice on the phone ask you to do?"

"They told me Carson had gone rogue and was talking to subversives. They wanted him out of circulation for a while till they could check out how much damage he'd done."

"Did they tell you that you might have to kill him?"

"No, never."

"This must have been a very high priority. You had quite a big team involved in the snatch."

"I have my little network. The simple plan got blown up when he wasn't alone. I called in some backup, and then we had to improvise—fast."

"We'll have the names of your accomplices that night. Now."

"Look, it got crazy when they rushed him off in the ambulance. My guys were just responding to a crisis. They didn't plan for a kidnapping. They didn't plan for a heart attack either. His heart was racing a hundred miles an hour when we got him. I'm surprised he was still alive. I don't know how he did that, but he was clearly trying to avoid me."

Liam smiled. "One of the tricks in my little back bag. Shall I get it out of the car?"

Sean looked at Liam wide-eyed, then it dawned on him. "I don't think we're going to need a lot of physical encouragement to get Mr. Bennet here to tell us all he knows. Give me the names. Now."

"If they have any brains, they're long gone," he said, but he rattled off three names, which Sean wrote down.

Then he asked, "What happened after you got Carson here?"

"He calmed down. A couple of days later, I got instructions to get him hooked on heroin." "Didn't that tip you off that something was fishy?" asked Sean.

"I've been asked to do that kind of thing before," answered Bennet, shifting in his chair.

"By the FBI?" asked Sean.

"Well, no. It was in Iraq."

"And the light still didn't go off in that supposedly sophisticated, worldly brain of yours?"

"Who was I going to contact? I had no way to contact the guy who was calling me."

"You didn't try your other contacts at the FBI?"

Harry looked away. "It had been a while."

"Tell me who you have done work for there in the past. All of them."

Bennet came up with two names.

"That's all?" scoffed Sean. "Seems like your story of big-time relations with the agency is bullshit."

"I could go out and get my little black bag," said Liam.

Bennet almost jumped out of the chair, forgetting he was tethered to it. "Look, I told you all I know. I don't know anything about

Chinese. I don't know anything about what Carson was doing or who they thought he was talking to."

"What about Nixon? Have you talked to Nixon?" asked Liam.

Bennet's face was blank. "Who is Nixon?" he asked.

Sean took the lead again. "How much did you get paid for the snatch and addiction?"

"Twenty grand. I had to pay my team. I put the repairs for the SUV on the debit card I have for expenses."

"Is that why you used Carson's for the dope?"

"Yeah, my expense card is empty."

"Exactly when did the twenty grand get deposited in your account?"

"December sixteenth."

"At what bank?"

Bennet stiffened. "Are you going to confiscate my money?"

"No. I'm going to assume that at least some of the money there was righteously earned for the benefit of the United States. I'm not even going to ask you for the name on the account. I want the name of the bank and the last four digits of the account number."

Bennet weighed his options. If he gave them the information, maybe they would end it here. They couldn't take his money, and he had other accounts. As far as he was concerned, the CIA was a bunch of lying bastards. And he didn't need to be taken somewhere and waterboarded. He looked glum when he said, "I'll give you that info if you turn me over to the FBI."

Sean replied, "In due time, assuming what you tell us checks out."

"It's the British Colonial Bank in the Bahamas. The number ends in 6446."

"Okay, we'll keep you with us for a while to see if there are any holes in your story. If there are, we have a nice quiet place for further conversations, and my friend will certainly have his little black bag with him. Is there anything else you want to tell us?"

"I don't know who the guy is who calls, and I sure don't know nuthin' about any Chinese."

Sean said, "We'll see." He got up, opened the door, and called the guards inside. "Take him to the dungeon. Don't let him talk to anybody. I'll have more instructions in a day or so."

The guards took Bennet off, carefully shackled.

"What are you going to do with the bank account?" asked Liam.

"I'm going to add it to the job I gave Matt with your account information. I need to find out where that money came from and if both came from the same place. Good move mentioning the black bag. The thought seemed to scare the shit out of him. I wonder what kind of stuff he saw in Iraq."

"So now you're feeling sorry for him?"

"No, but he probably thought he was too smart to be used. Now he realizes he's been used and has no idea who's doing it."

Sean drove Liam back to get his car at CIA headquarters. "Get some sleep. I have a feeling that will be in short supply over the course of the next few days."

Liam was willing to try, but when he got home, he found a message from Matt. It said that Nixon had put his house up for sale at a bargain price. *Sounds like he's getting ready to run. Or maybe just retire?* Sleep was slow in coming.

Chapter Fifteen

Though still a little groggy, Liam got up early to stake out Nixon's house. The man's driver did not show. Instead, a van marked "Foreman's Estate Sales" arrived, and a man and a woman carrying clipboards got out. Nixon welcomed them. An hour and a half later, the couple emerged and began to root around in the back of the van. After about fifteen minutes, they posted a white sign about three feet square with big blue letters saying, "Estate Sale," under which was the date: Saturday, January 3, 10 a.m." *Nixon is indeed moving swiftly to end his connection to DC.*

Liam called the general to impart this bit of news and update her on the Carson situation.

She had some news as well. "The FBI has reached out to Greenpeace and convinced them that causing panic in Times Square on New Year's Eve would be 'counterproductive' for the organization's image. They got the message. Several of us are driving to DC tomorrow to meet with Jesse and the FBI director. We would like you and Sean Doyle to attend as well. We need a plan to end this insanity."

Liam replied, "I can't speak for Sean, but I'm not interested. I'm working hard at flying below the radar, remember?"

"You are a key piece of this puzzle and have a lot to lose if the plot can't be destroyed and all its participants scooped up."

"I also have a lot to lose if my identity and some of my past show up as headlines in the *Washington Post*. That would also expose my daughter to a lot of risks as well. No thanks."

The general was quiet for a moment. "I'd be naive if I said there won't be any publicity, but I think we can keep your name out of it."

"Ha!" scoffed Liam. "Why have you inserted yourself into this thing anyway?"

"That's all your fault, Liam. You called the Society a bunch of toothless tigers and then asked for our help. You woke the sleeping tiger."

"Well, go back to sleep. I'm not going to any meeting."

The general said, "One o'clock tomorrow at the marine headquarters at Quantico. Be there." She ended the call.

"Shit, shit, shit," shouted Liam to no one there. *This thing has gotten way out of hand!*

The next morning, as Liam sat in his car down the street from Nixon's house, sipping his coffee, there was a tap on his window. He looked up to see a marine in fatigues with Sergeant Major's stripes on his sleeve and a sidearm on his belt standing there. He took a quick look out the passenger window and saw another marine.

The sergeant major gestured for Liam to lower the window. He did so.

He smiled and said, "Mr. Sweeney, I understand you have a meeting at Quantico at lunchtime. We're here to provide transportation. The traffic can be quite bad at any hour on 95. We wouldn't want you to be late. Please get out of the car. That will be safe here."

Liam sat there with his mouth open for a moment. The marine opened his door. Liam gathered his laptop and got out. *This fuckin' general is turning out to be a major pain in the ass.*

The traffic was bad. They didn't get to Quantico until almost noon. The sergeant led him to a small conference room in the basement of the headquarters building, and they sat down. "My partner will get us some sandwiches."

It was clear that his jailer was not going anywhere until the general and her friends arrived.

Liam nibbled on his sandwich and sipped his coffee while the two marines enjoyed theirs and argued vociferously about whether the Redskins would get to the NFL playoffs. They snapped to attention and saluted when the general and a tall man with eagles on his shoulders—and the craggiest eyebrows Liam had ever seen—entered the room. It seemed as though his eyebrows were longer than the hair on his close-cropped head. Both wore class A uniforms: she of the army, he of the marines. "As you were," she said and then turned to Liam. "Ah, Mr. Sweeney. I'm glad to see you were able to make it."

Liam found himself standing too. He had no idea why and no idea what to say. *Is the Sweeney charade going to stay in place for the whole meeting?*

The next to arrive was Sean, who looked at Liam and struggled to hide his laugh. Then Senator Jesse Richardson and the director of the FBI walked in and bade everyone to sit down.

The marines saluted again and left.

It was not a big conference room. There were only eight wooden chairs at the plain oak table. Even though Liam sat at the far end, he could still reach out and touch the marine colonel, one chair away.

Senator Richardson said, "Sorry to have this meeting in such Spartan accommodations, but we're far less likely to attract attention down here. This meeting is completely off the record." He studied Liam for a full minute and then said, "I remember you from the sidewalk in front of the restaurant, Mr. Sweeney, is it? I suspect you told me a tale about living in the neighborhood."

Liam just shrugged.

The director said, "All right, let's get down to business. Sean, what's with Carson?"

"It's not good. His withdrawal has been very difficult. Our docs have had to strap him down and try their methadone magic to wean him off the poison. It's liable to be weeks before he's fully rational."

"Are you sure you've got the best docs on the case?"

"Director, with all due respect, our guys know a hell of a lot more about this stuff than anybody, but if you want us to call in some consultant you recommend, we'll be happy to."

The director sighed. "He's our only witness to anything. Let's see how it goes for a couple of days, but keep me up-to-date."

"Done," said Sean.

"As I understand it," said the director, "you're trying to track down where the money for the kidnappers came from."

"Yes, and the million dollars deposited in a bank account in... err...Mr. Sweeney's name as a down payment for the murder. In addition to our in-house experts, we've hired an outside hacker to work the question. So far, no progress."

"Mr. Sweeney, tell us about all your contacts with these people since your meeting with Carson," ordered Richardson.

Liam wondered how much to share at this meeting. He decided to spill most of it. "I had a phone call from a man with a distorted voice, demanding to know how my plan to do the job was coming. That was just after the Electoral College voted. I ignored it. A couple of days later, I got another call asking the same question. I diverted that into a demand for a down payment. The bank account got set up after that, but it was structured so I could only verify how much money was there, not take it. I gave Sean the info as he reported."

"A million bucks is a sizable investment in the reality of the scheme," said the marine colonel.

"Yes," said the director, "but if we can't find out who's putting up the money, we don't have anything. Have you had any contact with Nixon, Sweeney?"

"Not that I know of. As I said, the voice on the phone was disguised."

"Yes, but you followed him to a couple of his meetings. Why?" asked the director.

"By that time, I knew that Nixon had ordered Carson to corner me at the football game and demand the assassination."

"How did you find that out? "asked the director.

"I had a chat with Carson just before he was kidnapped."

"And how did you find out about the meetings?" asked Richardson.

Liam looked at Sean, who shook his head ever so slightly. He said, "I have a confidential source."

The colonel said, "Cut the bullshit, Sweeney. Who told you?"

The general put her hand on her comrade's arm. "Easy, John. We're still working in the civil arena."

"Yes," said Richardson, "but I can testify that Nixon gradually got more fired up about preventing the inauguration as legal efforts kept coming up empty. Congresswoman Hahn seemed to have a stomach for violence as well. Nixon never mentioned any contact with the Chinese Embassy."

Liam said, "I saw Nixon and a Chinese drive away from the meeting the night I talked to you and met for coffee the day after. The day after that, the bank account for the down payment was opened."

The colonel said, "So it seems that Nixon got the Chinese to put up Sweeney's down payment."

"That's speculation," declared the director. "In fact, all we have on Nixon, or anybody, is speculation. If I were him, I'd argue that the whole thing was a plot to ensnare somebody he thought might be thinking about an assassination. Maybe he was spreading the word that an assassin was available to see who crawled out of the woodwork."

"I think it was a lot more serious than that," said Liam. "After I got the first phone call, I got a message that two men were following my daughter's group in Africa. I sent Carson an email threatening an unpleasant visit if those guys didn't depart from my daughter's trail. Two days after that, the two were found murdered in their hotel room."

"Who were they?" asked the general.

"I have no idea. I assumed they were meant as a message to me because I didn't return the phone call. Whoever sent them apparently didn't think they would keep their mouths shut if questioned."

"Now we have money and murder," summarized Richardson.

"Let me throw in another tidbit," said Liam. "Nixon's house just went up for sale at a bargain price. He's having an estate sale on Saturday."

The director said, "Well, he's over seventy. Some people retire a lot sooner than that."

"Or maybe he's fleeing the coop and trying not to make headlines about it," said the colonel.

"We still have nothing," said the director. "Sean, find out where the money came from, and maybe we can put these pieces together." He stood up. The meeting was clearly over.

The colonel leaned over and whispered something in the general's ear. They cornered Liam before he could escape.

The general said, "We've decided that a private chat with Mr. Nixon might be helpful for resolving the situation. Would you care to join us?"

"Sure, but how are you going to arrange that?"

"You can leave that to us." She handed him a business card with an address in Springfield written on the back. "We expect to invite him tonight, say seven o'clock. Would that be convenient?"

Liam had to laugh at the formal, businesslike approach to what had to amount to a kidnapping and interrogation. He was all for it.

"See you there."

Chapter Sixteen

Liam found his way through the shopping malls around the exit from 95 and got to the house in Springfield, just about dark. He had his "little black bag" with him. It was a residential neighborhood; many houses were still decorated with Christmas lights. The houses were split levels and Cape Cods with small front lawns. They were a cut above his house in the district but a long way from upscale. He drove around a few of the streets to get a feel for the area and came away with the impression of a working-class enclave that moved around by car, many of which were parked at the curbs of the narrow streets. The one-car garages were clearly overflowing. He found a spot on the opposite side of the street from the house, parked, and settled in to await the arrival of the general's entourage.

At about the same time, Nixon's driver sat in their car with the motor running. He was listening to the news in the executive parking area behind the FBI headquarters. Nixon liked the car warm when he got there, and his arrival was imminent. He was startled when three men in camouflage uniforms suddenly surrounded the car. The guy with the most stripes on his sleeve pounded on his window and gestured for him to get out of the car. When he hesitated, the man pointed a big pistol at him. *A carjacking at FBI headquarters? That's crazy*, he thought, but he got out. The guy with the gun handed him a twenty-dollar bill and said, "Go home. We'll drive your man tonight."

"What the hell is going on?" he said.

Rather than answer, the man nudged him a couple of steps out the driveway with the nozzle of his gun. The driver got the message and scurried away.

A figure in a black overcoat matching the driver's emerged from the shadows and got behind the wheel. It was the general. The men in camo slipped into the shadows she had come from.

Nixon emerged from the building a few minutes later, eased into the back seat, and removed his hat, revealing a narrow head devoid of hair except for a fringe around the side just above his ears. "Ah, nice and warm," he said.

"You haven't seen anything yet," came a voice he didn't recognize from behind the wheel.

"Huh. What?" he said.

Just then, he was joined by the colonel in the back seat and the sergeant major in the front passenger seat.

"What is this?" he demanded in a commanding voice.

"We're going to have a little talk, someplace private," answered the colonel. "Just go with the flow. There's nothing else you can do. Give me your phone, put your hands in your lap, and keep them there."

After a quick analysis of his situation, Nixon complied with a smirk as if he still thought it was a bad joke.

Nixon's car pulled into the driveway of the house Liam was watching a few minutes after seven. It was followed immediately by a nondescript sedan, obviously a rental. A man dressed in camouflage got out of the sedan and opened the door for the general. The rest of the car then emptied. The colonel had a firm grip on Nixon's arm. The group entered the side door of the house. One light flared on the first floor. Then Liam saw lights peaking from the basement window wells along the driveway. He picked up his bag and walked to the side door.

The door was opened by the man who had driven the rental car. He studied Liam's face for a long moment and then gestured him toward the stairs leading down to the basement. As he descended, he felt the chill creep up his body. The place was lit by a row of fluorescent fixtures and had cement block walls and a concrete floor. The ceiling was unfinished, showing a bevy of pipes, sheet metal ducts, and wires. The heating unit was at one end but was not lit.

The general, the colonel, and the sergeant had Nixon sitting in a chair at the opposite end of the space. He was an austere man; light reflected off his bald pate, and he sat as erect as a Buckingham Palace guard might have if he wore a black suit and white shirt. They had Nixon's coat, cell phone, and briefcase on a table near the side wall.

Nixon started the conversation in a calm voice, "All right, you got me here now. Who are you? What's this all about?"

The general answered, "We believe you have the answers to some important questions, so we thought we'd have a private chat to clear the air."

"In the cellar of a house in some rundown corner of the world? After you kidnapped me? That hardly sounds like a chat. I'll have your asses."

"Nothing like a little bravado to stir the pot," said the general, "but we know you're getting ready to flee the coop. Now you can give us the answers to our questions the easy way with information we can verify, or we can do it the hard way. The New Year holiday starts tomorrow, and no one will miss you for three or four days at least. Which will it be?"

"I have nothing to hide but am not going to give away classified information."

"Good. We know that you have hosted several meetings aimed at preventing the president-elect from taking office. We also know that you initiated a plot with Mr. Sweeney here to assassinate the man before he takes office. We know you have collected money toward those ends. Now we want to know who is behind all that, where the money is coming from, and who else is involved. You might even find a way to take credit for exposing a major plot."

Still rail straight in his chair, he said, "I don't know what you're talking about."

The general was quiet for a long moment, and then she said, "What is your reading of the situation you're in, Mr. Nixon?"

Nixon looked around but said nothing.

"We've shut off your cell phone. If anyone is tracking you, they'll have nothing to follow. What does your situation look like?"

Nixon glared at the general and then snorted, "Like some would-be militia has gone crazy."

"So here you are imprisoned in a basement by a bunch of crazies with no possibility of help. That can't be too comfortable to think about. Do you still want to play the hero?"

"What did Nathan Hale say?"

The general interrupted, "We know full well what Nathan Hale said. Do you have his courage? Are you ready to deal with the hard way?"

Nixon sagged just a bit in his chair. "I am a patriot," he said, looking at the floor.

"Sergeant, where's the tape?"

Liam spoke for the first time. "Before we tape him to the chair, let's get his clothes off."

Nixon's head jerked up. The general twisted to look at Liam. The colonel nodded. The sergeant shrugged and started to take Nixon's jacket off. The man stiffened and hissed, "What are you, barbarians as well as crazy?"

"No," said Liam, "but I'm the guy with those special skills, remember? You can take your own clothes off, or the sergeant can tear them off. Your choice."

Nixon refused to stand up. The colonel grabbed one arm, the sergeant the other, and dragged him erect. The general started to untie his tie. "Bastards!" he shouted, slapped her hands away, and started on his tie. Slowly, he opened the buttons on his shirt, his eyes on the ceiling.

When his chest was bare, he stopped.

"Keep going," snapped Liam.

"Have you no class?" he pleaded. "There's a woman here."

"Are you ashamed of your package?" scoffed the colonel.

Liam ignored the crack. "Keep going," he repeated, "unless you want to sit down and start answering questions."

"I'll never give up classified information," Nixon said.

The general said, "Sergeant."

The sergeant stepped around in front of Nixon, grabbed his belt, and unbuckled it. When he started to unbutton Nixon's pants, the man screamed, "Stop!" The sergeant did and looked at the general for guidance.

"What do you want to know?" asked the tormented man, hands in front of his fly.

"Let's start with you," said Liam. "Sit down. You're the big patriot in the room. Presumably you didn't profit from all this anti-inauguration activity. Which banks do you use?"

"Chase."

"What about the offshore banks?"

"I don't have any," he said, but his face was locked in a scowl.

Liam snorted. "Who the hell are you trying to kid?" he said. Liam dug into his bag and brought out a metal block with wires connected to it. One of those could be plugged into a wall socket. The other split into two with alligator clips at the ends. He said, "This little beauty works equally well on the balls or the nipples. Want a little demonstration?" He plugged the power wire into a wall socket and brought the two alligator clips close to each other. A flash of sparks like lightning leaped between them.

Nixon turned ghostly white. "Okay. Okay. I have an account at the British Colonial Bank in the Bahamas."

Liam opened his laptop, found an Internet connection, and handed the computer to Nixon. "Dial up that account. Let's see the last three month's activity."

Nixon looked at him, then at the wires, and sighed. After a dozen keystrokes, he handed the laptop back to Liam. The general and colonel crowded around to see what it said. The sergeant stood in front of Nixon.

"Interesting," said Liam. "A million-dollar deposit at the end of October, another in November, another a week ago, and then a transfer of a million right after that to an account in the Cayman Islands. Surprise, surprise. That account number corresponds to the one opened for me as a down payment. Where did the money come from, Nixon?"

"I don't know."

The colonel turned on Nixon with as fearsome a scowl as Liam had ever seen. "Stop the bullshit, you traitorous bastard," he said. "Who sent you the money?"

"I mean, I'm not sure which was which. The money came from two places."

"And those were?" said the general, sounding like a mother trying to find out how her son got the clap.

"George Swoyer, Congresswoman Hahn's supporter, and… err…the Chinese."

"You are a fuckin' traitor," screamed the colonel and lunged for Nixon. He bounced off the sergeant and staggered a couple of steps to the right to regain his balance. The general held up her hand and said, "John." That stopped the man in his tracks.

Liam asked, "I assume the Chinese money came from the embassy guy you have coffee with. What's his name?"

"Henry Choi. It's a more complicated name than that, but that's the name he uses in his contacts here. He's a commercial attaché."

"Did your money men really want the president-elect assassinated?" asked Liam.

"I think Choi did," admitted Nixon. "Swoyer may have just been suffering a passing reflex about losing the election to a bully."

"Tell us how this all went down," demanded Liam.

Nixon looked down at his feet and started talking as if a valve suddenly opened. "Congresswoman Hahn came to me after the election, distraught at the thought of having a man she thought was a criminal and was bought and paid for by the Russians as president of our country. She correctly thought that I might feel the same. She said she had this billionaire supporter, a big importer, who was willing to put up money to fund street protests and try to coerce electoral college delegates to change votes so that the popular vote winner would ultimately be declared president. She thought I could help line up some people to do those things. I agreed to give her some contact information."

"Harry Bennet?" asked Liam.

"Not then. Just some radical Greenpeace and social activists I'd been keeping an eye on. There was this group of Russian gangsters up in Boston, but they were just that, gangsters, and I wanted a coup to justify my job, so we took down a couple of their leaders and gave the Irish mob the rest of the info so they could win that turf war."

Nixon shifted in his chair as far as he could with the big sergeant's hands on his shoulders. "Hahn said there were several other congresspeople who wanted to see if they could prevent the inauguration. We made up a list, made some calls, and scheduled the first meeting. As the meetings went on, enthusiasm for the task grew, but the tactics didn't seem to be having the desired effect. This was especially true of the Electoral College delegates. They were holding fast to their charge."

"Is this when the Chinese got involved?" asked the general.

"Yeah. We got word through Swoyer that his mainland contacts wanted to start a backup plan. He introduced Choi to the group. With the Secret Service all over the president-elect, accidents or things like anthrax seemed impossible. Choi said his backers would put up millions to be sure he never got inaugurated."

"How did Choi get a couple of million from his government?" asked the general.

"He had a connection up the line, but I have no idea who that was. The money may not have come from the government directly. Perhaps it came from Chinese manufacturers who saw billions in lost business on the horizon."

"And what was your role in plan B?" pressed Liam.

"We had always kept loose tabs on former 'black ops' agents in case we ever needed one here. Your background looked like you might be forced into the job. I sent my hound dogs to find you. I never thought it was a real possibility, but I went along to see where things would go. The next thing you know, those things got out of hand."

"Did Choi hire Bennet and his thugs?" asked Liam.

"I assume so. I kept him up-to-date on every detail, but I had nothing to do with Bennet."

"So Choi was the guy who sent two men to shadow my daughter in Africa and ordered their murder," concluded Liam.

"We believed you were over there somewhere, and Choi thought you would do to them what you're doing to me."

"How did you let that happen?" asked the astounded general.

Nixon looked at the general and then at the floor. "Things don't seem to follow the regular order anymore. Everybody thinks their way is the only way. I guess I've lost it."

"This Choi is one nasty bastard, and you did nothing to stop him. Just great," said the general. "Sergeant, keep an eye on Mr. Nixon while we caucus."

The group moved to the other end of the basement, next to the inoperative furnace. The general summarized. "None of what we learned tonight will stand up in court, and Choi has immunity. We need a creative thought."

The colonel, his shaggy brows knitted together to form a gray ridge over his steel-gray eyes, said, "What about the 'leak strategy'? The suits use it all the time."

"What exactly do you mean?" she asked.

"We put out a story that a Chinese embassy put up millions to hire someone to assassinate the president-elect. Some members of Congress were suspected of supporting the plot. The FBI infiltrated the organization and broke it up. Nixon could play the hero."

"And he gets away free and clear, the guy you called a traitor?" asked the general.

"Of course, he would retire. Once out of the public eye, law enforcement might investigate him. If he flees the country, that might cause him serious pain."

"What about the money?" she asked.

The colonel smiled. "Think about the irony of using that money to help with the cost of the inauguration."

Liam said, "Choi would be deported. We should see to it that that happens immediately to be sure he doesn't leave orders for more mercenaries to do mischief."

"Suppose we get Nixon to write the facts down, spinning them to his own advantage," suggested the general. "We can go see the director and Doyle tomorrow to see if they buy in. We could even ask Swoyer to comment on the story to see what reaction we get."

She looked at the colonel and Liam. Both nodded. *I do see how she ended up a three-star*, thought Liam.

"Sergeant," she said. "Get the equipment out of the car, please."

In a matter of minutes, he returned with a wide-screen laptop and a printer.

Liam asked the colonel, "Did you guys know it would turn out this way?"

"Semper fi and simper prepared," replied the colonel with a smile.

Nixon didn't think long before starting to write. After the signed documents were in the general's hands, the two marines drove Nixon's car back to his house and spent the night there to "ensure his safety."

Chapter Seventeen

At eleven o'clock on New Year's Day, the group arrived at the office of a somewhat grumpy director of the FBI. Sean Doyle was there before them. The military officers were in class A uniform, Nixon in his dark suit, and Liam, Sean, and the director in casual clothes. They sat at the round conference table without coffee. The director had given his secretary the rest of the week off. Still, everybody was all business.

After studying the documents, the director said, "This is quite a story, Angus. Are all the facts here?"

"Yes, sir."

The director looked at the general, who nodded in agreement.

"All right, we'll get this in the hands of our contact at the *Post* to be published in Friday's edition. That will give them time to see whether either Hahn or Swoyer want to comment. Now, about the money. You can transfer the two million you got from wherever to the inauguration expense fund right now. Here is the account number."

He slid his neat little laptop across the table to Nixon. There was silence in the room except for the click of keys for several minutes. When the money arrived in the inauguration account, the director said, "I have the President's authorization to deal with the details as I see fit. There are two more things. First, you will arrange one of your coffee klatches with Choi for tomorrow afternoon. He won't make it there. We will pick him up on the way with the necessary papers for deportation. Someone from the embassy will come to state to plead his case on Friday, and we'll deliver an angry message and a copy of the *Post*."

He reached for the telephone in the center of the table and placed it in front of Nixon.

Again, there was total silence in the room until the task was completed.

"Very well, Angus. I hear you're leaving town. Where to?"

"I'd prefer to keep that confidential," he said, his face stiff, looking at the floor.

"Well, we need to know where to send your pension checks."

"The same place you send my paychecks: my Chase account."

"Social Security will want an address."

Nixon raised his head, looked the director in the eye, and said, "When I get settled, I'll contact them and sign up."

After a moment of silence, the director said, "Okay. The marines will be with you until we pick up Choi tomorrow afternoon, and then you'll be free to do as you please. How did you get involved in this shit, Angus?"

Nixon sat up straight. "I guess I got my political sensitivities and patriotism mixed up and didn't have the strength to straighten things out."

Everybody stood. The director said, "It's a shame your long years of service had to end this way, Angus. Unfortunately, one bad decision can be all it takes. I hope you can enjoy retirement." He did not offer to shake Nixon's hand. "Happy New Year to all," he said and went to open his office door.

Outside, the general shook Liam's hand and said, "Liam, or Jerry, or whatever name you choose tomorrow, it's been a pleasure to work with you. We're going back to our sleepy village, but we're not going back to sleep. You may hear some stories about the Society in the future. Keep in touch."

Liam laughed. "I'll send you a Christmas card, but I'll be doing my best to ensure you never hear anything about me."

The colonel shook his hand and winked, and they went their separate ways.

As expected, all hell broke loose on Friday. To the relief of the principals, neither Liam nor the Society was named in the press. Liam hoped one of those nosy reporters did not keep scratching in the dirt. He and Sean sat in Mahoney's Saturday afternoon, sipping martinis. They were watching the TV coverage of Choi being led across the tarmac at JFK to a loaded China Air flight that sat there with the engines running. Sean summed up the status of the loose ends after the plane's doors closed.

"Bennet threw his buddies under the bus in exchange for a lighter sentence for the kidnapping. The FBI even caught the guy who sold Bennet the heroin. Carson is going to make it, but it will take a while before he's fully rehabbed. Hahn and Swoyer left yesterday in his ocean-going yacht for an undetermined period. That will give the real FBI plenty of time to figure out what to charge them with. Matt found that Bennet's money and two of the three million that went to Nixon came from a bank in Macao but got no further. Incidentally, the deep web site he set up for you is no more."

"Well, that's as good as it gets, I guess. I wonder what will happen to Nixon, but I'm not going to worry about it. I'm driving up to New York early tomorrow to fill Cathryn in and thank the lads you arranged for."

Sean finished his martini and stood. "And whatever you do, and whatever you call yourself in the future, stay the hell out of more trouble, will ya please."

"I'll do my best, old friend."

They shook hands and walked out together.

A little north of Baltimore on I95, Liam got a phone call from Sean. "Guess what," he said. "We don't have to be concerned with whatever Nixon does anymore. There was an explosion at his house early this morning. They just identified his body an hour ago."

"An accident?"

"Doubt it."

"You think it's Choi's legacy?"

"Could be. I wouldn't chase the Irishmen away from Cathryn too quickly."

"Shit."

"Drive safely."

An hour later, Liam got an urgent call from Brian. "Liam, we've fecked up bad."

"What? Has she snuck off?"

"No. Much worse. There were two guys waiting in her room. I don't know how they got in, but she's a hostage. They want you to join them."

Liam was quiet for a long moment. "What's the situation?"

"They called my mobile. They will kill her unless you come and trade places with her. I told them you were not in town. They said they would wait. They had nothin' else to do."

"I'm a couple of hours out. Do what you can to keep things calm. I'll think of something. Give me an update if anything changes."

"Aye, Liam."

Liam didn't think his old Honda could go as fast as it did up the turnpike and through the Lincoln Tunnel. He drove into the hotel parking garage in an hour and forty minutes.

There, he dressed for the party: He wore his Kevlar vest underneath a loose-fitting denim shirt, and a small .38 in a spring-loaded holster was on his right forearm and another .38 in an ankle holster.

He had run through ideas as rapidly as he drove. He had a plan, a hope, really. It all hinged on getting Cathryn out of the room before the shit hit the fan if that was possible. He didn't think the bastards wanted to shoot up the hotel. There would be no chance to escape if they did that, but maybe they were desperate now that all their support was in jail.

Liam met Brian and Devlin, Brian's older brother, in the hall. They were dressed in ConEd coveralls. Liam laughed. "Where did you get those?"

"One of our lads works for that big boy, ya know."

"Have there been any changes?"

"No. Devlin slipped one of his fancy peeping tom cameras under the door. The men are Chinese. One is propped on the bed. They are all watching the TV. Cathy is in the chair by the desk. The other bad guy is at her side, maybe five feet away." Brian's face looked as if he were ninety years old. "Liam, I'm sorry."

Liam held up his hand to silence the man. "It is what it is, Brian. No time for apologies. They still calling for a trade?"

"Yeah. They want you to come in with your hands up. Once you're in, they'll let Cathy go. I'm to call when you're ready, and one of them will open the door."

Cathy? thought Liam. No time for that now. "Look, it's entirely possible they won't release Cathryn. I don't think they want a shootout in the hotel. Two hostages would be better than one for an escape. I'm not gonna let that happen. If you hear any shots, just bust in, and do the best you can. Got it?"

"Aye."

"Make the call."

After the call, the door opened about six inches, and a Chinese guy holding a .45 looked out. He saw Liam standing there with his hands on his head, backed up, and gestured with his gun for Liam to enter. Liam did, but he made sure the door did not lock again.

Inside, he found his daughter and another Chinese standing on the far side of the king-size bed. He stood within reach of her left arm with his gun in his left hand near his belt. The other guy backed up to take partial shelter behind the TV cabinet.

Liam said, "OK, I'm here. Let her go."

The guy with his gun near Cathryn's head smiled. "U kiddin', right? Turn around. Hands behind back."

Liam said quietly, "You have to be kiddin'. Your guns are useless in this room. If one shot goes off, my two men in the hall and a dozen police will be in here shooting before you can say, 'Oh, shit,' in any language. Put the guns down. We'll talk about this."

"Turn around!" shouted the man partly behind the TV cabinet.

Liam said, "Are you guys on a suicide mission? Some guy at the embassy got sent home, and he wants revenge on me? You will never get out of here alive if you shoot either of us."

The guy near Cathryn snapped, "Shut up and turn around!" He then grabbed Cathryn's arm and brought his gun to about a foot from her head.

Liam turned slowly to his right, putting his body between the men and his right hand. He pressed the release on his belt with his left hand, and the .38 slid into his right. He whirled and squeezed off two shots, which hit the man holding Cathryn's arm in the face and drove him over backward.

The second man shouted something in Chinese and fired two shots, which struck Liam in the chest, knocking him back until his back hit the wall, and his momentum caused him to sit down. Cathryn screamed. An instant after the first shots, Brian and Devlin rushed through the door, shouting, and fired at the shooter, hitting him in the shoulder, the force straightening him up from his lunge to get behind the bed. Liam put his elbows on his knees and squeezed off a shot at the diving man, which entered through his left eye and blew out the back of his head. Cathryn dove across the bed, landing on her hands and knees at her father's side.

"You're shot. Oh my god!"

The noise in the small room was horrendous. Liam could not hear a word that Cathryn just said. He was sure that she couldn't hear any answer he might give, so he did not reply. The stink of the gunpowder almost made him gag. It had been a long time.

Devlin leaped onto the bed to check on the Chinese and then jumped off on the other side to kick their guns away. He came back across the bed to lift a gasping Liam to his feet. Brian helped Cathryn up, smiling widely.

Liam found it hard to breathe but said, "You guys better find some pipe to work on. An army of police will be here in a minute. And thanks. You made it possible to get the second guy." Then he handed Brian the short-barreled .38 from his ankle holster. "Please take care of this for me. No point in giving the police any distractions."

Brian said, "No problem, Liam. It was our privilege to be of service." Then he turned to Cathryn. "Perhaps I'll see you around and about, lass. Take care of your Pa."

With that, the two of them slipped out the door and down the stairs. Liam groaned and sat down on the bed. "I'm getting too old for this shit," he said. The room smelled of blood, as well as the gunpowder and something else. He indulged in a big sigh, which hurt like hell. Cathryn just stood there with her mouth open. She had no idea what to say, much less what to do to "take care of her Pa."

"They hit my Kevlar vest, Cathryn. That .45 packed a wallop, though. I'm going to be sore for days."

Liam searched his daughter's eyes. "Did they hurt you?"

"No. I went down for breakfast this morning, and when I came back, they were sitting in the room with that big gun pointing at me. They sat me in a chair, took my phone, and called Brian. Until the last minute, they never touched me."

"Thank God for that anyway. I'm sorry for all this. It got nasty before I had a chance to end it. He handed her his phone. Call Sean. We can't let the newspapers make a big deal out of this. Sean will find a way to prevent that."

"Of course, you had to do it yourself." He felt the frost returning to their relationship.

"No, I had a lot of help and needed it."

She said, "I was terrified when you came in. I thought they were going to shoot you right then."

"I had to try to get them to release you first. My guess was that they planned to take me somewhere else. I don't think they wanted to shoot up the hotel. There would be no escape if they did that. I guess they were just a revenge detail, a suicide mission. All the big guys behind the plot are either in jail or fleeing the country. Apparently, our president-elect scared the hell out of some people in China, and they found a couple of zealots here who let their frustration numb their brains." He lay back on the bed with a groan.

"What am I going to tell the police?"

"The truth, except that I am a member of the security team you need for your travels in Africa. Your captors called me from your phone, and I came to negotiate your release. They wanted money, nothing else."

Cathryn grabbed the only chair in the room and dragged it into the hall. "Come on," she said. "We have to get out of this hellhole." She took her father's arm and helped him to his feet, out into the hall, and into that lone chair.

*****

RESURRECTIONS

That's where the mob of police that arrived a few minutes later found them. The group included the hotel security guy and was complete with a SWAT team. They blocked off the hall with yellow tape. After they ensured there were no more people in the area, they let the med techs in. One went into the room to check on the Chinese, and the other started poking at Liam. The police and the security guy wanted to question Cathryn at length, but she first insisted on getting her savior into the ambulance. "Which hospital are you taking him to?"

"Bellevue," replied the medical tech with the gurney.

Cathryn shouted after him as they wheeled him toward the elevator, "I'll see you at the emergency room." Then she laughed. "Shall I ask for Sweeney?"

Liam felt warm all over for the first time in twenty years. "Yeah. Sweeney will be around for another day or two. O'Hara is waiting in the wings. It's time for me to start a new life."

Cathryn told her story to the authorities several times. The hotel manager promised to have a room for her that night on a different floor. He had trouble believing that two foreigners could have gotten into her room but did admit that one of his housekeeping staff had failed to return from her lunch break. He also had some suspicions about some men with caps that had been seen in the hotel in recent days. Cathryn said they were part of her team. Eventually, the newspaper people showed up and wanted her to tell the story all over again. She refused and went to the hospital. They followed.

Cathryn found Jerry Sweeney in the Bellevue emergency room. It was a huge space buzzing with activity. He was lying on a gurney in a hospital gown, waiting to be transported upstairs, his chest wrapped in an elastic bandage. His toys, excluding the gun and his shirt, were in a plastic bag on the shelf below him.

A nurse said, "He's got a cracked rib, nothing serious. We're going to keep him overnight to be sure and give him some more pain meds. The detectives want to talk to him first thing in the morning, but after that, we'll let him go. Of course, I have no idea what the police will want to do."

Cathryn found her father woozy from the medication. She said, "I got the rundown. What did they give you? You look drugged."

"I am. Don't know which way is up, but I don't hurt. Stick my phone in that plastic bag if you can. I'll call you when the cops leave."

She stuck the phone in the bag beneath him. "Okay," she said, "and thanks...Dad. I'll see you tomorrow."

He mumbled, "Thank you," and then closed his eyes.

The next morning, he declined the offer of more pain medication and cranked up the bed to face the detectives. He was in a room with two other men next to a window that looked out over the East River. One of the other guys had his leg in a cast, suspended a foot above his bed on a pulley. The other had his head wrapped in a bandage and was asleep.

One detective was a big black guy; the other, a dapper Asian. The black guy asked, "Jerry Sweeney?"

"Yes."

"You told the hospital you live in DC."

"That's where I live."

"What were you doing in New York?"

Liam looked the detective in the eye. "I am part of Cathryn's security team. She works for an NGO on projects in Africa. I function as her liaison with the government, contacts, visas, that sort of stuff."

"Where did you get the gun and the fancy spring-loaded holster?"

They're left over from my government career. I'm sure you've been through my wallet and found the permit."

"A federal permit," said the Asian detective. "So you think you're legal anywhere?"

"Yes."

"What did you do in your government career?"

"My job title was 'field agent.'"

"That's not what I asked," retorted the detective. "I asked what you did with all this artillery and a Kevlar vest."

"I am not at liberty to talk about anything I did."

"That 'it's classified bullshit' ain't gonna cut it," snapped the big detective.

"It's all you're gonna get," replied the man they called Jerry.

"We can label you a POI and hold you if that's what you want."

The 'we'll throw you in jail' bullshit ain't gonna cut it for sure. Let's talk about what you really want to know."

The two detectives looked at each other, and then the Asian one said, "We spend a lot of time at Bellevue because a lot of guys who get shot get brought here. Sooner or later, we find out why they got shot. Why did you get shot?"

"I was driving back from DC when I got a phone call from one of the would-be kidnappers. They wanted ransom for Cathryn: 100K. I was on her speed dial, so these thugs thought I had the key to the bank and that these charitable NGOs were sitting on bottomless pits of money. They laid down the rules. I followed them—up to a point. When they let me into the room, one guy was standing behind Cathryn with a gun pointed at her head. The other was trying to use the TV cabinet for a cover with his .45 pointed at me. They laughed at my demand that they release Cathryn before I sent the money to their bank. They demanded that I turn around and put my hands behind my back. I sprung my .38 loose and shot the guy holding Cathryn. The other guy shot me. Twice, right in the center of the Kevlar. Knocked me back against the wall. Cathryn dove out of the way. The shooter dove for the floor but wasn't fast enough. The crime scene report should square with all of that."

The two detectives looked at each other again. The big guy nodded. The smaller one said, "You were down in DC. Did you have anything to do with the mystery plot that got the Chinese embassy all riled up? Maybe these thugs were looking for revenge."

"Whoa! That's a stretch. I heard about that. The FBI did all of that. I have never had any connection to the FBI."

"Who did you work for?" asked the other detective.

Liam paused a moment for effect. "The CIA. But you can't put that in any public document."

"There's still one loose end," said the big guy. "When they brought you in, you were wearing an ankle holster, but it was empty. What happened to the gun?"

"The gun is in my house. I took it inside to clean and forgot to return it to my car."

"Why did you need to clean it?"

"Target practice."

"Do shoot often?"

"Not often, but enough."

"So it would seem," said the Asian. "All right, Mr. Sweeney. We may have a few more questions in a day or so."

Liam pushed the button to summon the nurse.

Cathryn came, bearing a new shirt as the paperwork was being finished. "Can't let you walk out of here with two bullet holes in your shirt," she said. "Somebody might think you're a ghost."

A cab was waiting to take them back to the hotel, where Brian and Devlin led them into the dining room.

After they had ordered, Brian said, "This one's on you. We lads eat at the golden arches."

Liam said, "I guess a celebration is in order, but I do need to get back to DC."

"How do you propose to do that?" asked Cathryn.

"My car is in the hotel garage. How else?"

"After all those pain meds in the hospital, we need to talk about that."

"Come on, Cathryn. I'm a grown man. I know what I can do."

She answered, "You are also sixty-five years old with a cracked rib. Not a good combination for a four-hour, high-speed drive."

Liam did not know how to respond to that. In his mind, it was much too soon for his daughter to turn into his parent.

Brian saved him from the potential of a major screw-up. "You know well, Liam, that some rest after a bit of action is the right thing to do to preserve one's edge. Why not stay here tonight and see if you're really up to speed in the mornin'?"

"You, too, Brian? Have you and Cathryn been plotting together?"

"Just a bit of logic, lad. And maybe a reminder."

"Of what?"

"Tactics."

Liam thought, *Does young warrior carry the wisdom of the ages too?*

"All right, Brian. You ride shotgun with me and fly back in the morning."

"Not gonna work, Liam. That leaves Devlin here alone to guard Cathy for twenty-four hours straight. The other lads have to go back to their real jobs."

Devlin said, "I'd be fine, Brian," but his face said otherwise.

Liam had a thought. He sat up straighter in the comfortable dining room chair. "Okay. Then the three of us can go. You two can take the Acela Express back tomorrow morning."

Cathryn made a face. "I have a fundraiser luncheon here tomorrow at noon. I need to be sharp."

Liam said, "I'm sure they run those express trains every evening as well. Pull out one of your fancy phones and check the Amtrak schedule."

Brian did and reported that there was a train at seven that got to New York at nine thirty.

They both looked at Cathryn. She said, "If there are no cock-ups, that would be fine."

"There's a backup train at eight," added Brian.

After a moment, Cathryn said, "Okay."

Liam pulled out a credit card and asked, "Can you buy the tickets over the phone?"

"Of course."

Their food arrived just as this was finished. Liam left the card on the table since he was buying lunch as well. The food was excellent, and all enjoyed it—except Liam. He was wrapped up in what, to him, were sad thoughts. *Shit. I have now accepted my daughter turning into my caretaker. And Brian seems to be in on the plot with her. And "cock-ups." Where did she get that term from?*

"Well, I'm glad nothing bad happened to her. Maybe this will keep other bad guys from trying such things. She must have been scared to death."

"This woman is not your daughter?" She locked her eyes on his.

"My last name is O'Hara. I can show you my ID if you want."

She smiled slightly. "Well, at least I know your last name now, but you remain a mystery, Jerry O'Hara. I shall continue to investigate."

"You may not like what you find."

"My instinct tells me that won't happen. Of course, you could just disappear on me."

Liam had to smile. *This woman is a piece of work.* He said, "I'm up for the challenge."

"Will I see you tomorrow then?"

Liam eased off his stool. "We'll see."

But he had to visit with Sean the next morning, though Mary was still on his mind. He found him behind his desk talking on the ever-present phone. Sean held up one finger and gestured him toward a chair. After a grunt and a couple of *okay*s, Sean hung up.

"Our hero returns," greeted Sean. "Are you okay?"

"Forty-five packs a hell of a wallop, but I'm getting there. Where do we stand on the publicity, secrecy, and such?"

"So far, nobody, except the FBI, has connected all the dots. The Feebees are all over the explosion at Nixon's house and demanding to talk to everybody Choi talked to before being ousted from the country. Our people in China and elsewhere are carefully playing their cards to find out where the money came from and who might have initiated the whole thing, including the Nixon explosion. We are not getting anywhere and probably won't. Neither you nor your daughter have surfaced in anything so far."

"Any signs of any more hitmen out there?"

"Not so far. I'd keep the lads on the job for a while, though."

"We'll do that. Cathryn has changed hotel rooms and has learned to tolerate Brian and Devlin well. I owe you a ton, Sean, especially for the lads. They were the ones who saved my ass, you know."

"I heard."

"Is there anything else I need to do?"

"Just keep your fucking head down for a while. I'm spending more time on this bullshit than on my job. You got me out of a ton of shit that night when I got drunk in Iraq and not only lost track of our target but also got captured by his friends. Still, I need to fill this chair for a couple of years more to get the girls through college and start to make it up to my wife for all the running around the world I did on the job."

"I've started a new life. Meet Jerry O'Hara, who maybe even has a girlfriend and has his daughter talking to him again."

"I feel sorry for those ladies, but wish you luck."

"Thanks, Sean. If you hear anything from the general or her friends, don't let me know." He stood slowly, carefully, threw Sean a salute, and left.

He managed to walk a mile that day with only tolerable pain and resolved to attempt his usual routine of a morning run tomorrow. *Does this mean a trip to the diner?*

That night, Liam got a call from Brian.

"Liam, old son, as the need for protecting Cathy has wound down, I wanted to let you know we have had dinner a few times. I think we have a bit of a thing going on."

"Ha. I thought I saw a hint of that coming that day at the hotel. Are you asking my permission to date my daughter?"

It was Brian's turn to chuckle. "Hardly, Liam. We're much too old for that, and as you well know, Cathy is far too independent to put up with anything like that. I did want to give you a heads-up on the possibility that I will be going to Africa with her next time, for security, ya know."

"I admit that possibility eases my mind about her safety over there. Won't that mean complications for you getting back into this country, though?"

"Our friend, Sean, is working on a strategy to deal with those formalities. He's confident he can make the appropriate arrangements."

"So I just gave you permission to shack up with my daughter."

"Remember that independent streak, Liam."

"Yeah, yeah. I trust you will be a gentleman."

"Aye, Liam. I'll keep you up-to-date."

Morning did bring a trip to the diner, even though he was sure that his pain after a curtailed run was obvious. Mary greeted him with that beautiful smile. "Good morning, Mr. O'Hara. You look a little worse for wear today. What's wrong?"

"I went for a run this morning but had to stop. My ribs hurt like hell with big breaths. I'm getting old."

"Did you hurt your ribs somehow?"

"Yeah." Then, after a long moment, he said, "I got shot."

Her jaw dropped. The smile disappeared. "Oh my god! Sit down. Do you want to tell me about it?"

"I guess I had better since I've let the cat out of the bag. My guess is that you'd get me to tell the story sooner or later anyway. It was my daughter who was involved in that New York shooting."

A momentary light of triumph appeared in Mary's eyes, but she said nothing, waiting for the rest.

"The would-be kidnappers wanted me and were using her to get me there. I'm sure they meant me no good. I went into the room to get her out. They shot me in my bulletproof vest, but they didn't have any of those. The bullet didn't break any ribs but bruised the hell out of a couple. I don't heal as quickly as I used to."

Mary was quiet for what seemed a full minute. Then she said, "I have a million questions, but know you are a very private man. Tell me what you're willing to share, and I'll keep my mouth shut."

"Thank you for that. I'm sure it took a lot of resolve. I was involved on the fringes of all that Chinese activity you read about down here. The Chinese wanted revenge on everybody who helped expose the plot. They got desperate. I was just saving my own ass."

"And what is your daughter going to do?"

The man she knew as Jerry shrugged. "I'm sure she will continue with her Africa trip later this month. I'm hopeful that we have gotten past the big chasm between us and that we can have a more normal relationship even if she spends a lot of time in Africa. Maybe I could even accompany her on one of those trips. Speaking of daughters, did yours get to church on Christmas?"

Mary laughed. "She did. I feel a little better about her after that. We are still on different life paths, though. When I was only a year older than she is now, I was married and working twelve-hour shifts as a nurse. Every parent wants life to be better for their kids than they had it, but maybe I went too far. Maybe some of that was my husband's doing because we moved so much, but it is what it is."

"Moved so much?"

"My husband was on the football team at Rutgers, but not good enough to have a scholarship. He joined the ROTC to get free tuition for his last two years. We met while I was working in the college cafeteria and going to nursing school at night. He was a mechanical engineering major, got commissioned at graduation, and had to serve five years. He took the incentives offered to re-up for another five and get a second promotion. We moved seven times in those ten years. Lucy got spoiled rotten."

Liam found himself enthralled by the story. There were many parallels to his own early marriage, except that instead of moving, he would go off on one assignment or another and leave his wife to raise Cathryn. She was determined to get Cathryn an Ivy League education and dragged the young girl through all the application-padding steps that admission required.

Just then, four laughing women entered the diner. They looked to be in their midthirties, were well dressed, and seemed to be on holiday. Liam thought, *Tourists? Young mothers on R and R? A bridge club?* They settled into a booth.

Mary sighed. There would be no table waitress for an hour when one would arrive to help with the lunch crowd. "Duty calls," she said and got off her stool. Liam got off his and walked past the ladies to the door. He paused to look back at Mary and give her a smile and a thumbs-up. Then he was gone.

*****

The next morning Liam, now Jerry O'Hara, showed up at the diner at nine thirty. Mary was able to join him immediately.

"The ladies yesterday were going to the matinee at the Kennedy Center. They were very excited."

"It's nice some people have the time to do that. I might try it sometime if I ever get over my fix on football."

"I'm hooked on football too. That came from watching the man who became my husband play his limited minutes on the college team and then drag me to as many pro games and homecoming games as we could squeeze in."

Liam probed, "You were telling me about your life and family when the ladies arrived."

"Ha. Do ya think I'll tell ya all my secrets without hearing any of yours?"

"I'm not interested in your secrets. Just in how you got to be the charming, curious, and beautiful lady I see before me."

She smiled. "So now it's the blarney, is it.? Do I look like a gullible lass? I'd have thought you'd know me better by now."

"I do. But it's a joy to see you smile."

"My husband always said that too. He even got me to smile when he told me about his reserve unit being called back to build bridges in Iraq, just when he was making good money at a government think tank, and we had settled here."

"I'm sorry I triggered that memory. I know what being called on to leave my family and go overseas is like."

"Do I have to ask you to tell me about your trip?"

"There were many trips, Mary. They were more like your husband getting orders to move so often when he was on active duty. As you said yesterday, duty called, and I just went, at least until one too many came along."

"What happened on that one?" Her face showed she knew that the answer, if it came, was not going to be pleasant.

Liam took a deep breath. Today, that didn't hurt. He blurted, "Ten years ago, my wife got killed in a terrible auto accident while I was on assignment in some shitbag Balkan country. I did not make it home in time for the funeral. My daughter hated me for that. Might still. I got the hell out of that job and began a life under everybody's radar. I was not going to be in any reserve unit."

That stopped Mary in her tracks. He could see the questions blazing in her eyes but overshadowed by something darker. Her brow was furrowed. She shook her head. "That's terrible, Jerry. If that's your real name, I assume your last name is Martin, like your daughter's, but you don't have to tell me your real name if you don't want to."

The momentum overwhelmed Liam. "It's Liam, Mary. Liam Martin. You, Sean Doyle at the CIA, and my daughter are the only people who know that. I'm living as Jerry O'Hara these days and need to keep it that way."

He thought, *What the hell am I doing? This is crazy. Am I losing it altogether?*

Mary just sat there, looking at him. Her face was a mask as if she were reading his thoughts. "It's okay, Liam. I'm honored that you trusted me enough to share this." She got off her stool, stepped to his, and hugged him hard. They could each feel the other's heart pounding.

They clung together until the lunchtime waitress arrived and said, "Excuse me."

They laughed and untangled themselves. Mary looked at the clock. "You're ten minutes early, not that we knew what time it was."

The waitress blushed. They all laughed a little more, and then the women started preparations for the lunch crowd. Liam left to walk off his bewilderment.

Chapter Nineteen

Many changes in Liam's life began in the next weeks and months. He went back to his normal habit of running first thing in the morning and going to the gym to lift in the afternoon. Even that changed in several ways. He bought a car, a modest one: a Honda Civic. On Sunday mornings, when she was off, he ran with Mary. She could keep up if he slowed just a little. He was still traveling some but was rarely gone for more than a month, the artifacts of previous plans. He found himself filling Mary in on his plans so she might anticipate his appearance at the diner. He still felt the need to find several random local gyms to preserve his ritual of not being noticed at any one place. He also shifted his focus to heavier weights to build more muscle. After all, Mary had been married to a football player, and he didn't want to seem relatively puny.

He accompanied Mary to Mass on Sundays. She preferred the cathedral at Catholic U, but he insisted they go to random churches for the same reason he went to random gyms. In time, she even helped with the weekly choice as she explored the differing characteristics of churches in the DC area.

After about a year, they no longer met regularly at the diner. They traded phone numbers and home addresses like normal couples, but they were different from normal too. Their social life was isolated: They did not go out with friends. Liam had none except Sean, and he knew Sean had his own things he did not share with his family. Neither man was willing to have any of those come up in casual conversation over dinner. Mary's friends tended to be church ladies, some of whom were also widows or elderly. She did drag him monthly to volunteer at a soup kitchen, where he did his assigned tasks with energy but little interaction with the rest of the volunteers.

Their daughters were not part of their picture either. Cathryn was preparing for another expedition to Africa, and Mary's daughter, Lisa, was deep into preparing her dissertation. They communicated with the young ladies the modern way: text messages. Phone calls were rare, which suited Liam. He wasn't sure how to explain the changes in his behavior to Cathryn, even though she seemed interested in his life these days.

As the months passed, another thing that changed was the decoration of his house. Mary took him shopping for some "warmth." They bought a few paintings for his living room and a wooden crucifix, which contained the oil for the last rites, for his bedroom. He didn't want to face up to the implications of those acquisitions. When he did, he realized that he was already splashing in the deep end of that pool.

After about a year of their still budding friendship, at a dinner in one of the small local restaurants they had come to prefer, Mary started to explore his reactions to his changed lifestyle.

"How do ya feel about being pretty much in one place for all these months, Liam?"

"I'm comfortable, Mary. There seem to be no signs that people are paying attention to me. I appreciate your going along with the changes my paranoia has imposed on your life, including your calling me Jerry in our limited public life."

"And going to Mass, Liam. How do you feel about that? Is that just another social event, or are you beginning to feel God's love?

"There you go, trying to save my soul again, Mary. I'm beginning to believe there is a God who loves us. I don't experience that on an emotional level, though. I feel comfortable about going to Mass, about praying with you at my side, but I'm a long way from a committed evangelical. I can identify with Catholic teachings in most things and see some practical examples that demonstrate them. You, our relationship, for example. You may not be an angel sent from heaven, but you've had that impact on my life."

"Liam, Jerry, don't be puttin' such a heavy weight on my shoulders. I'm just Mary, your friend, doing what I can to make both our lives as good as they can be."

"If that's not an example of God's love, I don't know what is. Enough of this. The Redskins have a game this Sunday, maybe the last Redskin game ever. Would you like to go?"

"You know I'm a football nut. I'm supposed to work, but I'll get someone to fill in for me at the diner."

"Great. We'll go to ten thirty Mass and sample stadium food for lunch."

"The only ten thirty Mass is at the cathedral."

"I know. This is your day."

In a break with his tradition of sitting with the visitor's fans, he got good seats on the Redskins side even though he had to pay exorbitant prices on the Internet. The cost didn't bother him. Over the course of his career, he had had many opportunities to collect some "spoils of war," and he had taken those. Dead guys didn't need money. He wasn't sure how that fit in with his newfound thoughts about Christian behavior, but that was a problem for another day. A lot of things had changed in the year since he confessed to being shot in New York to Mary.

The January Sunday dawned cold but sunny. Mary had a hamburger and a beer for lunch. He chose the Caesar salad, the most exotic thing available, and a glass of white wine.

As they took their seats ten rows up from the field on the forty-five-yard line, Mary asked, "How did you get these seats on short notice?"

He laughed. "Determination and a little money. Maybe one of the team's fans got tired of waiting for them to change its name."

"All that PC stuff annoys me too. I used to enjoy watching my guy play on his college team. He got in the game only when they used five defensive backs. He weighed 185 but said he used his brains to steal a step and surprise the bigger guys."

Liam said, "I have a soft spot in my heart for the smaller guys too. Of course, at this level, they all weigh two hundred or so. The

Dallas quarterback is supposed to be something special. We'll see how he does against the Redskin D."

"He was good but not good enough. The Redskins won the game, but they were not good enough to make the playoffs in 2018, so their season, and perhaps their tradition, was over."

During the walk from the Metro to Mary's apartment, they stopped at a Thai restaurant for takeout. The curry went well with the bottle of Merlot Mary had saved for a special occasion. They drank it all and settled on her couch to watch a CNN special on climate change.

After about fifteen minutes of the same old "the sky is falling" message with nothing added or explained, Liam put his arm around Mary, and she leaned against him. Soon, they kissed. They had kissed before, but tonight, it was deeper, longer, and more sensual. Soon, their tongues played, and Liam got hard. He reached up to caress her breast. She took his hand away and pulled back. She said, "We'll have none of that tonight, lad."

"Mary, we're not just irresponsible teenagers."

"All the more reason to behave ourselves until we find our feet."

"We don't have an infinite time left."

"God will give us the time we need to understand His plan for us. I trust Him, and I trust you. I believe you trust me. What we have is much more serious than sex. In the last ten years, I'm sure you've had some experience with sex and can tell the difference between that and how we feel about each other."

"Yeah, but—"

"No *but*s," she interrupted. "I'm not immune to your charms, but we're not going to bed together anytime soon. Can you live with that?"

What a woman, he thought. *She must have been tough to live with sometimes. Can I live with those rules? I feel like I'm starting part of my life over. Can't quit on that now.*

"Yes…I guess."

"Good. Let's say an Our Father, and then you'd best go home."

They did, and he did, deciding to walk the almost two miles to try to clear his head.

Chapter Twenty

While all this was going on, the revivified Linonian Society was meeting regularly in Williamsburg. All members were present. At their first meeting in January, which was just after the inauguration of the new president, they were discussing rumors they were hearing about a small group of extremists beginning to build a network of militia groups across the country. The group didn't seem to care what motivated each militia. White supremacists, free rangers, anarchists, antitaxers, and neocons were all welcome. The members of the society were concerned that this smelled the same as the start of Hitler's "movement" in the 1930s in Austria.

"Where are these rumors coming from?" asked the general.

The retired Marine Corps colonel who was active in bringing down Nixon and friends answered, "A couple of my remaining master sergeant contacts reported some rednecks whispering in the ears of young corpsmen in the bars around our bases. They were looking to recruit servicemen to a 'Resurrect America' movement, touting websites like Paler et cetera. They quote groups like the Oath Keepers, whose sales pitch is, 'America's veterans truly are like a sleeping giant. It is time to awaken them and fill them with a terrible resolve to defeat the domestic enemies of our Constitution.' A lot of the emphasis involves the riots in the streets and looting that the opponents of our current president perpetrated after his election. All the BS about systematic racism adds fuel to the fire. The base commanders considered making the bars off-limits but could not close down all the bars around the bases and didn't want to start a game of whack-a-mole, so they passed the word to me."

RESURRECTIONS

"We have a first-amendment issue here," said the retired JAG major, the legal advisor to the society.

"You would say that," snapped the colonel.

The general stepped in to preclude the nascent argument. "There are a couple of things we can do now. I can alert our senator, Jesse Richardson, to needle the FBI on the possibilities. We can monitor the websites, and John here can keep plugged into his sergeant's network. In a few months, we should know whether these are just the wet dreams of a few wackos or something somebody needs to do something about."

"I'll follow the websites," said the lawyer.

"Done," said the colonel.

The retired major who once ran the army's MP corps said, "It's good to be doing something, not just flapping our gums."

The general looked at him. "Well, don't strap on your sidearm just yet."

They all laughed but left with a little more energy than when they arrived.

The next month, the Linonian Society met to assess the status of what they decided to call "the potential insurrection" situation.

The former JAG officer reported that there had not been much traffic on the websites he'd monitored, and there was nothing on Twitter over the last month.

The marine sergeant network reported a drop in bar contacts.

Their senator reported the FBI was on the job, would remain alert, and welcome any info they collected.

The general asked, "Have they gone underground?"

She got a round of shrugs in reply.

"Okay, let's keep our noses to the grindstone and get together next month unless anything pops."

*****

Sean Doyle had a couple of CIA agents on the border in McAllen, Texas, looking for known foreign agents among the immigrants slipping into the country. Looking at hundreds of thousands of photographs of would-be immigrants was deadly boring, so like all agents, they kept their eyes open for other things they thought were illegal as well. Over the course of several months, they reported seeing dozens of the fancy Colt pistols favored by the drug soldiers being carried back into Mexico by the returning *coyotes*. Sean was exploring what to do with that tidbit with the FBI since his people were not supposed to be working in the United States.

Meanwhile, his agents contacted their compatriots at the embassy in Mexico City to get data on the source of the guns recovered at crime scenes in that country. Most of them came from the United States. They passed the data on to Sean.

Still bored, they spent the next couple of months getting the Border Patrol to let them see the results of the drone surveys they were increasingly using. They found no foreign agents but noted a building on a street full of bars that had an unusually large heat signature. They decided to do a little surveillance.

The bar was the largest one on the street and the only one with a parking lot behind the building. Many of the cars sported American flags in the rear windows and "America First" bumper stickers. The agents spent the next couple of months taking random photos of the people coming and going at the bar. They shipped those to Sean as well.

Sean handed all the photos over to the FBI, taking some heat over what his agents were up to. He got almost immediate feedback. Several of the pictures matched photos of known members of the Proud Boys, Oath Keepers, and other extremist groups. A couple of those were still on the FBI wanted list. Now he got thanks for hints about where to find them. However, that meant that the FBI insisted on taking over the task and doing things on their time frame. Sean organized a peaceful transfer from his people to the FBI. In time, the FBI informed the Society's friend, Jesse, the senator from Virginia, of the activity.

The general called another meeting of the Society. When everybody was settled over their coffee, she filled them in on the new info.

"Do we know anything about this bar?"

Their self-appointed computer watcher, the retired JAG lawyer, was pounding on the keys of his laptop. "Hang on a minute. I may have something. Yeah. The property is owned by a George Armstrong. He apparently inherited it from his father, Grant. Google says that Grant ran for city manager a decade ago. He was defeated by a lawyer named Jeremiah Brown and claimed fraud, but nothing ever came of that."

"So the son of a disgruntled loser is hosting some insurrectionists at his bar, which just happens to also have an unusual heat source," summarized the colonel. "I'd like to be a fly on the wall in that place."

"Do you think that the FBI could plant an undercover agent in there?" asked the former military cop.

"I'll ask Jesse to suggest that to them," said the general. "Do we have anything else?"

All the assembled heads shook.

"Okay, let's keep on keepin' on, and we'll talk again next month."

The month went by with nothing much seen on the Internet and no word from the FBI. The general scheduled the next meeting for a weekend and convinced the senator to attend to share some details about his interactions with the FBI and anybody else he'd been talking with.

The senator was happy to meet with his loyal constituents the next month and show off a little of his influence in the halls of power. "The FBI is fully engaged in surveillance of the bar, sometimes twenty-four hours a day. So far, they've seen five people on their wanted list come and go. Some nights, cars remain in the parking lot until well after the bar closes for business. Power demand goes up late at night as well. The FBI thinks this place is a gold mine for catching fugitive rioters and wants to keep watching the place and tracking its visitors. One day, they hope to round up a dozen insurrectionists there."

"If they watch long enough," said the colonel from the chair next to the general, "they can just welcome them to DC."

"What about the idea of getting an undercover agent in there?" asked the former MP.

"They think that would be too risky. The group is too tight-knit. An outsider would raise red flags and drive the flies away from the honey. In addition, it would be personally dangerous for the agent. Look, I know your concerns about this group are growing, but let's let the pros handle it. That's what we pay them for, and they're good at it. I'll make sure they don't fall asleep at the wheel and keep you up-to-date."

The general put her hand on the colonel's arm and squeezed. After a moment, she said, "Thanks for all your time and effort, Jesse. We are going to stay on this. You can count on that."

Things were very quiet on the Internet for the next three months. There were only a few taunts tossed back and forth about which town's high school football team was the best. There were bets placed on whether McAllen's team would win the state championship in their class.

"Do you guys think this is just some kind of code?" asked the general at the Society's December meeting. "Have the militia leaders gotten suspicious?"

The retired marine colonel said, "No. As I remember my days stationed in Texas and surrounding states, football is king in the fall. I doubt there is much going on right now."

Chapter Twenty-One

Back in DC, Liam got a call from Cathryn on a Friday night in January, a year after he and Mary had gone to the Redskin game and struggled with his physical awakening.

"Just wanted to say goodbye. We're leaving on Monday for Africa via Brussels. We'll probably be gone for six months, maybe more, depending on how much cooperation we get."

"I had hoped to have dinner with you one night before you left."

There was a moment of silence. Then she said, "I'm really up to my eyeballs in these last days before we leave. I'll tell you what. Our charter is leaving from Teterboro in New Jersey at ten o'clock Monday night. We're having a team dinner at the airport at six. Why don't you come? You can meet the team and maybe feel a little more secure about my safety."

"That sounds like a great idea. I'll be there."

"Great. Look forward to seeing you. Is everything okay with you?"

"Yeah. I'm staying in one place these days. Running around constantly didn't prevent the bad guys from finding me."

"I hear you have a lady friend."

"Who told you that?"

"Sean called to check on whether there had been any suspicious activity lately. He wanted to be sure it was safe to call off "the lads."

Liam fussed in his chair. "He's grossly exaggerating a casual mention of the waitress at the diner around the corner from my house. She dragged me to church on Christmas."

"If you say so, Dad. Gotta run. See you Monday."
Is Sean just pulling my chain, or is he wiser than me?

*****

Liam flew to Newark on Monday and rented a room at the same airport hotel at which he had been attacked just before Christmas. He took a taxi over to Teterboro and found the group in a small private dining room where the round Formica tables were covered with paper cloths. There was a bar set up in the corner and a long buffet-serving table along the wall opposite the door. There were six tables in the center of the room, each set with six chairs and a long rectangular table against the end wall. The bar was crowded with thirty-somethings in high spirits. One of those was Brian.

Cathryn came to meet him and begin the rounds of introductions. There were six engineers of various specialties, one of whom was a black woman from MIT, a half dozen craftsmen: pipe fitters, welders, electricians, and a nurse who served as their EMT, just in case. In addition, there were a few media types, including a cameraman and a couple of translators. Brian was the only man who looked like a security presence. Two of the pipe fitters looked like they could hold their own, but one of the others was a woman.

Liam asked, "Are you going to be building something over there?"

"No, Dad. The technical people are trainers. We are working on the 'teach a man to fish, and he has food for life' theory. Often, we have to get hands-on to demonstrate. Of course, we have to document what we are doing for the people who fund us, and leaving videos behind preserves the lessons and spreads the word."

"You've got quite an operation, Cathryn. Congratulations. Brian is going along?"

She blushed, but only a little, and only for a moment. "He did such a good job after you forced him and the rest of the lads on me that I thought it might ease your mind about our security."

Liam smiled. "Nice," he said. "I take it Sean was able to defuse any potential reentry problems."

"Yes."

"I'm sure he'll earn his keep. It looks to me that that he might train a couple of those pipe fitters as additional security forces."

"The female fitter is trained in martial arts as well."

Liam said, "You were right about tonight. I do feel better about the personal safety of your group."

He sat at one end of the head table and Brian at the other. Liam watched his daughter lead. She reminded the group of the required procedures and itinerary. Every eye was focused on her. Liam came away convinced that she could take care of things a lot bigger than a little sex. Dinner was Italian and ice-cream cake. They would not be seeing any of either on their trip.

Dinner over, Liam and Cathryn hugged briefly.

"Be safe," he said.

"I will, Dad. Don't worry. Stay out of trouble yourself."

Liam felt good during the entire taxi ride to his hotel.

*****

A week before the next scheduled meeting of the Society, Senator Richardson called the general.

"The FBI has been searching the dark web for sites, especially new sites, that are potentially troublesome. They found two. Both were encrypted, but they hacked into *Infowars* and found somebody trying to organize trouble. There were no geographic limits and no limit on the range of extreme ideas. There is yet no measure of how many wackos are involved. They are secretly monitoring the sites and working to track down the physical location of the biggest sites. It looks as if you and your buddies are on to something. I'll send you the URLs and passwords."

"What is the FBI going to do next?"

"Watch and search. The search is starting with the electrical grid, but the Bitcoin miners complicate things because they suck up a lot of juice too. I'll keep you posted. Don't do anything rash."

"Jesse, you know us better than that."

"I thought I did, but then you went and kidnapped a very special FBI agent."

"Well, there is that. We are meeting next week."

"Eleanor—"

"Have faith, Jesse. I didn't earn three stars tilting at windmills."

The next Society meeting got a little heated. The old lions were eager for a kill.

The Internet watcher reported that the new site was on a recruiting spree. "They are repeating all the complaints one has ever heard about life here and the failings of our government. 'We are turning socialist. The LGBTQ+ people and the people of color (the fags and you know what in their parlance) are taking over the country. Our grandchildren will be in debt forever. If you've had any success, you are a racist. The commie teachers' union wants to teach the white students to be ashamed. Et cetera, et cetera, et cetera.' There is a strong theme of support for our current president. I saw no specific plans or gatherings."

"We have to do something to shut this down," said the colonel.

The former MP said, "If the FBI won't put somebody on the inside, can't we get a listening device in there? They must get deliveries of beer and food. Maybe we could bribe some truck driver to drop something off."

"And how would we ever get the output? We're a thousand miles away," scoffed the former JAG lawyer.

"Have you got any better ideas?" replied the MP.

The general tapped her coffee cup on the table. The men shut up. "Look, men. We are no longer in control of anything. We need to rely on the FBI for action. Do you have any ideas about what more they can do other than watch and take pictures?"

"They could sneak in the listening device and collect the results," proposed the MP.

"One listening device in a bar room isn't gonna get us much," said the JAG.

"Maybe they could bug the owner's telephone," said the colonel.

The general said, "I can't imagine the FBI doesn't have more sophisticated technology than we know anything about, and I have no idea what a judge would say about what we just talked about."

"I'm told that crooks can steal credit card numbers off gasoline pumps and even from the keystrokes on computer keyboards," said the colonel. "Can't the FBI do that too?"

"Don't forget about the judge," warned the former JAG lawyer.

"There are special courts for that," said the general, looking interested. "I'll give Jesse a challenge for his influence with the Feebees and maybe the whole justice department. In the meantime, we wait."

After a few minutes of silence, the general stood. The other members of the Society got the message and started to file out.

*****

Despite the beautiful spring weather in Williamsburg and the flowering azaleas and crepe myrtles, the senator was reluctant to attend the next meeting of the society, but he came, bringing with him a document that he hoped would dilute some of the abuse he anticipated. He had achieved nothing with the FBI. He started the meeting with an apology. "I was unable to get the FBI off their position of watching and waiting. Their leadership feels other priorities are more important."

"What the hell could be more important than saving our democracy?" snapped the colonel.

"I'm in no position to critique their judgment on where to spend their resources," replied the senator. "The one thing they did do was get the detailed floor plan for the bar." He unfolded the document in his hand and spread it on the dining room table so everybody could see the page. The one thing of interest was the location of the owner's office at the very back of the building, just inside the wall adjacent to the parking lot. There was one window in that wall. There was also a rear door to the building leading into a hallway that ran past the restrooms and kitchen into the main bar area.

"Pretty basic," said the MP. "I wonder if there are alarms."

"Why are alarms of interest?" asked the JAG retiree.

"You're kidding, of course," replied the MP veteran.

The general interjected, "Senator, you may wish to leave."

"No way, Eleanor. If you guys get involved in something illegal, I need to know about it to protect my own ass. I surely don't want some aggressive reporter sandbagging me in public. I need you to trust me not to divulge anything that might involve the Society."

"You've already told the FBI of our concerns," growled the colonel.

"No, I haven't. The society is just a group of my 'concerned constituents.' Neither it nor Eleanor has been mentioned in my conversations with the FBI."

The retired marine would not be mollified. "So you diluted the strength and credibility of our concerns to cover your own ass in case some remote hypothetical comes up."

The general said, "Easy, John. That won't do any good. Senator, we will take some action soon to penetrate the veil of secrecy the FBI refuses to address. Whether that action is technically legal or not remains to be seen. You can assume that if anything you wish to disavow hits the headlines, we'll understand. By the same token, whatever we do will be what we think is the right thing, regardless of your worries. Meeting adjourned."

The retired JAG officer sighed deeply, just as he had as the plan for the Nixon kidnap had developed. After the others had gone, the colonel asked, "What are you going to do?"

"Call Sean Doyle. He must have a bunch of criminals at his beck and call."

Chapter Twenty-Two

While the Society schemed, Liam and Mary were getting more involved in each other's lives. They ran together on Sunday mornings before Mass. There, they held hands during the Our Father and kissed at the sign of peace. They participated in two 5K charity runs, proudly wearing the T-shirts that signaled participation. More importantly, they "came out," that is, became blatantly obvious, as a couple to the church ladies and soup kitchen volunteers.

They called themselves *friends*, rejecting the term *partners* for its sexual inference. They also rejected the term *relationship* for the same reason. Sex was still off the table. They often had dinner at either his house or her apartment. Liam even cooked simple stuff like shepherd's pie or chili.

Liam maintained his multiple gym routine and ran by himself most days. Since he was no longer roaming around the country, he needed other activities to fill the time. He and Mary signed up for Georgetown University's Lifelong Learning program and audited a university course in creative nonfiction, where fifteen undergraduate English majors studied that genre. They read published memoirs written by people they never heard of who seemed to be living in a different world.

When it came time for each student to write a personal essay, they ran into some problems. They were amazed as the undergraduates casually confessed to sex, drugs, and cutting themselves. Mary wrote about the pain of losing her husband in Iraq. Liam constructed a series of lies about traveling the world for an unnamed government agency, filled out with vignettes from his visits to little-known tourist sites. They were amazed at the frequent use of f-bombs by the students, not only in their writings but also in class. Well, they came to learn something, and they did.

Every few months, they would go away for a day or so to celebrate something. The first of these was a weekend in Nashville for a folk music festival in honor of Mary's birthday. She was two years younger than Liam. He knew nothing about that kind of music but enjoyed it. They spent two nights in a nice hotel—in separate rooms.

The next trip was to New York to catch the Bruce Springsteen show on Broadway. The cost of a hotel room in the Big Apple was so extreme that Mary's conscience would not allow her to demand a separate room. They slept in one room, in separate beds.

One Sunday afternoon, they were baking chocolate chip cookies in Liam's kitchen when he advanced an idea he'd been thinking about for some time. "We spend so much time together. You should just move in here. You'd save a bunch of money in rent, and we could share the drudgery."

"Not going to happen, Liam. I'm not going to live in sin."

"What sin? We hardly touch each other."

"Scandal, love. Everybody will assume we're sleeping together."

"Who is everybody, the church ladies?"

"I don't know. Maybe it's me. The way I was brought up. Maybe it's my daughter. I don't know what she's doing, but I don't want to be an enabler for things I don't approve of. What about your daughter?"

"I confess I never thought about that. I'm pretty sure she'd be happy for us being happy, but at this stage of our resurrected father-daughter relationship, we've never had any serious conversation about you and me. That is not a subject for emails."

"So thank you for your offer, but my finances are fine, for the moment, at least."

Liam had tried to get her to quit her job once or twice, but the job was like an umbilical cord supplying some of her needs for social interaction, and as yet, she knew not what the future held with Liam.

*****

While all this peaceful development was going on with Liam and Mary, the country was undergoing a lot of disruption. The president that Liam had refused to assassinate was raising hell. Almost daily, he had a row with the press, calling them liars on Twitter for things said that he didn't like. He enraged some allied countries by criticizing their feeble financial support of NATO. He abandoned the Kurds who fought ISIS in Iraq. The opposing party initiated impeachment proceedings. However, the economy was starting to grow, and some were happy with his tough stance against China.

Then the George Floyd murder and COVID-19 came on the scene. Crowds marched in the streets around the world, bringing with them the inevitable passel of looters. The president sent Federal agents to troubled cities and threatened to take over their management if the existing leadership, which happened to be from the opposing party, did not shape things up. The president downplayed COVID-19 despite the rising death tolls and touted unproven medications. Everything he did, everything he said, aroused a storm of media criticism on some channels and a storm of support on another. All this added urgency to the general's efforts.

There were groups calling for hard-core suppression of the BLM marchers, just as there were groups calling for the president's ouster. Division in society was rampant, pitting brother against brother. Social disparities were inflamed by opposition to the local lockdowns taken to control the spread of COVID-19 and the resultant destruction of children's education. At the national level, nothing was being done to calm the situation, and the president refused to wear a mask.

Though he was not paying much attention to politics these days, Liam sometimes wondered how life would have been different if he had carried out the mission the zealots had demanded of him. He had been told that the vice president would have been installed as president. The VP was a religious man. He opposed abortion and had been vilified for that when he was governor of a Midwestern state. He had a reputation for integrity. He was, however, behaving as a loyal follower of the president in his role as VP. How would he behave if he were president?

Liam had no regrets about breaking up the assassination plot. He still harbored anger at those in the government who used him and Sean badly during their service to the country, but he never had any thoughts about usurping the will of the voters. He considered himself a loyal citizen, if not a zealous patriot. He did think he would do things differently if he were in charge. He had enough of violence and disruption.

In his isolated travels, Liam had seen a lot of what he considered "good stuff" going on in the country. The people doing it probably thought nothing of what they were doing, but those things looked important to an outlier. There were many soup kitchens like the one he volunteered at. Boys' clubs, police athletic leagues, and CYO groups worked to keep kids out of gangs. Civic groups put up billboards fighting discrimination, and college students tutored disadvantaged kids. There were a lot of "golden rule" things going on, which helped draw the country to appreciate the things everyone believed in. Those things did not get much visibility on the TV news networks, where the talking heads blathered mostly about disagreements and disruption. Liam didn't think he could do much about all that. He'd just keep working at the soup kitchen.

*****

The general called Sean early one morning. "Top of the mornin' to ya, Sean."

Sean sighed and then said, "The Irish don't talk that way, General. Has something gone wrong with your dealings with the FBI?"

"Let's just say that they don't seem to understand the urgency we see in the situation."

"Why are you calling me?"

"I am hoping you can help us off the books. We want to hire a contractor to sneak some listening devices into that bar and record what is said. I suspect that you have access to both equipment and talent."

There was a long silence on the phone. Then Sean said, "You know, of course, that the CIA is not allowed to carry out operations within the United States."

"Of course. We don't want you to do anything except point us to a trustworthy contractor and maybe lend us some equipment."

"Contractors cost serious money, especially for clandestine projects."

"The Society has access to funds."

Sean laughed. "How much is your husband worth?"

"You can get that information from *Forbes Magazine*. I haven't checked lately."

"General, Eleanor, you're asking me to wade into a swamp. Have you got any hard evidence that your fears have substance?"

"There's a lot of recruiting on a dark web site. All kinds of crazies are being invited."

"Have any of them signed up?"

"We won't know until we hack into the owner's email."

"I don't think that would work. You'll probably need a keystroke copier and someone to decode the messages. The cost keeps going up."

With an edge creeping into her voice, the general said, "If we're right, the cost to the country will be astronomical and include countless lives."

"If you're right."

"We know how to retreat when it's called for. Your name will never be involved. Unless you want to take a bow after we prevent an insurrection."

"Let me explore some possibilities to see if there is a safe path to do something. I'll get back to you soon."

"Tomorrow!"

"These things can't be rushed, General. Soon."

When Sean hung up on the general, he went outside for a few private calls. The last of those was to Liam. "How are you doin', boyo? Gettin' laid yet?"

"Cut it out, Sean. Every time you call, you ask about my new life. A gentleman doesn't talk about his love life."

"Love, is it? Oh my. I'm just pullin' your chain a little. I called to warn you that the general is on the warpath. She's pissed off at the FBI for not moving fast enough on the Society's concern that some guy in McAllen is trying to line up a bunch of wackos to stage an insurrection and convert our current president into a king. She came to me for some 'off the books' help. There's some possibility I can do that safely, but the odds are fifty-fifty. If I can't help, she may come to you. Forewarned is forearmed."

"Thanks for the heads-up, Sean. I am officially and irrevocably retired. She's one tough broad, but I'm not about to disrupt my current peaceful life for any call to duty."

"I thought you might have gotten bored with domestic life by now."

"No. A run with Mary on Sunday morning before Mass has gotten to be quite comfortable. I don't miss roaming around the country at all."

Sean took a deep breath. "Before Mass? Oh my goodness, this is serious. Look out, Liam. You're running down the road toward typical senior citizenry."

"Que sera, sera, Sean. Thanks again for the warning. I'll have my defenses ready in case you fail to help."

Chapter Twenty-Three

That night, Liam had a nightmare, the first one in five years. He jerked awake in the pitch dark at three in the morning, sweating. A faceless general wearing a dress uniform complete with medals had been chasing him through the woods, cracking a whip at his heels. He had been barely able to dodge the lash, which tore small branches off the trees he passed. *Was it General Townsend or some ghost from his past?* He tossed until dawn and then got up.

Later, he went to the diner for the first time in weeks. On Saturday, the breakfast crowd was much thinner, and Mary could get to him quickly. She greeted him with a smiling comment, "Well, this is a surprise."

"Yeah. I had a very bad night. Needed a little TLC and a serious breakfast."

"This is the place for both. The usual?"

"Do you still remember that?"

"I remember everything about you."

"Yes, to the food. I hope you will say yes to what I'm about to ask. I need to find some peace. I can often find that with a day at the ocean. I've booked a B and B in Ocean Beach for tonight. I dearly hope that you will come with me. We can have a nice dinner and run on the boardwalk in the morning, sit on the beach, and listen to the waves in the afternoon. How about it?"

"I'm not really a beach person, Jerry. My skin burns too easily, and the ocean in May is still too cold to swim in, even for an Irishman."

"I'll rent an umbrella, or we'll cover you up. I didn't say anything about going into the ocean. I just want its rhythm to soothe my brain. I haven't had a nightmare in years, but I had a doozy last night, and I'm still twitching."

She looked into his eyes for a long moment and then said, "I'll be happy to help you soothe your brain."

He took her hand in his. "Thanks. Can I pick you up at one?"

"Yes."

*****

The ride to Ocean Beach, Maryland, took a couple of hours. Mary didn't probe about the nightmare or what might have caused it. She did search the Internet for a church in their destination.

They pulled into the small parking lot at the B and B, which was just one block off the ocean. "This must have cost a pretty penny," said Mary.

"One pays for value, love. Let's check in."

The facility had four rooms, only two of which were booked. They and their overnight luggage were led to their room through quiet, carpeted halls, the walls of which were decorated with paintings of lighthouses and ships. It was a big room at the end of the building, with windows on two walls and an elegant, old-fashioned bathroom.

Mary said, "It's lovely, but there is only one bed."

"It's a very big bed. The same size as two single beds. They are just pushed together. Have no fear, my dear. There will be no hanky-panky here."

She kissed his cheek gently and said, "Shall we tour the place? It looks interesting."

"Sure. They serve 'tea' at five, which mostly means wine, and by then, I'll have a dinner reservation. There is a concert on the beach at dusk. Should be fun."

And it was. All of it. Liam was not a fish fancier, but the fresh crabs were great, and the band played mellow jazz, ala Dave Brubeck. It got cool on the beach at dark, but they were prepared and got back to the room at about ten. They took turns in the bathroom, where Mary got into long silk pajamas. Liam climbed into bed in a T-shirt and his tidy whiteys.

Mary asked, "How do you feel, Liam?"

"I'm good, Mary. A good meal, some cool music, the rhythm of the sea, and having you here beside me have given me peace."

"I'm honored that you came to me for help. To be trusted by such a strong and private man when he is vulnerable is a wonderful thing. At first, I wanted to cry, but then I realized that I was so happy I was just filling up with emotion."

"Mary, your support has been my strength these last months. I call it love, the senior kind, deep and encompassing the whole person. I worry, though, that you don't have the same kind of trust in me."

"I do trust you, Liam, but at the same time, I know that there is a part of you that I don't know, those things you can't, or just won't, talk about. There is this little lingering fear that what you have buried deep inside you will spread like cancer and change you. That would break my heart, not only for my loss but also for yours."

"I can't imagine anything that would make that happen, Mary. Have faith."

"Speaking of faith, there's a church about two miles north on the beach road. Mass is at ten o'clock."

"Good. I have a lot to be thankful for," said Liam.

"And I, as well."

They kissed once, had a nice long hug, and turned back-to-back to sleep. There was no repeat of Liam's nightmare.

They woke early and went for that run on the boardwalk in a cool breeze under a cloudless sky with the tide a third of the way up the beach. They had time to shower before the hostel's breakfast at nine.

And a marvelous breakfast it was: pancakes, eggs, sausage, homemade blueberry pastry, and excellent coffee. The couple who rented the other room was young, bubbling with love and energy.

The young lady said, "It's nice to see an older couple doing something romantic. Is it your anniversary?"

Mary blushed. Liam laughed. "Sort of," he said, "not a milestone, though."

The couple looked a little puzzled at that but went on to explain that this was their first wedding anniversary and that they lived in Maine and could afford only a short trip because they both had to be back at work on Monday. They got up and headed for the door. The woman said, "But we're gonna make the most of it, even if we have to drive all night to get home in time."

"Good luck to ya," said Mary, "and best wishes for the years to come."

Mary and Liam looked at each other and laughed. There was nothing to say, however. They went to Mass, sat on a bench on the boardwalk, and drove home. Neither had any room for lunch.

*****

Sean called on Monday. "I thought I'd relieve the suspense for you. I've put together a very small and very discrete crew for the general."

"What do I need to know about it?"

"Not much. It's Devlin, Brian's brother. He hung out with the IRA as a kid. Learned all sorts of fancy techie stuff."

"I remember he had the Peeping Tom camera in New York. No backup?"

"Shouldn't need one. He's just gonna sneak into the bar's office one night, bug everything, including the computer keyboard, and pipe it all to a recorder outside. He'll mail the recorder's thumb drives to the general. I'm out of it."

"Sounds neat. Hope it works. Thanks for the info."

Liam hoped he sounded businesslike about the news, but it was truly a big relief for him. The summer arrived warm and sunny, like the evolution of his friendship with Mary. They went back to the beach once in a while: Mary in her one-piece green suit and he in his floppy shorts. They gave up running in the heat, choosing to swim laps in the municipal pool for their exercise. There were evening concerts in the parks where they picnicked and an occasional trip to the Kennedy Center. Life was good, and it was peaceful.

*****

The general and the colonel met with Devlin at the Marriott Hotel at Newark Airport a week later. Their coming to him seemed like the right protocol.

After introductions and a cup of tea in the hotel's coffee shop about midmorning, they got down to business. Devlin wore an alligator polo shirt and carried a leather briefcase. Eleanor and John were in long-sleeve shirts and khakis. They all looked like the rest of the tourists in the place. The guys in the suits had already departed for their planes or trains.

"Are you sure you know exactly what is needed?" asked the general.

"Yes, ma'am. Sean was quite specific. He faxed me the drawing of the building. I'm quite prepared. All the equipment I need is in this case, along with spare batteries."

"I'd prefer General or sir rather than ma'am. Are you confident you can handle the job?"

"Yes, General. I've done this kind of stuff a dozen times from quite a young age. It's just a question of finding the right time to enter. A few nights' observations should solve that."

"And your fee will be what?" asked the colonel.

Devlin laughed that full-bodied Irish roar. "Am I in a bidding war?"

The colonel blushed—only a little, but Devlin saw it, and the colonel saw he saw it. He looked down for a moment and then into Devlin's eyes. "Okay, I could have asked the question better. We just want to be prepared. This is not a cash-in-thirty-days kind of a job."

"Aye," said Devlin. "It's two thousand for the incursion, a hundred a day before and after, plus expenses. I'll email the expenses weekly. I gave you the bank account number in the Caymans. You tell me when you've got enough, and I'm out of there."

Eleanor and John didn't even look at each other. "When will you start?" asked the general.

Devlin smiled. "General, sir, I'm on the bird to McAllen tonight. What is the best way to contact you?"

The colonel took a phone from his shirt pocket. "Just push the green button on this for either verbal or text. It's scrambled. We'll plug it into a computer at our end. The data will come on thumb drives via the mail?"

"Aye, probably FedEx, but I'll send any urgent contents to the phone. In an emergency, or if circumstances change, you have my mobile number. Barring any emergency, you should hear something from me every Monday morning."

That was it. They all stood and shook hands, and the colonel muttered, "May the wind be always at your back."

The general said, "Fire against fire, John. Let's hope it works."

Chapter Twenty-Four

Devlin

It was hot when Devlin woke up the next morning in his room at the Holiday Inn—McAllen. Much hotter than any Irishman would like, unless, of course, said Irishman had trained in Africa with some people who wanted to blow up Protestants and their tanks back on the old sod.

The border crossing from Mexico at McAllen came across a toll bridge. The road split into four lanes leading to four customs booths, then combined into a giant traffic circle with exits to the highways and local streets. The first local street led to a grassy square at the right side, of which the Holiday Inn took up an entire block between two east-west running side streets.

One of these was a quaint, cobble-stoned street named "Saloon Alley." The reason for the street name was obvious: six connected, three-story saloons graced its north side. Each building had a painted brick facade, with colors ranging from the tan shades of the desert to a bright blue reminiscent of Europe. Small windows pierced the front walls high enough to preclude looking in to see what the place was like.

The entrance to each establishment was through a solid wood door at one side, painted a different color from the facade. It was one step up from the sidewalk and provided with handrails on both sides. At the opposite side was a street-level door providing access to the apartments above. The buildings extended back from Saloon

Alley almost to the street behind but left room for a small backyard between the buildings and the street.

The opposite side of the street contained a row of similar buildings. These held commercial establishments typical of an older residential area: a pharmacy, a bakery, a butcher, and a small coffee shop. The storefronts were glass, except for the entry doors and the door to the apartments above. The street was a tourist attraction of sorts.

Devlin put on his touristy-looking shorts and a sleeveless muscle shirt and went to survey his environment. The target building stood out. The establishment was stand-alone at the end of the street. It was one story, with a walkway on each side, which connected to a small parking lot behind the building. A man-sized American Flag stood on a movable pole to the right of the main entrance. The back wall of the building was lined with foundation plantings. *Boxwood*, Devlin thought. The parking lot could hold perhaps half a dozen cars and was lit only by the streetlights on the street behind.

Devlin wandered into a random saloon to hydrate and ask a few questions. In the late morning, it held only three customers. The place smelled of stale beer, had sawdust on the floor, and a brass rail for one's feet while sitting on a bar stool. In short, it was a classic American bar, not at all like an Irish pub. When the bartender asked what he wanted, Devlin laid on the brogue and said, "I'm told that in Texas, I should drink Lone Star beer."

"That used to be true, but now, there are more choices. We have a local IPA that tastes more European. That may be more like what you're used to."

"That's kind of you, but I'll try the Lone Star."

"Sold," said the barman and went to fetch one.

Devlin tasted it and smiled. There might be a little more to it than Coors Light, but it was piss even compared to the Irish lager, Harp.

"Say," he said, "how did that fancy new place down the street get added to this row of traditional-style pubs?"

"The original owner tore down an old bar like this one, bought an apartment house next door, and built it. Tossed six families out on the street to do it and didn't give a damn. Now it's a hangout for bikers and other rednecks. Once in a while, a guy in a shirt and tie will stop in there. I think the FBI is keeping an eye on the place. Our neighbors like the traditional saloons just fine."

"It seems there are enough rednecks, as you call them, to keep the place goin'."

"Oh, yeah. After all, this is Texas, but some of the license plates on the bikes say they're from pretty far away. I saw one the other day from New Mexico."

"Interesting," said Devlin. He chugged the rest of his beer, such as it was, gave the bartender a salute, and went out to look at license plates. He didn't see any from New Mexico, but Alabama, Arkansas, and Arizona were there, and there was even one from New York. There were none from Texas and no cars in the lot. There must be some locals who like the place.

Devlin studied the place for the next three nights. It was open for business until midnight, and the lights were on for the cleaning crew for another hour. After 2:00 a.m., the place was dormant until about ten. The lights from the street behind left the back wall of the building in shadows. He would need about an hour to accomplish his plan. He scheduled it for three the next morning. He dressed in black, put his lock-picking tools and a penlight in his shirt pocket, and double-checked the electronics in the briefcase.

It took him less than two minutes to defeat the deadbolt on the back door to the building, holding the penlight in his mouth. There was no alarm inside the door, so he relaxed. This was going to be easy. The office door was locked, but it was a simple bathroom lock opened by pushing a pin through the center hole in the outer knob. He put a bug in the telephone handset and a listening device in the overhead light fixture. The computer was a desktop located vertically in the knee space under the desk with a wireless keyboard on top of the desk. There was no cell phone in sight.

Installing the device that recorded the keystrokes on the computer took a little time. He had to dismantle the back of the keyboard to do that, and getting the tiny screws back into their holes with only the pen light proved to be a challenge, but he overcame that. All these devices would export the data wirelessly to the recorder he hid in the foundation plantings. The recorder saved the data in replaceable thumb drives. As a backup to the listening device, he stuck a transponder to the outside of the window glass. It was a two-part device that sent a laser beam from one side and a reader that translated the changes in the frequencies of the laser light from the minute vibrations in the glass caused by the voices inside back to the words spoken. Its signal would be weaker than that of the listening device, but Devlin had an amplifier in his bag of tricks.

Devlin used his mobile to call the office phone and talked for twenty seconds in a whisper. He found the brief soliloquy faithfully recorded outside. That would have to do with any cell phone conversations as well. He packed up and left but did not try to relock the deadbolt. It was five minutes to four.

Devlin slept for four hours and then sent a text to the general: *Package installed* and added a list of the *toys* and where they were installed.

He got back into his tourist garb, blue-and-white plaid shorts, and a white polo shirt and went to the target bar just before noon. It was much cleaner than the neighborhood place he had visited yesterday and smelled better. The bar was mahogany and occupied the entire wall opposite the door. There was no brass footrail. Instead, the place featured an immaculate mirror the whole length of the wall behind the bar. It would be easy to see anyone entering the establishment without turning one's head. At each end of the mirror was a meter-wide TV showing a replay of the Houston Astros game from the night before. At the right end, two men in jeans and orange T-shirts were watching the game. Their arms were covered with swirls of tattoos.

Three men, also in jeans, had their heads together in serious conversation at the other end of the bar. One of those was a guy about six five and 250 pounds with a shaved head, wearing a muscle shirt. It had no sleeves and had big arm holes to show off his lats and broad chest. The three watched Devlin in the mirror when he approached the bar and took a stool near the middle.

The middle was the home for six elongated handles for the beer taps. Each had a foot-long ceramic hand grip at its top with the name of a beer engraved on it. Devin didn't recognize any of them. When the barkeep approached, Devlin saw he had a gun strapped to his hip. It looked like a Glock police special. After a deep breath, Devlin asked. "Which of these beers would you recommend to a stranger?"

"Judging from your accent, I'd say try the dark one, the Mexican Umbro."

"Okay, I'll try that."

The man picked up a glass from a shelf below the bar top and began to draw the frothy tan liquid into it. The beer did look like a bit of home to a guy who had not been there for three years.

"I wonder if I could get a bit of food to go with this."

"Right now, all we have is Texas chili. Our cook doesn't get in until later. It's a little spicy."

"I'll have a cup and some crackers if you have them."

As Devlin munched, the big guy from the end of the bar approached. "Mind if I ask how a guy from Ireland got so far from home?"

"Curiosity," answered Devlin.

"Curiosity?"

"Aye. Texas is famous all over the world. I had a chance to see it and couldn't resist. Can I buy you a pint?"

They looked at the bartender. "Would you say that's a pint, Joe?"

"No, Josh. We know it's twelve ounces. He didn't ask for a pint."

Devlin, who knew a pint when he saw one, wondered what this bullshit was all about. He said, "Sorry for the confusion. Just a habit, I guess. The offer stands for a glass."

"I don't drink that brown piss."

Devlin addressed the barkeep. "Joe, may I call you Joe? A glass of his usual if you please."

Josh took the beer and sat on the stool next to Devlin. It was clear he was not finished asking questions. Devlin waited.

"The only foreigners we get in McAllen are the Mexicans. Why did you pick here?"

Devlin decided to cut to the chase. "Are you saying I'm not welcome? That the renowned southern hospitality doesn't apply to Irishmen?"

"Er, no. An overflow of curiosity, I guess."

"I picked this pub because it was the nicest one on the street. Do you live in the neighborhood?"

Josh was not happy at having the tables turned before witnesses. "Why do you care where I live?"

"As you say, just curiosity. I saw several motorcycles with number plates from other states when I took a stroll last evening."

"Yeah, well, a lot of veterans stop by here in their travels." He finished his beer and got up. "Thanks for the beer." He started back to his friends. As he walked away, Devlin saw a big gun, probably a SIG Saur .9mm, stuck in his waistband at the small of his back. His group put their heads together again.

"Joe, is Josh head of security or something?"

"No, but he's good friends with George, the owner. They were in the second Iraq War together."

Devlin asked, "I've seen several people on the streets carrying guns openly, but I was a little surprised to see you wearing one. Doesn't that put off some of the customers?"

"Nah. Almost all of the customers, even the women, are vets. A few are still on active duty. And this is Texas. We have an 'open carry' law here."

Devlin made a mental note that this guy, Josh, was probably trouble. He turned on his stool and looked at the relatively few people in the bar at noon. There were no women. The men looked to be about forty and still fit. It looked as if Joe's description of the clientele was accurate, but then a man in a coat and tie came in and went down the hall toward the toilets without stopping at the bar. No one seemed to pay him any attention.

Devlin's *toys* worked well. He had a good spot in the bushes for the recorder. For the first week, he went every night after the bar closed to harvest the thumb drive in the recorder and put in a fresh one. The harvest was not great, however. The recruitment of militants was going well, and there was some chatter about the chances of the current president losing next year's election, but there was no talk of anything specific being considered.

Long, hot, boring days were not Devlin's cup of tea. He decided to spend some time taking photos of the number plates on the vehicles in the parking lot during peak hours. Those might serve to identify some of the regular customers at least. The rest of the time, he went to movie houses and watched old westerns. He cut back the frequency of his harvesting trips to every other night. The payments were coming to his bank promptly. That eased his frustration somewhat, as did memories of seemingly interminable surveillance assignments in his early IRA days.

Toward the end of August, high school football games took over the social life of the city on Friday nights. Devlin had never seen an American football game and became captivated. Secondary schools in Ireland had European football teams, but attendance was scant because the best eighteen-year-old players were already members of professional teams. Here, the players, some of whom were huge, donned their armor and tried to maim one another while a mob of their mothers, fathers, sisters, brothers, aunts, uncles, and probably grandparents cheered them on, often lubricated by a few beers at a pregame picnic in the parking lot. In those parking lots, youngsters threw the strange, pointy balls around with abandon, often abusing one another if something went awry.

After the games, the bars were also crowded. Devlin found his harvesting trips more complicated. Die-hard fans would stand in the parking lot, rehashing the highlights of their game for extended periods after the bar closed. All manner of people seemed interested in the outcome of the silly game: guys in T-shirts and shorts through men in dark suits with shirts and ties. Waiting to do his brief chore did not sit well with Devlin.

And the harvests were getting more abundant. A big attachment to a private email to George, which he printed out, held the names of two hundred men in Arizona who had volunteered to do something if the president was not reelected. A man in Virginia offered the barn on his farm as a place to hide weapons. Oath Keeper clubs around the south offered their members, though no numbers were mentioned. Devlin went back to daily harvests.

*****

Back in Williamsburg, the general and the Society were getting excited. They had been collecting Devlin's findings, hoping to assemble a pile of evidence big enough to get the FBI's attention. Now they thought they had it. The general called Senator Richardson with the news on Tuesday morning.

"Where did you get all that stuff? How did you get it?" he demanded as soon as the general stopped for breath.

"Why does that matter?" asked the general. This is intelligence, not evidence. You know the FBI director. Put the pile on his desk and demand he get his troops in action."

"All of that is true, Eleanor, but I have to be sure that all this stuff is legitimate."

"You have my word on that, Jesse. We have an asset in place with some fancy toys. All the info came straight from the horse's mouth."

"You've bugged them?"

"Just a key player and his closest troops."

"I don't know, Eleanor. This is pretty crazy stuff."

"A weapons cache in a farm in Virginia? That's your turf, Jesse. Can you take a chance on ignoring a thing like that?"

"All right. I'll come down this weekend and pick it up."

"No, Jesse. John and I will drive the package up this afternoon. Can't see wasting any time at this point. Look for us by three." With an order given, the general hung up.

*****

The senator greeted them cordially, bade them sit, and took the two oversized manila envelopes to his desk. For half an hour, there was silence in the room. Then he picked up his phone and pushed a single button. "Elizabeth, I'd like to come over right now with the package we discussed this morning." After a long minute, he went on, "Okay. It will take that long for me to get there anyway."

He turned to the general and said, "Okay. You got your wish. I'll call to report what happened this evening."

He didn't call that night but did early Wednesday morning. "Sorry about last night. I hung out in the director's office until he finished organizing the agency's response. They are going to mass some manpower to check on the people and groups on the list and the owners of the vehicles you gave plate numbers for. Soon, they will want to take over the monitoring of the bugs your guy has placed. I assume you have a means to communicate, so that can be arranged. They will put the Virginia farmer high on the priority list. You got everything you wanted. What are you going to do?"

"We'll continue to accumulate the data Devlin collects while we wait to hear from the FBI. If something urgent pops up in the next few days, you will hear about it instantly."

"Good, Eleanor. I'll keep you up-to-date on the Virginia aspect. Have a good weekend."

Chapter Twenty-Five

One Friday night after the football game at the local high school, Devlin went to harvest the data on the recorder outside the bar. As usual, on Friday night, there were a couple of guys standing in the corner of the parking lot, shouting about the exciting plays in the game. Devlin had come to ignore these folks as harmless.

As Devlin bent over to retrieve the recorder in the bushes along the back wall of the building, he was suddenly aware he was not alone. He felt the cold, hard steel of a gun muzzle pressed into his back. He froze.

"There you are, caught in the act," growled a husky voice. "My friend was right. He thought he saw someone messing in the bushes here last Friday night, and look what I found: somebody who shouldn't be here doing something he shouldn't be doing. Surprise, surprise, it's the Irishman."

"What are you doing here, Irishman? Come along now, and we'll have a little conversation about what you were up to."

Devlin said nothing. He had not prepared for this.

The man grabbed Devlin by the back of his shirt and propelled him toward the street. His car was parked fifty yards or so away from the entrance to the parking lot so as not to be obvious. He cracked Devlin over the head with his pistol, causing a small flow of blood, and thrust him into the back seat of the car. Then he tied Devlin's hands behind his back with Devlin's own belt.

Devlin knew he was in deep trouble. His foggy brain could not identify his captor. He was dragged into some dark building where he could smell jet fuel. It was a bare metal building with a concrete floor. A bit of moonlight came in from a skylight on the roof. That was enough for his captor. The guy found a chair in a corner and some rope on a shelf above the sink and tied the still-groggy Devlin to the chair. Both feet were tied to the legs of the chair, and his hands were tied together behind the back of the chair.

Devlin had been interrogated in Ireland as a youth when he had some personal friends to protect. Still, he was reluctant to confess anything here because Sean had provided an escape from his troubles in Britain, and he had developed a loyalty to the United States during his years of the good life here. On top of that, the general was a friend of Sean's and seemed to be right about some guys being willing to stage a coup if the upcoming election didn't go their way. He struggled to create some bullshit story that this thug might believe.

The interrogator was crude. He started by slapping Devlin's face—hard.

"Alright, Irishman, tell me what you were up to and who put you up to it. Whatever it is, it's over now."

Devlin said nothing, still assessing the situation. He had no idea who this guy was.

The man swatted his face again. "You don't look so tough to me. You'll tell me sooner or later, so make it easy on yourself. You know that I've got some Irish blood in my veins and don't want to make this any worse than it has to be. You'll be helping your adopted country."

The silence continued. The guy waited a full minute, thinking.

Then he punched Devlin in the stomach, causing him to bend forward and almost retch. The man kept asking the same questions. Devlin said nothing. In fact, he had no idea what to say. To give in to this brute was against his Irish nature, but the blows hurt.

The silence infuriated his captor. He cursed and paced the floor, as his anger management class had instructed, but it did no good. Five steps from the chair to the back of the building and five more past it to the front did nothing to calm him. Each time he passed his silent prisoner just poured a little more fuel on the fire in his brain. He didn't know what to do next.

The world started to speed up for Devlin's captor. Scenes of the Irishman standing in front of a group of skinny tan people wearing white shirts and ties flashed across his mind. To his horror, they all ran to a big letterbox labeled "Vote here" and emptied boxes of envelopes into it.

He smashed Devlin across the face with the barrel of his pistol. The blow knocked out two teeth and tore his upper lip. Blood flew everywhere.

Just then, another man entered the building and stopped, awestruck. It was Donnie, Josh's bar buddy. He yelled, "What the hell is going on here?"

The guy seemed to recognize Donnie. He said, "If you don't wanna know, get out of here."

Donnie said, "You can't go around beating up people like this. It will tip off the whole world about the operation."

The guy shouted back, "This guy is spying on us. That could destroy the whole operation. If you don't want any part of this, maybe you don't want any part of the operation. It ain't gonna be for wimps."

Donnie just stood there.

The guy resumed pounding Devlin's body. Soon, Devlin was unconscious. He screamed, "Looks like this Irishman is a pussy!" He shoved the chair over backward, leaving Devlin on his back, his hands caught behind the chair, blood running down his cheek to the floor. He started pacing the floor again. Donnie tried to intercept him but was shucked aside as if he were a child. The guy walked for almost fifteen minutes, still getting angrier each time he passed the unconscious body. Finally, he went to the sink in the corner of the warehouse, stuck his gun in his waistband, found a bucket, filled it with water, and splashed Devlin's face repeatedly until the Irishman started to resume consciousness.

In a grim whisper, the guy said, "All right, Irishman. I'm out of patience. Talk now, or you're done."

Devlin said nothing, but when he focused on the guy's face, he knew the man was right. He was done. He said, "Our Father who art in heaven…"

This infuriated the guy, who kicked Devlin's head and screamed again. "What the hell were you doing out there? Who do you work for?"

The only response he got was, "Hallowed be thy name, thy kingdom come…"

The guy shouted, "You bastard!" He pulled the gun out of his waistband and shot Devlin twice in the chest.

"God!" screamed Donnie.

The guy whirled to face Donnie, still consumed by a red fog. He fired two shots. The first tore through Donnie's neck just below his jaw, causing a spurt of blood. The second caught him in the chest, driving him to the floor. The blood continued to gush for a few seconds, and then the body was quiet. *Good,* the guy thought. *He wanted no witnesses, whoever they were.* He would go back to the bush after dawn to see if he could figure out what the Irishman was up to, but he first had to get rid of the bodies.

Despite the fading light from the moon, he found a dirty tarp in a corner of the building, wrapped Devlin's body in it, and tossed it into the back seat of his car. He opened his trunk, dragged Donnie's body to it, and dumped him inside. He looked up at the sky. It was past 3:00 a.m., and his time was running out. He drove south to the shore road and then east until he came to the spot he had been told about where illegal immigrants had beaten a path through the scrubland and swamp grass from the river to the road. He dragged the bodies through the path to the riverbank and tossed them into the water as if they were so much garbage.

Chapter Twenty-Six

Early Monday morning, the retired JAG officer who had appointed himself the Society's computer watchdog pounded on the general's door.

When she opened it, still in her robe, he said, "General, I have some terrible news. The McAllen newspaper website reported this morning that after a serious rainstorm Saturday night into Sunday, two bodies washed up on the American shore of the Rio Grande. They were both shot in the chest. One was a local man. The police were able to identify the other body because his fingerprints were on record with Interpol. It was our man, Devlin Quinn. He's dead, General. He's dead. Of course, there is no information on where or how all this happened. He was likely caught in the act of harvesting the data from his listening devices. Whether they found a recorder or the devices, we don't know."

The general sagged onto the steps that led upstairs. "Oh my god!" she said. "None of us ever thought it would come to this. Have you told anyone else about this? Does the colonel now?"

"No, General. I came straight to you. What are we gonna do?"

After a moment, she said, "I don't know. I just don't know. Maybe the first thing to do is to call Sean because Devlin was his guy. I wonder if Devlin had any family."

Although she knew Sean got into the office early, especially on Mondays, she waited until eight thirty to call. He snatched up the receiver on the first ring as usual. She said, "Sean, it's Eleanor."

"Eleanor, it's not that I don't like to hear your voice, but if you're calling me at this hour, it can't be good news. You got the FBI all fired up. Wasn't that enough for a week?"

"I'm afraid it's more than bad, Sean. It's terrible. I don't know how to say it. I was never very good at writing those letters when one of my supply troops hit an IED."

"For Christ's sake, Eleanor. Spit it out!"

"Devlin Quinn has been murdered."

"Shit!" After a long silence, Sean went on, "That's my fault. I misjudged his capabilities. He was not renowned for his patience, much more for his skills and action. He said he had matured, and I was fool enough to believe him. I suspect he got a little cocky with early success and made a mistake. Obviously, the FBI needs to know about this immediately."

"Done. Does he have a family?"

"A younger brother, Brian, is all I know about. Brian is currently providing security for Liam's daughter on her trip to Africa. I'll contact him."

"I'm sorry, Sean. We never thought about this possibility."

"Neither did I. Let me get to work."

The FBI volunteered immediately to *help* the McAllen solve the murders. They were still reluctant to try to put an undercover agent in play, however.

A couple of days later, Liam's phone started playing Beethoven's Fifth. It was Cathryn calling from Africa.

Liam almost jumped out of his skin. "What's going on? Is everything okay?"

"Everything is okay here, but there is big trouble in Texas."

"What trouble? For whom?"

Brian broke in. "Devlin has been murdered. He was doing some spying for the general in McAllen. There was this guy, Josh, whom he was suspicious of. He must have done it. I'm heading for Texas."

"And what are you going to do? Go down there and waste Josh? The cops and the FBI will handle it. That's their business, and they're good at it."

"You know that's not how the Irish work, Liam. An eye for an eye. It's personal."

"Cathryn, where are you now?"

"We're on our way to Niger."

"Niger. Isn't that where Boko Haram is just killing women and children for fun? Brian, you can't let her go there."

Brian laughed. "Liam, you don't seem to know your daughter very well. She says that's where they need us the most, so that's where we're going. Besides, I need to get to Texas."

"Not so fast, Brian. The cops have been working on this for almost a week. Let me get a current update. I'll get back to you by tomorrow morning your time."

After a moment of whispered conversation, Brian said, "Okay, but in the meantime, I'm going to arrange transport."

Liam ended the call with his teeth grinding. Reluctantly, he searched his phone for the general's number. She answered on the first ring. "Liam. This is a surprise. I guess you heard about Devlin."

"Yeah. Brian called me from Africa. He's getting ready to go to Texas for revenge. Apparently, Devlin was suspicious of a guy called Josh."

"Don't let him do that. We're told the McAllen cops know Josh as a bully. They also think he's cunning. There is no proof of anything. Their theory is that the second body belonged to a witness to Devlin's murder, so he had to go too. The FBI is all over Josh and other regulars at the bar. They are optimistic, but that could just be their ego. They are giving me daily updates, sub rosa."

Liam said, "I'll call you tonight to get the latest. I promised to get back to Brian first thing in the morning their time."

"Good."

Liam spent the day in thought. He even thought about going to a church to pray on it, but that thought fled.

His call to the general provided no new information. No one had uncovered any proof that Josh was the murderer, and the FBI still felt that it was much too early to take the risk of trying to insert an undercover operative. Of course, the FBI was also very much interested in dealing with the longer-term implications of the whole scenario.

Liam called Brian at the time he calculated the group would be having breakfast in Niger. His calculations were correct. Brian was finishing his coffee when he answered the phone. "Yeah?"

Liam wasted no time with small talk. "The FBI and the McAllen police have no proof that Josh was Devlin's murderer. However, they are working on the theory that he did it and killed the other guy they found washed up on the riverbank to eliminate a witness. Josh is still around town, and the owner of the bar, who is the son of a man who narrowly lost an election for mayor ten years ago, is standing up for his character because of their service together in Iraq."

Brian growled. "So there's no progress. I'll be on a plane tonight."

Liam said, "If another Irishman shows up in McAllen, it will be a red flag. Let me offer you an alternative."

"What's that?"

"I will go to Texas and try to infiltrate the organization. I can be there tomorrow. It will take you two days to even get to the United States."

There was a long pause on the other end of the line. Liam could hear bits of whispers but could make out no words. Then Carolyn came on the line. "Still trying to be the hero, Dad. Didn't you learn anything from your last attempt at that?"

"We're all here, aren't we? And have you forgotten all the stuff I told you about my past work?"

"That was twenty years ago."

"It's like riding a bicycle, Cathryn, and I Just exercised some of those skills only a couple of years ago, and if I need them, I'll have contacts in the FBI."

There was another long silence. Then Brian got back on the phone. "All right, Liam. I'll give you a few days. I'll want a daily update."

"I'll ask the general to do that. She can meld the FBI report with mine and maybe give you some insight into the body language."

"Done."

"Now tell me what's going on in Niger."

"Nothing now. There have been no raids for the last two weeks. There is a small army of constabulary at the hotel, and much of that will travel with us. They do appreciate our efforts here. From what I've seen, they need all the help and wisdom they can get. We're leaving now to start that. Talk to you tomorrow."

Liam sat down and took several deep breaths. The task he had volunteered for in McAllen did not trouble him, but explaining his decision to Mary frightened him. He was too tired to attempt that tonight. He'd catch her when she came off shift at lunchtime tomorrow.

*****

Liam was waiting for Mary when she came out of the diner after her breakfast shift ended. Her white blouse showed a few brown spots where a splash of coffee had escaped her apron. When she saw him, she said, "Oh, Lord. This looks like more trouble. Did you have another nightmare?"

"Not the conventional kind, love. A small bump has come up in our road. We'll get through it just fine, but we do need to have a serious, private talk. Do you want to eat?"

"No. Let's go to the cathedral. It should be very private there. If this is going to be so serious, maybe He will help us."

That choice was a surprise, but he took her hand, and they started to walk. "A couple of reminders. Do you remember the female general who was involved in the big Chinese issue back around the first of the year?"

"Yes. She and her Society got lots of ink."

"Well, she's back on the warpath. The Society thinks they are onto a plot by a bunch of militias to keep our current president in office even if he fails to get reelected. Next, did I tell you about the two Irishmen who helped me rescue my daughter in New York?"

"Yes, but you never told me their names or anything about them."

"Sorry. They were brothers: Brian and Devlin. Brian is now serving as part of my daughter's team in Africa. I think they have a thing starting. The general hired Devlin to spy on what they think is the headquarters of the leaders of the potential insurrection."

"What does any of this have to do with us?"

"Devlin was murdered in Texas last week. Brian has his blood up and is threatening to abandon Cathryn, go to McAllen, and get revenge on the guy Devlin told Brian he was suspicious of the last time they talked."

"That's crazy."

"For two reasons: Brian will go to jail for life, and Cathryn will be without her best protection just as they enter the most dangerous place on their trip, Niger. That scares the hell out of me."

"Soooo?"

Just then, they arrived at the cathedral. They entered a side door near the back and slid into a pew at the very back of the giant nave. A huge rose window over the altar caused the sun to pave the center aisle in a pink haze. Dark wooden beams stretched from the stained-glass windows running along the top of the side walls and reached across the thirty-foot-high arched ceiling to the opposite wall. A priest was arranging something on the altar, but otherwise, the place was empty.

"So I volunteered to go to Texas to help with the investigation. I figure I'll be gone a week, maybe two."

"That's crazy too. How are you going to help the cops' investigation?"

"I'm going to pretend to want in on the action and see if I can dig up some proof about this guy Devlin was worried about."

"Liam, you told me that all that kind of stuff you won't talk to me about was behind you. That you could not even imagine anything that would get you to go back to it."

"And that still goes. This is different. It has nothing to do with my past, and I'm telling you all about it up front."

"It smells the same to me."

"Mary, this is not some superior officer giving me an order to do something. This is personal. I need to help Brian and make it as certain as possible that my daughter is as safe as she can be."

"So Daddy comes riding to the rescue to build up his renewed relationship with his daughter. I can see you wanting to do that, but

I thought I was part of that new life too. You decided on all this heroism without a word to me."

"You are part of my new life, Mary—the biggest part of it. I believed you would understand."

"You took me for granted. I thought I had found the companion I could spend the winter of my life with in peace—our peace. I believed it would be grand. I believed you were a grand fella. I even talked to a priest here about sleeping with you. It was all a damn pipe dream."

"No, Mary. No!"

She grabbed a handful of his shirt and glowered into his face. When she spoke, it was in a vicious whisper that sounded like the hiss of a rattlesnake. Spittle splashed on his face. "You, bastard! You, lying bastard!" She jumped up and stormed out of the church.

Liam put his hands over his face and bent to put his face on the back of the pew in front. *What have I done? What was I thinking? What can I do? Where can I go? Am I really an adrenaline junkie?*

He stayed there for what seemed a long time. The priest was no longer fussing at the altar. The place was silent except for the sound of his sighs. He was startled by the slamming of the church door. He looked up and saw Mary standing there. She said, "You're still here. I thought you were going to Texas."

"Do I have any reason to do anything else?"

"No. I'm just here to confess my insane anger to Him." She gestured toward the giant crucifix hanging over the main altar.

Liam had a sudden thought. "I have things to confess as well. Do you want to hear about all those things I have never talked to you about? Telling you will either help you understand why Texas is different from those things or cause you to hate me even more."

"I don't hate you, Liam. Hate would be something else I would need to confess. I just feel terribly betrayed. I pray He will go with you." With that, she started up the side aisle toward the confessional set into the wall of the church.

Chapter Twenty-Seven

Liam left to prepare for his trip. First, he poked through his dresser drawers to find all the T-shirts that showed patriotic messages: flags, quotations, ads for veterans' groups, and the like. The more colorful, the better. That done, he called the general to tell her about his trip and get the list of bugs Devlin had installed and where he put them. Then he called Sean and wasted no words.

"Sean, old buddy. I'm off to McAllen. The FBI needs some help in tracking down Devlin's murderer, and I need to keep Brian in Niger to protect Cathryn. On top of that, I owe those lads."

"That's crazy, Liam."

"I know, but it's what I'm gonna do. Will you have my back if things get rough? I plan to infiltrate whatever group exists and see if I can up some clues, just like we used to do."

"That was a long time ago, Liam. Do you think you're still able?"

"I'd better be."

"What name are you using on the trip?"

"Jerry O'Hara."

"Does it have to be Irish after the Devlin thing?"

"It has to be one I have a legend for. Besides, I don't sound like him."

"Who are you going to be in contact with?"

"Mostly the general. She's connected to the FBI. If needed, I'll call Brian."

"All right, Jerry. Be careful, and don't get cocky."

"Thanks, Sean. I may be needing for you to back me up again."

"Always there for you."

*****

Liam, calling himself Jerry O'Hara, arrived in McAllen that night and took a room at the same Holiday Inn at which Devlin stayed. The hotel called itself "The Luxury Hotel in McAllen," probably because it was the only one with a coffee shop and a self-serve, coin-operated laundry room tucked in beside the ice machine on the first floor.

His room was on the second floor, overlooking the city green. It was a very standard room, no sign of luxury, except for the queen-size bed. The door to the bath was just inside the entrance, opposite a narrow closet enclosed by an accordion enclosed door. There were the usual appliances, a small desk, and the brown drapes that matched the comforter on the bed. It was just like a hundred other hotel rooms he had occupied in his travels.

Following his normal routine, he went for a run first thing on a gray, soggy morning. He ran down Saloon Alley, catching the stale beer smell coming from the open doors, and then around the corner marked by the America First Bar, and back along the street behind it. He jogged through the empty parking lot and paused briefly to inspect the bush under the window where Devlin had hidden his recorder. It was still there, tucked down among the stalks of the bush and camouflaged as a wasps' nest by a piece of gauzy cloth. *The bad guys hadn't found that, and perhaps not the bugs either. Good.*

He spent the rest of the day checking out the neighborhood and watching the customers come and go to and from the bar. Among them were two youngish, lean guys in khakis whom Liam pegged as FBI agents. In late afternoon, he went back to the hotel and pulled on a red T-shirt with an American flag and the letters *USA* emblazoned on its front. He added a pair of navy-blue shorts and went to the bar.

An American flag secured in a heavy bronze stand guarded the door. He stepped past and stood inside the door for a couple of minutes, trying to adjust to the South's typically frigid indoor air, and took in the view. The bar, which looked to be mahogany, stretched the full length of the far wall. A spotless mirror, bookended by flat-screen TVs, filled the backbar wall. There were eleven stools, also mahogany, lining the bar. Each was covered by a tan cloth decorated with some writing.

There was no stale beer smell in the America First Bar. It was late morning, but the kitchen hadn't opened yet, so Liam took a second to develop his own perception of the natural fragrance of the place. To him, it smelled of leather with a slight hint of body odor—a man's place.

A few tables lined the inside of the front wall. Only one was occupied. A couple of mature women in camos looked to be at home there. The bar itself held five customers, anchored by two men in black T-shirts at the left end. Most of the customers were white men, about forty, who still looked fit. Many of them and the bartender carried pistols in holsters on their hips and wore boots. This was Texas.

One of the men in black T-shirts glanced up at the bar mirror and noticed him standing just inside the entry door. Stitched on the front of the T-shirt was the message "Donnie, RIP." The guy did not turn to look at Liam, but they locked eyes for a second in the mirror. Liam walked to the bar and took a stool near its center, leaving one stool open on each side of his. The legend on the seat of that stool said, "Freedom demands responsibility." He decided to claim that stool as his primary resting place in the establishment. He asked the bartender for a Lone Star draft beer and a menu.

The bartender said, "The cook is just getting things started up. It will take a few minutes."

"No sweat. I'm in no hurry," Liam replied. He started on his beer and ordered the BBQ sandwich. It went well with the beer.

Just as he was finishing his meal, the stool on his left was taken by the bigger guy in the black T-shirt. Their eyes met in the bar mirror again. The man said, "Welcome, stranger. Can I buy you another Lone Star?"

"That's very kind of you, sir. To whom am I in debt?"

"Folks around here call me Josh."

"Nice to meet you, Josh. I'm Jerry."

"Jerry, who?"

"O'Hara."

"An Irishman?"

"Not really. My great-grandfather got off the boat about a hundred years ago, but the genes got diluted over the course of all that time. I'm just plain old American."

"What brought you to McAllen?"

"Just a bit of tourism. I saw many countries around the world when I was in the service. Now that I'm retired, I thought I'd see more of my home country."

"Many of us here were in military service and were shipped out. What branch of the service were you in?

"It was not the military."

"What then?"

Jerry put on his most charming smile, turned to face Josh, and said, "As they say on television, if I told you, I'd have to shoot you."

"So you were a spook."

Jerry said, "Field agent is a better description."

There was silence for a long moment while Josh rolled all this around in his head.

"Josh, is there something going around at this place? I saw a cop car sitting just down the street while I was out running this morning, and that young guy sitting in the corner nursing a bottle of beer smells like FBI to me."

"Yeah, the cops are on our case. A few days ago, the bodies of two guys who used to hang out here washed up on the shore of the river. They'd been murdered. One of them was a friend. All the regulars have been interviewed at length. Now the cops just watch the place almost 24-7. As a new arrival, you may find them wanting to talk to you."

"I wouldn't like that. I heard I'd be among friends here."

"Where did you hear that?"

"A website."

"Which one?"

"Parler."

Josh grunted and then got up to return to his original spot at the end of the bar. There was a pistol with a fancy bone handgrip stuck in his belt at the small of his back. Liam called out, "Hey, Josh, a quick question."

Josh turned.

"Where'd you get that fancy pistol? That's pretty cool. Everybody in McAllen seems to carry, but no one has a class piece like yours."

"Ha. There's a gun shop about a block past the border crossing that specializes in these things. Tell them I sent you if you want."

Josh then continued to the end of the bar. Liam signaled to the bartender for a refill. When it came, he asked, "I wouldn't have thought a guy like Josh would go for a fancy pistol. Has he had it long?"

"No. Only about a week. For years, he carried the SIG Saur he brought back from Iraq. He and George, the owner, served together there. He was proud of that and claimed he'd killed a couple of 'rag heads' with it. He seemed to have an attachment to that piece."

Interesting, thought Liam. He then relaxed and enjoyed the rest of his beer. As he walked back to his hotel, he thought he was being followed. A stop in a store doorway and a couple of turns off the direct route confirmed his suspicion. It was quite a first day on the job.

About dawn Texas time the next morning, he called the general. "I'm here and have started the process. Nothing happening yet. I did find that Devlin's recorder is still in place. Are you getting data from the FBI on what it captures?"

"Not yet. Their theory is that Devlin was captured while he was harvesting the thumb drive. They're looking for a safer way to retrieve the data. Their lab is cooking up a more remote collection system. Maybe even a drone."

"How long is that going to take?"

"God knows."

"Shit. I need to know whether Devlin's toys are still in place and functioning. Can they tell that much yet?"

"I'll find out."

"Thanks."

It was too early to call Africa, so he lay down for a nap. As he dozed off, he wondered what Mary was doing at this particular moment. No. He could not let his mind be distracted by romantic wanderings. Any loss of concentration could be fatal. He learned that decades ago. Maybe something like that caused Devlin's loss.

Somewhat refreshed after an hour of semisleep, Liam dialed Cathryn in Niger. "Did I wake you up?"

"Hell no. We're working our butts off over here. The hotel is okay, and there are lots of soldiers around. The hotel is just north of the main road that runs east-west between the hotel and the parallel river. There's a patch of farmland just north of the hotel, which is divided up into small personal plots. The owners of these tend to camp in shacks along the road that leads back there, working 24-7 to fight off the wasteland that starts about a hundred yards farther north. That's the Sahara Desert, and it keeps moving south. The country is big, but the desert is eating it up. This is critical because the population keeps growing with no land to live on and very limited land to grow food on. The birth rate is high, and refugees from Nigeria, Burkina Faso, and even Libya keep coming here, even though lots of kids are starving. Essentially, all the water is in the south of the country with the river and Lake Chad, which is on the border with Chad.

"There's a water pipeline from the river that runs up to the hotel's water treatment plant. We're working on a project to extend that supply farther north to irrigate the farms. Ultimately, they might be able to extend it about another mile to an abandoned uranium mine and possibly recover some of that land for living and farming."

"You sound tired."

"I'm exhausted. We will have done what we can do in a week, and I'll be very glad to get on a plane back to civilization for some R and R. We've taught a couple of people to weld and will leave our welding machine here with the instructional videos. In a week, we will have helped the locals build enough piping to carry water to the farm patch. Twenty-foot-long sections of pipe just appear every morning. I think they stole it from the oil company's materiel yards in Nigeria. Whatever. We've built a couple of pumps and taught a gaggle of women to connect and maintain them. It's all we can do.

"If they can get the water to that old uranium mine, they'll have some space and infrastructure to farm. Maybe they can grow some of the sweet potatoes we brought the seed for. Some of the natives are up for the task, but the government is noncommittal. Time will tell. I suppose you want to talk to Brian."

"Not yet. What else is going on with you?"

"I spend my days directing, cajoling, and negotiating with sergeants who laugh at us behind our backs. It's wearing. Here, talk to Brian. He's holding his breath."

"Hello, Brian. I'm not sure what I have to tell you is worth holding your breath for."

"Well, tell me anyway."

"I've connected with Josh, the guy Devlin was suspicious of. He seems to have appointed himself the security guard for what, if anything, is going on there. The FBI is setting up some fancy, long-range spy equipment, and Devlin's toys still seem to be operating. I have an idea of a way to use that to worm my way into their hearts and see what lurks there. Meanwhile, I'm gonna go to the high school football game Friday night and hope to dissect it with Josh in the bar afterward. He just bought himself a new gun. Everybody down here has a gun, but maybe he got one because he had to dump the murder weapon."

"I seriously doubt he'll confide anything like that to a stranger."

"No, but you never know what tidbit might pop up to a trained interrogator between the lines."

"Good luck and stay safe. This place is a fooken hellhole. I can't wait to get out of here. We're goin' back on commercial flights, and we hope to be able to stop in Ireland for a couple of days. I haven't seen my family in years."

We? Liam asked himself. "Okay, Brian. Have a great trip. I'll be in touch."

Calm down, old man. Cathryn can take care of herself, and it's time for you to go to bed.

Liam went to the gun shop on Friday morning. Josh was right. The owner had dozens of ornate pistols for sale. Most were stainless steel or chrome plated, and all of them had bone or intricately carved and stained wood handles.

The owner came over with a big smile. "Beautiful, aren't they?" He was a man about Liam's size, Hispanic, but clearly had been in the United States a long time. His English was perfect, and he even had a slight Southern accent. His name was Eduardo, Eddie to his customers.

"They are. Where do you get them from?"

"My son and I make them here. The base is just a standard Barretta, which we strip down and fancy up. We love being artistic with the grips and can even build a short extension to the handle to increase the clip capacity from nine to twelve. The bone and exotic wood come from Mexico. Some Mexicans order them online and give them as birthday presents."

"They look expensive."

"Moderately, but we have a discount for the people Josh sends up. We are a little off the beaten path, and he's been nursing that old SIG Saur for ten years, so we use him as an advertisement for upgrading."

"Did you take the SIG in trade, sort of a case history?"

The man laughed. "I never thought of that, but taking trade-ins would make a living with the gun laws, even in Texas, too damn complex. See one you like?"

"About six. What price range are we talking about, including the Josh discount?"

"The bone handles are about seven-fifty. The woods are a little more for the original artwork."

"That's a little stiff for my art budget, and I suppose there's a background check required?"

"Yes, but we can get that done in a day. There's no other waiting period here."

"The check is strike two. I'll think about it, but don't hold your breath."

"I understand. Nice meeting you."

*****

The football game Friday night was a doozy. McAllen was hosting Edinburg, home to Pan-American University and a regional and cultural rival. Edinburg scored a touchdown with three minutes left to go ahead 21–17. McAllen came roaring back, led by quarterback Tobias Brown, who completed three passes to put McAllen on the Edinburg thirty-yard line. Then there was a bad pass from the center that bounced away from Brown. He recovered the ball, picked and spun his way through a forest of large, speeding bodies, and broke into the clear in the center of the field. From there, it was a footrace to the goal line, and Brown won. They kicked the extra point for a 24–21 lead with ten seconds left in the game.

Edinburg did not fold. Their quarterback caught the kickoff and started up the left sideline behind what looked like a wall of blockers. With five seconds left, he stopped and threw a forty-yard lateral pass to their fastest running back, who was lurking near the right sideline with a single blocker. He leaped into high gear, sprinting for the goal line sixty yards away. He got halfway there before Tobias Brown, left in on the kickoff team by his prescient coach, slipped around the blocker to tackle him and end the game.

The TV sets at both ends of the bar were changed to show the president expounding his fears for the integrity of the future election at a rally in Ohio. Some of the crowd from the game surged into the bar, eager to relive the exciting finish. Josh was practically dancing when Liam caught up with him at the end of the bar he normally claimed. "A beer for everybody!" he shouted as he threw a fifty-dollar bill on the bar.

Liam said, "That Brown kid is a hell of a player," after Josh calmed down a bit.

"Oh, yeah! I wish we had a quarterback like him when I played," replied the big man. "I was the left tackle. The defense had to get through me to get to our quarterback, and that just didn't happen. Unfortunately, our guy couldn't throw worth a damn."

"I wonder where Brown will go to college."

"If he stays down here, they will convert him to a DB or a wide receiver, maybe have him run back kicks."

"Why would any coach limit him like that?"

"Obviously, you don't know much about football. Not surprising. You're too small to have played even in high school. There are two reasons: He's only six feet tall, and he's black. He'd never be able to lead the team."

"There have been several black quarterbacks at big-time schools."

"Yeah, but they are all six foot five or bigger. At that height, they can see over linemen who are six foot eight. They have had pro scouts lookin' at them since they were sophomores in high school. The scouts have connections to the college coaches. A bidding war erupts, which is why some superstars sign letters after junior season. The payoff for the scouts is that they get first dibs on the college coach's best graduates. There are dozens of six-foot-tall high school QBs like Brown."

"Well, I learn something new every day. With all this football talk going on, it seems strange to have the president shouting his fears about fraud in an election that's not coming for over a year. Every sitting president has his ratings go down as he ages in the job. I haven't been paying much attention. Is there something special going on?"

"The damn media criticize everything he does, and some local governments seem to be kissing the asses of the BLM rioters rather than putting them in jail. There's no telling whether those local guys will run a fair election or not. He's raising awareness about some really un-American possibilities. It's a good reminder that we have a big job to do, even while we celebrate a local victory."

"A big job to do? What is that?"

"Forget I said that. It's nuthin' for you to worry about."

"Okay. By the way, I went up to the gun shop this morning. He has quite a selection of fancy pistols. Eddie claims you are one of his chief converts from an old army pistol to one with some class."

"Yeah, my SIG was a long-time friend, but this beauty does have class. Did you buy one?"

"No. I forgot about the background checks. I'm not anxious to have the FBI poking around in what I've been doing since I retired."

"For an extra hundred or so, we can probably get him to forget the legalities."

"Nah. It's already a little rich for my blood."

He took a little different route back to the hotel that night. It was almost midnight. The temperature was twenty degrees cooler than it had been at game time. This route had more street lights, and a few more turns at where he hoped to get a glimpse of whoever was following him.

And someone was. It was a man in a T-shirt and jeans, a little taller than him but not much heavier. As he made one of those turns, he got a quick look at the man's face. It was Josh's buddy, the other guy who had been wearing the "Donnie, RIP" T-shirt the day Liam had first entered the bar. What was his name? Steve? Whatever. The guy had no idea about how to go about his chore. Liam began to consider ideas on how to take advantage of that. Steve, if that was his name, stayed on his tail all the way to the hotel and then sat on a bench in the grassy square across the street. Liam went up to his room and watched the guy sit there for twenty minutes. When Liam turned off the lights, he got up and left. *So he was alone and only interested in whether I was going to bed or not.*

Liam took his usual run just after dawn on Saturday morning. The sun was only a little above the horizon when he turned up the street behind the bar. The humidity was high, but the temperature was only about seventy, so there was little stress—until he got to the parking lot.

There, he saw Josh poking around in the bushes at the rear wall of the building. He jogged over and tried a joke. "Are you the landscaper too?" He jogged in place, looking down at the crouched man. Josh stood up, perhaps at what he saw as an insult for a man of his stature.

"Ha. That will be the day. My theory is that the Irishman bugged the owner's office. He must have hidden a recording device in these bushes somewhere."

"Have you hired a guy to sweep the place?"

"We don't have anybody to do that, and with all the scrutiny we're getting, George doesn't want to raise any more eyebrows. I'm trying to find some proof that somebody's spying on us so we can get rid of any spying eyes before we finalize our plans."

"For the big job."

"I told you to forget about my slip."

"The memory's fading. Look, if you and George want, I can do a crude scan for you. I have some experience with the old-fashioned types of this technology. It has gotten more sophisticated in recent years, but if your theory is right, a lone warrior probably didn't have access to the best. Let me know."

Liam was wearing his DAV T-shirt for Saturday. Josh came to him as soon as he got to the bar for lunch. "Come on back with me." He led Liam down the hall past the restrooms to George's office. The door was open, but Josh knocked on the frame before entering. George was sitting in a big leather desk chair behind a nondescript gray metal desk that held only a laptop and a telephone handset.

George said, "So you're the guy who's the bug expert."

Liam glanced at Josh. *What kind of lies had he told to arrange this meeting?*

"Jerry O'Hara, George. I'm nowhere near an expert, but I know something about older technology."

"Shouldn't you have a little box that goes beep when you find something?"

"Sorry. All I can do is look in the usual places where somebody would hide simple stuff and see if anything is there."

"Okay. Go ahead."

Liam pulled off the earpiece on the handset and found what he expected: a small black wafer. He showed that to George and Josh. Josh smiled and flipped his head at George.

Liam said, "This is a classic telephone bug, old-fashioned but still effective. There is probably a voice-listening device here as well. Let me look under your desk drawers and in the kneehole."

George got up. Liam felt around under the center drawer of the desk and inspected the walls of the kneehole. He found nothing. Then he climbed up onto the seat of the guest chair and removed the cover of the ceiling light fixture. There, attached to the base plate of the fixture by a magnet, was a cylindrical device about the size of an AA battery. It had a six-digit serial number imprinted on it.

"A general listening device. Again, old. There's gotta be a recorder someplace nearby. Josh, maybe you were right to be looking in those bushes outside."

Josh's smile lit up the room. George scowled.

Liam said, "Guys, what's going on here? I hear the president worrying about the election on TV, but all this spy stuff strikes me as over-the-top."

George replied, "There is a large and growing group of citizens who share the president's concerns. The 'America First' movement is coming together to make sure those who support the president come out to vote and motivate their friends to do the same. His opponents are socialists, plain and simple, and don't give a damn about law and order. These listening devices are proof of that. We intend to do all we can to ensure the election is fair and square."

"Wow!" said Jerry. "I never thought the situation was anywhere near that serious."

George snapped, "Well, it is. Let me make some phone calls to warn other groups about these things."

Back out in the bar, Liam cornered Josh. "Come on, big guy. What's really going on?"

"Jerry, we're just going to do everything we can to ensure our president gets reelected."

"Does that include planting bugs in the offices of the opposing party?"

"As all the bigwigs say, 'Everything is on the table.' We have lawmakers here and in other states tightening up voting laws and updating voter registrations. Some Southern states have formed a coalition to compete with those up in the Northwest. If that ain't enough, we'll be prepared for any problems that might come. We are building support among active servicemen as well. Right now, I'm gonna have a beer and go poke around in those bushes some more."

"Good luck. It's hot out there."

Liam left to call the general. After a minimum greeting, Liam reported, "There is something big going on here. The bar owner seems to be a prime mover in assembling a nationwide network of people who are dedicated to getting the current president reelected. They're working on getting the vote out and changing voting laws but say 'everything is on the table.' Lots of secrecy and code words."

"Have you gotten any insights into Devlin's murderer?"

"Not really, but someone followed me back to the hotel the last couple of nights. I plan to have a talk with him soon."

"Be very careful. The FBI has gotten their remote listening system operating and has promised to update me daily, more often if something that sounds urgent pops up."

"Good. I'll be in touch." He ended the call and thought, *I'd like to be in touch with Mary too, not having any luck. That's starting to feel more important than anything I'm doing here, and that ain't good. I need to keep focused. Am I really an adrenalin junkie, pushing off other things? I thought I was past that.*

He spent the rest of the afternoon taking a tour of the town and had a hamburger at the hotel for supper. He wondered whether he was missed at the bar.

Chapter Twenty-Eight

Sunday dawned hot and humid as usual. Liam got his run in as usual. It was very routine. So much so that he felt the need to go to Mass as he would have if he were home with Mary. When he asked the hotel staff about a Catholic church, he was shocked. The Baptists, the Evangelicals, the combination got the town fathers to forbid the bars from opening on Sundays. He also found that there was a small church with a large refugee hospice not far from the hotel. He went upstairs and put on khakis and a polo shirt to go to church, just as he would have in DC. The Mass would be in Spanish, but he felt he could figure it out.

And he did. He came away with an empty feeling, though. At the sign of peace, there were a couple of waves, some smiles, and a few nods, but he missed Mary's kiss on his cheek. He prayed he was doing the right thing here in Texas but wasn't at all sure that God gave a damn about what he did.

As he exited the chapel, he saw a white van back into a truck loading dock on the large refugee center next door. The logo painted on the side of the truck in pink said, "Feed the Hungry." He was impressed that a national organization was active in supporting a small rescue program in a remote neck of the woods.

Then he got a shock. The driver stepped out of the van. It was Josh! Josh opened the back hatch on the van, climbed up onto the loading dock, and punched a code into a box on the door frame. The roller door opened.

Liam walked over to the doorway. "Josh, I'm amazed to see you here."

"Jerry! What are you doing here?"

"I just came from Mass."

The van was crammed full of boxes and long plastic containers. Liam looked around, saw no one else coming, and said, "Do you want some help in unloading this stuff?"

"I can handle it."

"Of course, but I just heard a sermon about loving your neighbor. Would a little help be useful?"

"Yeah, okay. Pile the boxes on the right as you go in. The plastic bins go on the left, nearer the fridge."

Josh began dragging containers out of the van and placing them on the loading deck. Liam picked each one up and carried it into its appropriate place inside the building. When they had worked up a sweat, they stopped for a short rest. Liam asked, "How did you get this job?"

Josh did not answer for a long moment, and then he said, "It's a long story."

"We have time."

Again, the hesitation. "I was arrested for beatin' up a guy in a bar fight and was sentenced to one hundred hours of public service and an anger management class. This was the public service. The people were nice, the work was easy, and it kinda felt like I was back in the army, doing something good. When my one hundred hours were up, they offered me a job. I took it. Been doing this on Sundays for almost ten years. Occasionally, some other things come up that I can help with."

"That's a great story. I'm glad you told it to me."

A nun, with her habit covered by an apron, came to the door just as Liam was putting the last box on the stack. She said, "Oh, Josh recruited a helper today. He works so hard."

Liam said, "Glad to help out, Sister. I don't get much chance to do that these days."

"I'm afraid we take advantage of Josh. We usually have a list of other chores lined up for him when he gets here on Sundays. Most of those involve heavy lifting. A little help goes a long way."

She walked over to the end of the van. "Josh, there are just a couple of things today. Do you have a few minutes?"

Josh smiled, shrugged at Liam, and closed the van door. "Of course, Sister." The two of them got the door to start closing and walked into the bowls of the building.

Liam stood for a moment and then shook his head. He wondered who the real Josh was. The bully who set himself to intimidate strangers? The man who murdered Devlin? Or the man who willingly did chores for a diminutive nun?

Liam decided to live up to his image as a tourist today. He rented a car and set off to Brownsville to look at their famous zoo. It was interesting, as was the trolley tour of the town. Not worth a whole day, though, and he had paid for the day with the car, so he drove up to Edinburg for a look at the Pan-American University campus of the U of T. Then he went back to the hotel to face what was really bugging him: his need to talk to Mary. He called at seven. After five rings, it went to voicemail. Her invitation to leave a message ended with, "Have a good day." Though he did not know what he would have said to her, this had definitely not been a good day.

When he heard the beep, he said, "Mary, it's me. I'm okay. Hope you are too. With a little luck, I'll be home next week. Love you."

He exploded after he hung up. *Love you? What kind of greeting card bullshit is that? Are you so screwed up you can't even say I love you like a man? You sound like a fuckin' pimply teenager!*

Liam wanted a drink, a real drink, and there was nowhere he could get one in McAllen on Sunday night. The burning in his gut would not go away. He went down to the hotel restaurant but took only one bite of the hamburger he ordered. He went out for a walk, his mind spinning like the damn little blue circle on his computer screen that annoyed him so. Maybe the lack of access to booze was a good thing. Maybe there was a God watching over him. He remembered the time Sean had lost his cool, gotten drunk, and nearly gotten them all killed. He had pulled their fat out of the fire then, and he would do it now as well, although he could not shoot his way out of his troubles with Mary. He had to put that out of his mind. He knew damn well that if he didn't keep sharply focused on the task here, he could end up dead. After an hour with no solution in sight, he went to bed and, eventually, slept.

It was raining hard Monday morning, so Liam did not go out to run. The news reported that the rain was from the western fringes of a hurricane that had hit New Orleans. He went to the bar about noon, dressed in Sunday's green polo shirt. Josh greeted him with a fist bump and a half smile. Liam wondered whether Josh was embarrassed about his "good guy" side being exposed yesterday. He decided not to mention anything about it, especially since Josh's buddy, Steve, joined them.

Liam said, "I rented a car yesterday and did some exploring. I had been told the Brownsville Zoo was special, and it was, though I was not thrilled to get so close to all those snakes."

Steve said, "My kids love that place. Donnie's kids did too."

Nobody said anything for a whole minute. Steve said, "Sorry."

Liam resumed his travelogue. "Then I went up to Edinburg. The locals are still talking about the football game up there. The Pan-Am campus was interesting too. They had a platform where a skinny kid was ranting about how terrible it was for the president to be spreading fear about the possibility of election fraud. One of the kids in the crowd started to argue with him, and soon, there was a shouting match going on. It reminded me of a Sunday I spent at Hyde Park in London many years ago. Free speech. Wonderful."

Josh said, "Yeah, those college kids have been brainwashed by their socialist professors and just want to complain about everything the president does."

"Well, the other kid was not one of those. I thought he was going to climb up on the stage and deck the speaker."

"Man after my own heart," said Josh.

"At least they're free to tell it the way they see it," said Jerry.

"So is the president," said Josh.

"Yeah, but does it always have to get violent? What happened to civil debate?"

"The problem with civil debate is that it ends up being just a bunch of hot air. Nothing happens. We need action."

Jerry's cell phone went off. That was the first time that happened in the whole week. Liam's heart jumped. *Is it Mary?*

No. It was the general. He moved to the front of the bar for some privacy.

"Liam, I just got a call from the FBI listening team. Last night, there was a conversation about you in the owner's office. He and Josh have become concerned about how you found Devlin's devices so easily. They are also suspicious about anyone new to the scene, as are the leaders of some of the other groups George has been talking to on the phone. George wants you 'out of the way.' They could try something soon."

"Okay, General. Thanks for the heads-up. I'll take care of things."

He had another beer with Josh and Steve. The weather cleared, and he took his leave, saying he had to get his run-in. "I'll be back after supper," he said on his way out the door.

The walk back to the hotel was all the exercise he got. He used the time to generate a plan. He and Steve would have that talk tonight, assuming Steve followed him again. Back at the hotel, he collected some tools: his Swiss Army knife, the lock-picking tools he hid in one pair of his smelly running shoes, and his penlight. Then he took a nap, after which he showered.

He got back to the bar at dark, smelling of Irish Spring. Most of the talk was about the Monday night football game, which would feature the New York Giants and the Green Bay Packers. Liam knew nothing about either team, so he just cheered when one of his "little guys" made a good play.

The underdog Packers won, causing some money to change hands among the regular patrons and a lot of grousing. Not a bettor, Jerry laughed along with the good-natured banter and then took off.

As he anticipated, Steve followed him again. It was after ten, but some other football fans were spilling out onto Saloon Alley. This wasn't part of Liam's plan. He walked slowly, as one might who had taken a run in the heat only a few hours before. He stopped to tie his shoe on the rear bumper of a car parked near the corner of a side street. Out of the corner of his eye, he saw Steve lurking a block behind.

Liam turned quickly into the side street, put his back to the wall of the corner building, and waited. He felt the familiar rush of adrenalin as his heart rate revved up to "fight" speed and his senses to high alert. It was comfortable.

Steve came hustling around the corner, oblivious to danger. Liam was behind him and applied a chokehold before Steve knew what had happened.

The man Steve knew as Jerry said quietly, "All right, Steve, why are you following me?"

Steve was having trouble breathing but gasped. "Josh told me to see if you met anybody after you left the bar."

Liam relaxed the pressure a bit on Steve's windpipe and asked, "Why?"

"He and George are suspicious that you might be a spy like the Irishman. They want you out of the way so they can finalize their plans for the operation."

"'Out of the way'? What does that mean? Did they get the Irishman out of the way too?"

Steve said in a constricted voice, "I don't talk anything about what happened to the Irishman."

Liam increased the pressure on Steve's throat. He said, "This is a very useful hold, Steve. I can squeeze harder on your carotid arteries and put you to sleep, or I can squeeze on your windpipe and strangle you. What is this operation all about?"

Steve struggled for a big breath; Liam relaxed the pressure a little. Steve said, "I don't know much. I think that if the president gets screwed out of reelection, a bunch of America First groups all over the country are going to try to prevent the new guy from taking office."

"And how are they planning to do that?"

"I don't know. I heard someone was talking to the president's lawyers, but that's all I heard from Josh. I'm not in the inner circle."

"What have you heard about the murders?"

"Josh is glad the Irishman is gone. He thinks he was a spy and planted those listening devices. Josh thinks Antifa hired him, met with him that night, and shot him when he had nothing to report."

"Why would they kill their spy?"

"I don't know."

"And Donnie? How does he fit into that scenario?"

"I don't know. Maybe Antifa thought he was going to expose the Irishman as a spy. Maybe he was a witness to the shooting. I don't know."

"I got the impression the other day that you and Donnie were close friends," said Liam.

"We were brothers-in-law. We married sisters."

"And how are things going at your house these days?"

"It's hell. His wife thinks that I was involved in it somehow, and my wife is buying her suspicions. We haven't even talked in over a week."

"Would you like to get rid of some of those *I don't know*s? I could help."

"I don't know."

"There you go again. I promise you one thing, Steve. I'm not about to look over my shoulder anymore to see if you're following me. We are gonna end that tonight." He gave Steve's neck another squeeze.

"What do you want me to do?"

"Let's think about it a little bit. I have a different scenario about what happened. The Irishman was likely a spy for somebody. I think Josh found the Irishman poking around in the bushes at the back of the bar harvesting the recording from the listening devices he planted. I think Josh grabbed him and took him somewhere to find out who sent him. Where might that place be?"

After a moment's thought, Steve said, "Shit, I don't know. He wouldn't have taken him home to do anything like that."

"So where then?"

"I don't know."

"There you go again." Liam again increased the pressure of his grip and then released it.

Steve gasped. "We have this little warehouse down near the airport. George and Josh sometimes get shipments of signs and flags and other stuff down there."

Liam went on, "The other theory about the murders goes on like this: Josh can't beat any information out of the Irishman, goes crazy, and shoots him. Somewhere during the beating, Donnie shows up and witnesses the murder. Josh, still out of his mind, shoots Donnie to eliminate the witness to his crime. He then packs up the bodies and finds a place to dump them into the river."

"That's crazy!" Steve shouted, despite his limited breathing capability.

Liam asked, "Did anybody find Donnie's car?"

"No."

Liam lifted Steve's pistol out of the holster on his hip, released the choke hold, and pushed Steve two steps away. "How about we get your car and take a look at this warehouse?"

Steve was rubbing his neck. After a moment, he said, "You got the gun."

"Have you ever fired it?"

"Only in a couple of target sessions. I only carry it 'cause most people at the bar do."

"Well, we know it works, right?"

"It works."

"Good. Let's go get your car."

Chapter Twenty-Nine

Steve drove south on the road to the airport, which was labeled "International" but had only one runway and catered mainly to small craft. Two metal buildings were located at the southern end of the property, just outside the perimeter fence. There was a car parked outside one of them. Steve stepped hard on the brakes for a second when he saw the car.

"That looks like Donnie's car."

The building it was parked in front of had a roll-up garage door, a personnel door in the front wall, and two skylights in the roof. They parked in front of the garage door. Steve got out and inspected the other car.

"It's Donnie's, all right."

Liam said, "Let's look inside the building."

"I don't have a key."

"Who has keys?"

"Josh and George."

Liam asked Steve to shine the penlight on the lock in the personnel door while he picked it.

When they turned on the ceiling lights inside, they found a space about twenty feet wide and thirty feet long with metal walls, a concrete floor, and a sink in the back corner. There were some shelves against the back wall. A few unassembled cardboard shipping boxes leaned against the shelves, which were otherwise empty.

The middle of the room resembled a war scene. A chair was lying on its back, remnants of rope on its legs and back. It was surrounded by a circle of dried brown stuff. A bucket with a little water still in it stood next to that. Six feet closer to the door lay a second circle of dried brown stuff.

Liam said, "Well, well. We have the classic TV interrogation scene with two puddles of dried blood to mark the murder spots. Look, there are even a few spots in a blood trail leading toward the garage door. Don't touch anything."

Liam got out his phone and photographed everything. Steve just stood there with his mouth open.

Liam said, "There can be no doubt that this is the murder spot. Would Antifa have even known about this place, much less have a key for the door? Forget that last point. I just demonstrated how anybody with the skill could have gotten in. The bodies were dragged out and dumped in the river. Whoever did that must have some local knowledge to find a place to do that in the middle of the night. Have you heard of any local Antifa cells?"

Steve snapped out of his stupor and said, "No. I don't pay any attention to any of that stuff."

"Does anybody except George and Josh pay attention to that stuff?"

"I don't know."

"There you go again. How did you and Josh get to be buddies?"

"Donnie introduced me. He was a lot more interested in the 'America First' thing than I was. He got me to help with handling stuff at the warehouse with Josh, and we just sort of drifted into a threesome at the bar. I was never let in on the details of what Josh and George are up to."

"So you say."

"It's the truth. I have a good life: a couple of good kids and, up until Donnie's death, a loving wife. My father died in an accident on a drilling rig and left me a ton of money. With my army pension and what I get from selling real estate on weekends, I'm good for life."

Liam was quiet for a full minute, thinking, *Can I get this guy to help me find some evidence? He has a big incentive to clear his own name and now may be closer to the leaders of the plot, whatever it is.*

"Steve, I could use some help here. George and Josh seem to have gotten a bug up their asses about me; otherwise, why have you followed me? I'm enjoying my time on the Gulf Coast but can't go around looking over my shoulder all the time. We'd both be better off if these murders were solved. How about we work on that together?"

"I don't know, Jerry. What would I have to do?"

"Listen to everything Josh says. See if you can find out where he was the night Donnie got killed. See if there are any hints about what happened to the SIG Saur he carried around all those years and bragged about."

"Do you really think he did it?"

"Right now, he's my 'person of interest,' as the detectives on TV are prone to say, but I'm neither a cop nor on TV. It's just my guess. I hate to see my country caught up in another civil war."

"All right. I'll listen, but I'm not gonna stick my neck out."

"And you won't get your neck in any choke holds when you follow me."

"Yeah, that was a surprise. You're a strong little bastard."

"Don't forget that."

They shook hands. Liam used his handkerchief to wipe the door handle, and they left. Steve drove Liam back to the Holiday Inn. They left Donnie's car where it stood.

Liam texted his pictures of the crime scene to the general when he got back to the hotel. He would call in the morning.

The general answered promptly the next morning. There was no polite chatter. "Where did you get those pictures?"

"In a small warehouse-type building just outside the fence at the southern end of the McAllen airport. Apparently, the 'America First' group at the bar uses the place to store flags and some propaganda signs when needed. There was nothing there last night. Can you get the FBI to put a forensics team in there today before anybody returns to clean out the evidence? There has to be a slew of fingerprints as well."

"I'll do my best. Has anything happened with you?"

"The guy who was following me and I had a chat last night. He was the brother-in-law of the other victim. I think I recruited him to help a little. He's much closer to Josh, Devlin's suspect, than I am and may hear something helpful."

"Do you think that he was the only guy put on your tail? We don't need you getting hurt too. What shall I tell Brian if he, or maybe Sean, calls?"

"These guys are not at all sophisticated. I'll be alert. You can tell him that and that I'm getting close. The FBI techs could wrap this up quickly if they jump on the warehouse evidence. We'll see what happens today."

"Don't rush into anything risky."

Chapter Thirty

Liam went to the bar for lunch after a run in weather that was still much hotter than he liked it, even though it was a cloudy day. He didn't shower, though, just popped a dry black T-shirt with a "Wounded Warrior" logo over his toweled-off upper body. Josh and Steve were there, not talking much, and Liam did not join them. George came out to talk with Josh for a few minutes, with only a nod to Liam. Then he strode purposefully back to his office. Liam heard nothing of the conversation. The chili was a little spicier than usual after sitting in the pot all night, but Liam had a lot of time to kill while he waited to hear from the FBI or the general. Sitting around the bar trying to gather tidbits of information was boring as hell. Thoughts of Mary kept attacking his concentration. His nerves were tweaking.

He walked over to Josh and Steve and asked for the name of a gym they would recommend. Steve just shrugged. "How about you, Josh? You look like you still spend time with the weights."

Josh smiled. "Yeah, I do, but I go to a weight room a couple of miles north. Just heavy lifters there, and it's too far to walk."

It was Liam's turn to smile. "You forget that I run every morning. Walking a couple of miles would just be a warm-up."

Josh sniffed. With another smile, he said, "The place is called 'The Man Shop.' If you walk north on Tenth Street, you'll come to it. By the way, don't tell them I sent you." He looked at Steve and laughed. Steve faked a smile.

"Thanks, Josh. I haven't had a workout all week. This should be good."

Josh just kept smiling. "It gets pretty crowded in the afternoon. I usually go three mornings a week with a couple of buddies."

Liam thought, *And it will get me out of here for several hours. I wonder if he'll go up there to see if I really went.*

"The Man Shop" was a dump—a club for big guys who liked to show off how much weight they could hump around. There were racks and racks of free weights and none of those fancy multi-muscle group toning machines found in classier gyms. And the place smelled like an armpit. There were eight guys chatting and grunting in the limited expanse of the storefront.

The only guy in the place who was not a giant approached Jerry. He asked, "You lost?"

"We'll see. I heard this was the best place for serious lifting. I see that I'm in a different weight class from the rest of the troops."

"Yeah. By about a hundred pounds. Do you know what you're doing? I don't need any ambulances knocking on my door."

"Would I even have come in if I didn't know what I was doing? I've been sitting around for a week. I need a workout. Do you want my business or not?"

"For tourists, it's forty bucks an hour."

"Is that what these guys are paying?"

"They are regulars."

"What does a 250-pound regular clean and jerk?"

"About three hundred."

"I weigh 160. How much would I have to lift to become a *regular*?"

"150 would be good."

Liam slipped on his leather gloves with the fingertips clipped off. "I'll warm up with eighty."

The man pointed him to a weight bar leaning in the corner behind him. Jerry slid on four twenty-pound plates and tightened the end clamps. He did five reps and bounced the assembly. He stretched a little and realized he had an audience. The big guys had all stopped to watch. He did five more reps and bounced the weights again. He slid off the end clamps and added four more twenty-pound plates.

One hundred sixty pounds? Is my ego driving me again? Am I doing this to impress Josh? I have done 160 before, but it has been a while.

He set his feet, breathed a little, and took the bar to his chest easily. After another breath, he jerked the bar over his head without a hitch, held it there steady for several seconds, and then bounced the assembly with a bit of a flourish. *Adrenaline was a wonderful thing.*

One of the big guys punched his neighbor in the arm and shouted, "Pay up, Champ."

Jerry asked the manager, "How much now?"

"All the time you want. It's on Champ over there."

Jerry saluted Champ, who gave him a thumbs-up, and went to find some appropriate-size barbells to work his bis, tris, and forearms. He felt that all this was going to work out well after all.

But his confidence took a hit the next morning when he called the general. "The FBI says they can't get a forensics team into that warehouse for a couple of days."

"That's crap. Somebody might get in there any minute now and scrub the place down. Are they trying to sabotage the case?"

The general sounded chagrined when she replied, "I've got Sean and Senator Richardson on the FBI's case. I don't know what else to do."

"Shit, shit, shit! Do you have any connections to the local police?"

"No."

Liam ended the call and paced back and forth in his hotel room. No inspiration came. He went out for his run, still hoping for wisdom. None came. He showered and went to the bar for an early lunch. Steve was there, but not Josh.

"Josh went up to lift this morning. Did you go yesterday?"

"Yeah. I bet he's checking on what happened with me. That place is a zoo. Anything new happening around here?"

"No. The cops have even stopped hanging around."

Liam locked eyes with Steve, searching for any sign he was lying. There were none. "Steve, do you have any connections with the cops?"

"No. Why are you asking?"

"I don't know. I keep waiting for somebody to find Donnie's car or go into the warehouse. The shit could hit the fan if that happens."

"Yeah, but I ain't goin' anywhere near there."

"Good."

Just then, Josh charged into the bar. He came directly to the man he knew as Jerry. "You put on a show up at The Man Shop yesterday, I hear."

"How? I never mentioned your name."

"You're the only 'little old guy' I know who ever showed any interest in the place. You got the troops all stirred up."

Jerry laughed. "I didn't mean to upset anyone. I just needed a workout. I hope nobody will give you any shit."

"Don't worry about that. I never let on I knew you. I'm not sure I do know you. What other secrets are you keeping?"

"None, Josh. I run and lift to keep the 'old' part of that description from taking control of my life."

*****

There was no word from the FBI on forensics at the warehouse during the rest of the day. Liam's nerves were getting frayed again. He nursed two beers all afternoon, watched CNN for half an hour, and had to get out of there. He announced he was going to rent a car tomorrow and see the sights in Corpus Christi and left to arrange that.

But he didn't do that. Instead, he walked. He went down past the airport to the river and watched the cars come over the toll bridge and stop at the custom houses. The continuous flow of cars, the slowing for the toll, the stop at customs set up a rhythm in his mind and helped cool the fire beginning to smolder in his head. He walked along the riverbank, sat on one of the benches, and maybe even said a prayer as if Mary were there with him.

He thought as he sat. *This sucks. A year ago, I thought this self-focused life is what I wanted: free to do as I wished, when I wished. But that was before someone held my hand, bussed my check, and smiled that warm and lovely smile at me. Yes, that was before Mary. I feel empty, even cold in September in Texas. Today, it seems clear to me that those BM days were a shitty waste of what time I had left. I don't know how I am going to resurrect my friendship with Mary, but I know I have to do that. First, I have to clean up the mess here, which I have brought on myself out of fear for my daughter's safety. That is also nutty. I haven't worried about her for years. Is it really a contest between Cathryn and Mary? Or is it some kind of idiot hero complex in me?*

He was surprised when darkness engulfed him. Rather than go directly back to the hotel, he decided to stop at the bar. He was hungry.

Steve did not disturb his meal but followed him when he did leave for the hotel. He caught up with Liam on one of the darker streets with a message. "George read the riot act to Josh a little while ago. I didn't get it all, but it was something about whether the warehouse was 'ready for a shipment and maybe an inspection.' He'd had a tip that the FBI was getting ready to check the place out. Josh said he thought the place was ready for the shipment. There was more conversation, but the only thing I got was that George was going to take care of things in the morning and mad at Josh for not double-checking it already."

"George had a tip from the FBI?"

"I think that's what he said."

"How interesting. There's no telling who George is plugged into. He seems to have a lot of irons in the fire. Thanks, Steve. Keep your ears open. It's time for me to hit the sack."

It was midnight in Virginia, but he roused the general from her bed, making no polite apologies. "General, I have two things on good authority: First, George is going to 'take care of things' at the warehouse in the morning, and second, he got a tip from an FBI source that they were going to inspect the place. My source did not hear anything about pictures. I don't know which is worse news. Of course, all the bad news could be changed to good if the FBI caught George scrubbing the place in the morning."

To her credit, the general shook off sleep and jumped into action. "The listeners should still be on duty. I'll contact them, but it will require heroics on their part. There are no guarantees on that. Maybe one of them was the tipster. You'll know in the morning."

That was certainly true.

When he ran by the bar the next morning, the place was as calm and quiet as the stable on the first Christmas morning: no cop cars or men in suits and ties in sight. *Shit.*

It was Friday, but there was no football game in town this week. The team was playing at the opponent's school. The game was being live streamed via computer but was not being shown on the TVs in the bar. Instead, there was a tirade from the president about how his opponents were going to steal the election, and he was urging his poll watchers to be vigilant. He pleaded for 24-7 surveillance of remote ballot collection boxes, lest they be stuffed with fraudulent paper ballots. He added a list of other procedures he thought were necessary to prevent the election being stolen.

There was a lot of discussion among the patrons after the speech, some of which got heated. One guy with more gray hair than the others in his party jumped up from his chair, shouting, "That's bullshit!" He slapped a twenty down on the table and stormed out of the bar. His departure caused a moment of deafening silence before the buzz resumed.

Josh whispered to Liam and Steve, "That's Ed Rubin. He's been on the county Board of Elections since George's father ran a decade ago. He swears there's never been any cheating in this county."

Liam, dressed today in a white T-shirt with an American flag logo across the whole chest, said, "It doesn't seem like many people here believe that tonight."

Josh said, "Yeah. Our president is getting his message out."

"I wonder how Tobias Brown is doing tonight."

Joe, the bartender, had the game on his cell phone. He announced for all to hear that McAllen was winning 14–0 in the third quarter. That changed the tone of conversation in the room. There was applause and shouts of, "Way to go, Toby!" Despite the good news about the game, Josh didn't seem happy about the change of subject.

Liam called the general before her bedtime that night. The news was all bad. The general said, "The FBI did not get there in time. The place had been all scrubbed down before they arrived. It smelled of bleach. There was no blood, and everything looked normal. They did find a crumpled bullet, a .9mm they said, in a corner by the front door. That convinced them the place was a crime scene. They locked the place down and will return on Monday with chemicals, some special lights, and some swabs, hoping to find some bacterial residues. They apologized for the delay but then told me that they had fancy technology that could recover most of what had been cleaned up and maybe more. They gave me a long lecture on their sophisticated technology. They can determine if either victim's blood was on the bullet they recovered. They will use luminol, a chemical that glows in the dark when it contacts blood, to recreate the blood splatter on the floor. The splatter can tell them how it got there, the angle of the bullet, and whether the body was moved.

"They say that when you touch anything, you leave bacteria that will stay there for years. They can match it with the person who did the touching. A careful process is required with sterile swabs, and microscopes are used in the analysis. They're quite confident that they will find out who had been in the building, and that will lead them to evidence that can be used in court. All this will take time. Maybe a week.

"The bad news is that because of the leak, they are going to rescind the courtesy they have been giving me by filling me in on what's going on. The basis for that is that these tests involve murders and have nothing to do with a possible insurrection."

"Is that it? That's all they're going to do? Run some secret tests and not tell you the results?"

The general said, "They will still clue me in on what their remote listening system comes up with."

*****

On Saturday morning, it was raining hard. Liam slipped into his nylon rain jacket, took his umbrella, and walked to the bar, ostensibly to find out how the game ended. Today, he wore a T-shirt with the iconic picture of the marines putting up the flag on Iwo Jima. That got a "thumbs up" from Josh.

The game had gotten chaotic. The home team had scored one touchdown and was on its way to a second when the coach put Toby in on defense, and he made another spectacular tackle to end the threat. It seemed to Liam that Toby's high school coach was presaging his quarterback's conversion to defensive back in college, as Josh predicted. Or maybe he put him in there because he was the best player on the team. In any event, there would be joy in the bar today.

But there was no joy for Liam. His nerves were on fire. He could not sit still. He decided to go lift some weights. By the time he finished walking up to The Man Shop, he was wet from the rain despite the umbrella. There was only one other lifter there who was intrepid enough to brave the rain. He was not one of the guys who were there the last time Liam visited.

The manager said, "You're back. No audience for you to show off for today."

"That's great. I need to work up a good sweat and wash some knots out of my brain. Maybe then I can sit down and enjoy a college game this afternoon. The sun has got to be out somewhere."

Liam worked for an hour and was totally soaked when he was finished. The manager declined any payment without giving any reason. He walked back to the Holiday Inn, took a hot shower, and began to spin the TV dials.

He knew Mary would be home from work by now, but she did not answer the phone. And he couldn't find a football game on TV he deemed worth watching. Just another "Aw Shit" day for this would-be hero.

On Sunday, he went to Mass at the refugee center again and prayed for peace and progress in the coming week. He got no peace. He guessed that maybe his newly reawakened faith didn't have enough muscle yet to get him over that hill.

Josh came again with a van full of food for the center. Liam stayed out of sight. He wondered what Josh was thinking about these days. George had cleaned up the mess at the murder scene, but Josh had no idea about the FBI's super technology and the possible resurrection of evidence. Maybe he felt confident and redeemed by his charitable work. Liam wondered which was the real Josh. Liam did not feel at all confident, much less redeemed. He decided to go to the ocean.

Liam rented a car and started for Corpus Christi. On the way out of town for his two-plus-hour drive, he went past the warehouse. It was indeed locked down tight. A long yellow bar was bolted across the main door, and the roll-up garage door was padlocked to a ring cemented into the concrete. No one was going to get into that building unless he brought an oxyacetylene torch with him. The FBI techs would have their privacy tomorrow.

When he got to Corpus Christi, he drove down to the Padre Island seashore and sat on the beach. It was warmer there at the end of October than it had been at the end of May at Ocean Beach, though it did not feel warm to him. He thought back to those months ago when he and Mary had sat on the boardwalk, feeling close to each other and the warmth of their companionship. Now there was an empty space beside him, and a cool breeze blew through it.

The splash of the small gulf waves on the sand was gentler than those of the Atlantic in May but just as rhythmic. They eased his mind, even though Mary again did not answer his call. He was once again grateful to John O'Donohue, whose insight had led him to find peace and clear his mind by communing with the sea. Still, there was a hole in his life even communing with nature could not fill.

On the way back, he stopped to look at the full-size replicas of the *Nina*, *Pinta*, and *Santa Maria*. He was amazed that ships that small could cross the ocean safely. He concluded that anything was possible with the right expertise.

He was ready for bed when he got back to the hotel and slept immediately.

Chapter Thirty-One

Liam wandered into the bar at around 11:00 a.m. on Monday, wearing his last clean T-shirt with a patriotic motif. All seemed routine. Steve was there. Josh was off on his Monday, Wednesday, and Friday morning lifting routine. Liam and Steve lamented for a few minutes about the poor starts of the Dallas Cowboys and the Washington team, now known as the Football Club, as opposed to the Redskins. They clung to the signs that future results would be better.

Just after lunch, a dusty white van screeched to a stop in front of the bar. Its driver, a man with a scraggly gray beard, wearing a ball cap labeled CAT and bib overalls, stormed into the bar and went directly to George's office.

George shouted, "What the hell are you doing here?"

The man shouted back, "Where was I supposed to go after driving five hours? Your fucking warehouse is all locked up."

That was all anybody heard except for the noise of George's door being slammed closed. Liam would have loved being a fly on the wall in there but felt that even making a trip to the men's room to try to hear something would be too risky. The two remained closeted for almost two hours. Then the driver came out and sat at a table near the front door. Liam noted that the van had New Mexico plates.

Josh arrived half an hour later, got briefed by Steve, and brought two beers over to sit with the man in bib overalls. Their conversation went on in voices akin to respectful whispers in the front pews of a church. They ate lunch together, after which Josh went to talk to George. He did not return. The driver got up, moved the van around to the parking lot, and returned to sit in the same spot. He was the only person in the bar sitting at a table in the sparsely populated room.

Liam sat at the bar and nursed a beer. He watched and waited, wondering where Josh was.

In an hour, Josh returned, steam coming out of his ears. Before Liam could think of a way to approach him, Josh started to vent with Steve in a voice that carried. "The fucking FBI put bars on all the doors of the warehouse and put up a big sign calling the place a crime scene. I don't know what that's about, but they fucked up our plans to get a shipment of stuff today."

Steve locked eyes with Liam for a moment. He did not ask what the stuff was, but he did ask, "Did George's contact say anything about why they did that, especially now?"

"No. The guy is either not answering his phone or part of the problem."

"What are we going to do?"

"We ain't goin' to do anything. George has a plan in the works."

Steve said, "Okay. I have some paperwork to do today, but I'll be back later. If I can help, let me know." He caught Liam's eyes in the bar mirror and left.

At sunset, a battered, dust-covered black pickup truck pulled up in front of the bar. The last rays of the sun made the truck look like it was painted in desert camouflage. A young man who looked to be a Native American stepped inside the bar and looked around. Bib overalls waved him over. They chatted for less than a minute; then they exchanged keys. The first driver got into the pickup and drove off. The young man went back toward George's office.

A new driver for the van, thought Liam. I wonder what the new plan is.

Liam called the general. "A van load of something just went out of here with a fresh driver. It's white and has New Mexico plates. I have no idea where it's going. I just know it's very much involved with whatever George and his buddies are involved in. They were going to leave the stuff in the warehouse here but couldn't because the FBI has the place locked up."

"Interesting," said the general. "There was a rumor early on that a Virginia farmer had offered his barn to the militias to store stuff for future action. I wonder if the van is headed here."

Liam said, "At the moment, the van is over a thousand miles away. It will take a couple of days to get to Virginia, no matter how tough the driver is. Maybe the listening post caught some of the conversation in George's office while they were reworking their plans."

"I'll get the senator on this. It's his turf. Thanks for the heads-up. Anything new on the murders?"

"Locking up the warehouse has increased the tension around here a lot. George's FBI contact did not answer his phone. People are waiting for the other shoe to drop. I hope it's soon."

"Be careful."

Brian called from Africa a little later. It was morning there. It sounded like Brian was sipping his coffee between sentences. He wasted no time with cordiality. "Have you caught the bastard yet?"

"The FBI has found the murder site and is going over it with their best technology as we speak. In a few days, they should have a lot of evidence."

"In a few days? A lot of evidence? That sounds like a lot of bullshit—the 'innocent until found guilty' bullshit. When will they arrest the guy?"

"When they have the goods on him. It will be soon."

"We should be leaving here tomorrow. Cathy and I are planning to stop in Ireland for a couple of days on the way home, but I'll cut that short if I need to."

"To do what?"

"To get there and be sure justice is served, as they say. My brother's killer has to pay the full price."

"Do you remember what happened to the guy who shot the man they arrested for JFK's murder?"

"If I do it, it won't be in front of the TV cameras."

"They'll get you anyway. Come on, Brian. Let the system work."

"Liam, sometimes you got to bypass the system."

If you only knew, Brian. If you only knew.

"Right now I need you to concentrate on getting Cathryn out of that hellhole safely. I'll keep you up-to-date, but I'm not gonna help you commit murder and ruin the rest of your life."

Or *my daughter's, either.*

"Have no fear. I'll take care of Cathy. Do what you promised me."

Liam sighed deeply and hung up.

He called Sean early the next morning. "Christ, Liam, I haven't even tasted my coffee yet. The senator has got the firearms agency patrolling all the roads in Virginia 24-7 in search of a white van from New Mexico."

"Sorry about that. It's the general's fault. All I did was tell her there was a van out on the road. She thought it might be coming to Virginia. I need to talk to you about Brian."

"Yeah, I know. I found an email from him when I got up this morning. He's not sure you're gonna keep your promise in Texas."

"I'm not gonna help him start off on a career like yours and mine, especially since it looks like he and my daughter are bonding."

"Liam, get your head out of the sand. Why do you think I got him out of Ireland? He hasn't been an altar boy in a long time."

"Altar boys have to grow up. So do IRA members. Devlin made a mistake and paid for it. His murderer will pay for that too. The price for doing it Brian's way is the ruination of two lives. What's the sense?"

"Aren't you in the process of ruining two lives?"

"Huh?"

"Yours and your friend Mary's. You need to get out of there for two big reasons: You're destroying the new life you are building for both you and her, and your neck is now stuck way out. What do you think is going to happen if that van is really heading to Virginia and the firearms guys intercept it? It will take a nanosecond for the America First leaders to figure out you were the guy who tipped the feds off. The murder thing is being taken care of. Get the hell out of there now. There's nothing more you can do. I'll work on getting Brian to see that."

Is there really nothing more I can do on the murder case? Am I ignoring Mary in my adrenaline fit? There are also the pictures I took of the crime scene. If George's tipster tracked down where they came from, how would I BS my way out of that? Will that also put the kiss of death on Steve? The murders and the potential for insurrection are all mixed now because of the warehouse and the people. I sure as hell didn't want to get sucked into trying to save democracy single-handedly.

Liam rolled the murder situation around in his mind. He purged his mind of vans and drivers and focused. The FBI assured the general that the evidence they collected with their fancy technology would stand up in court. If he were some cattle rancher or oil worker on the jury, would he be convinced by a bunch of technobabble? He concluded that the guy would be more comfortable with the murder weapon covered with the shooter's fingerprints.

He caught up with Steve at lunchtime. "Do you know where Josh lives?"

"Yeah. Why do you want to know?"

"Just curious. He seems to walk here every day, so he must live close, but he drives to the gym."

"He lives above one of the bars up the Alley. The blue front, I think. Those apartments have mostly been remodeled. A lot of small families ask about them."

"Thanks, Steve."

Then he walked back to the hotel to get some equipment he would need to carry out the rest of the plan he was formulating, taking care to check out the building with the blue front. It had no door on the front to provide access to the apartments above. The building extended back from the Alley to within twenty feet or so from the street behind. The remaining space was fenced in to provide a small backyard. There was what looked like a tot's playhouse stuck against the side fence near the back door, which was located two steps above grade.

That evening, Josh came in through the back door and stopped at George's office before coming into the bar itself. He waved to the few regulars there, including Liam, and ordered supper. In a deviation from his normal practice, he sat near the center of the span, several stools apart from anyone. Liam thought he looked pensive. *Are these changes enough to derail my plan for the night?*

After Josh ordered his second beer, Liam decided to go ahead with his plan. He went out the back door of the bar and up the street to the gate into the blue building's backyard. It was not locked, and there were no lights showing in any of the windows on the back wall of the building. With the aid of his penlight, he picked the deadbolt on the back door quickly. Inside, the stairs at the back of the building that led up to the apartments were also dark, but there were windows on each landing. He tiptoed up to Josh's third-floor apartment, being careful to keep near the edge of each tread to avoid potential squeaks.

Josh's apartment door opened on the staircase. It had a window in it and another deadbolt, which quickly fell before Liam's expertise. No alarm sounded. The door opened into a small kitchen. He found a mixture of slovenliness and precision inside. There were two dirty coffee cups in the sink, and the trash can was overflowing. However, four pots were neatly hung on hooks above the stove, and dishtowels were similarly hung on the oven door. All the appliances looked new. A short hall led past a modern bathroom to the front of the building. A sparsely furnished living room was on the right, and the one bedroom was opposite it. Both had large windows overlooking Saloon Alley.

Two of the drawers in a large chest were partly open, showing jumbled clothes stuffed inside, but the bed was precisely made up—military style. Liam could have bounced a coin on the taught blanket. He remembered some general's advice about making beds: "Do it right first thing, and then if the rest of the day goes to hell, you will have at least done one good thing."

Liam thought, *If he hid the gun anywhere in this apartment, it would be under the mattress. Any mess in this bed would be a tip-off that someone had searched his place. Can I still make up a bed like that? Sure, I can.*

He studied the exact location of the pillows and folds, pried up one side of the mattress about six inches, and looked with the penlight. There it was! *Josh's* prized military SIG Saur. He could not part with it, even to destroy evidence of two murders. *How can I make sure that the FBI finds it if they search the apartment? Will they search the apartment? There are no guarantees.*

After a couple of minutes of thought, he dropped the mattress back, tightened the tuck of the blanket against the box spring, and tested his work by bouncing a quarter on the taught cloth. It was more than good. It was perfect.

Liam slipped back out of the apartment, taking time to relock the deadbolts on both doors. He had what he came for but still needed to figure out how to share the information with the law.

He got about twenty-five yards up the street when he heard the gate to the yard clank open behind him. That had to be Josh coming home. He was very clad: The relocking of the deadbolts had gone smoothly, or he would have been dead meat.

Safely in bed at the Holiday Inn, he considered the options he had to pass the information he had just collected to the FBI. *I could make an anonymous call from a pay phone (if I could find one) to the station chief. I could see if the general could pass it on. I could see if Sean could do it. I could wait and see if they came to arrest Josh. Waiting does not appeal because of the risks that Sean had listed yesterday. If I set a fire in Josh's trashcan tomorrow night, will the firemen or cops find the gun in the mess?*

Chapter Thirty-Two

Liam got part of his answer at six o'clock on Wednesday morning. He was awakened by a furious pounding on his hotel room door. He staggered to the door, rubbing the sleep from his eyes, and peeked through the spy hole. There were two men in FBI jackets and a man and a woman in the uniform of the local police standing there. The local policeman had a door breaker at the ready.

"Whoa, whoa!" he yelled. "Give me a few seconds." The pounding stopped. He undid the chain on the door and turned the lock. Only then did he realize he was standing there in his underwear. When he got the door open, he was greeted by an FBI guy with a gun pointed at him in one hand and a white paper in the other.

"What the hell is this?" Liam croaked.

"This a search warrant. I am Agent Scanlon. My partner is Agent Velasco, and the uniformed officers are detectives White and Suarez. We're here to carry out the search."

Liam threw up his hands and backed up two steps out of the narrow hall into the sleeping area. "Okay. Okay. Calm down and put the gun down. What is this about?"

"We'll ask the questions," said the woman, Detective White.

Oh shit, a woman cop trying to show she's tough. He backed up another step.

Agent Scanlon thrust the warrant into Liam's hand. "We're investigating a double murder that happened about ten days ago. Anybody who frequents that bar is a person of interest. With this warrant, we were able to collect your fingerprints from your room door. According to the hotel, your name is Jerry O'Hara. When we checked them with a bunch of databases, we found a match with a record at a federal agency, but there was no name associated with the prints, only a number. What is your real name?"

"The agency promised its agents' anonymity. That's how they do it. Jerry O'Hara is the name on the deed for my house in DC."

"So you're some kind of a mystery man," snapped the policewoman. "Where is your ID?"

"My wallet is on the nightstand over there." He gestured to the far side of the bed.

"Hold on. I'll get it," said Agent Velasco. While he was there, he opened the drawer in the nightstand. It was empty. He brought the wallet to Scanlon, who handed it to Liam. "There is a lot of cash in here. Remove the driver's license, please."

He inspected the small, laminated card with Liam's picture, held it up to the light, and handed it back. "The problem, Mr. O'Hara, is that despite your graying hair, you seem to have been around for only three years."

"So you've checked my credit card use. I prefer to use cash, except when it's too cumbersome. Hotels often get too cumbersome for cash. Look, I need to get some clothes on. Go ahead with your search."

"Hold on," said the woman. "We need to check the closet first."

"Of course," he said and sat on the end of the bed, waiting. They slid back the accordion door and found only a pair of khaki pants, two pairs of smelly running shoes, and an equally smelly bag of dirty clothes. They poked at the bag but did not empty it. Next, they rooted through the drawers where the rest of his clothes were. They never looked into the running shoes where Liam had stuck his lock-picking tools.

That finished, he slipped into his running shorts and a plain white T-shirt and sat in the desk chair to put his running shoes on.

There was very little for them to search, so it didn't take long. They did toss the mattress and look under it. That seemed to be the only reason Scanlon had brought the two local detectives. When they finished the physical search, they asked for the passwords for his phone and laptop. "We'll have to take these," said Scanlon, the lead FBI guy.

"There's almost nothing on them. Can't you examine them here?" He unlocked his phone and handed it to Scanlon.

Liam didn't want some techie to resurrect the crime scene photos he had deleted, especially if George's tipster would have access. The policewoman was immediately suspicious. Scanlon was scrolling through his contacts.

"Who are you calling in Africa?"

"My daughter works for a charity NGO. They are in Niger now. I really need to be able to contact her."

"And the general?"

"Eleanor Townsend. The first female three-star in the army. We worked on a joint project about three years ago."

"Sean?"

"Sean Doyle. My CIA contact."

"Is Mary your wife?"

"No. Just a friend from church."

"You have a long list of people you haven't called in a while. How would you describe them?"

"Detritus from my past."

"All right. Keep the phone. We'll take the laptop, though. Check with me in a day or so about getting it back." He handed Jerry his card, took back the warrant, wrote a note in the space provided on the last page describing the laptop, and signed it as a receipt.

Liam asked, "When I go to the bar for lunch, what am I going to find?"

"The regulars will likely be either pissed off or missing. You might think about eating downstairs. I assume you won't be leaving town without your laptop."

"I won't."

Scanlon gestured toward the door. The group started in that direction. "Have a good day, Mr. O'Hara." The policewoman looked unhappy.

She said, "Agent Scanlon, I have a lot of questions for this guy. We're not through here. Let's drag him into the house to get formal about all this."

Scanlon snapped back at her, "Look, I've got an insurrection case to work on. I don't have time to mess with a simple murder case you people can't seem to solve. We're done here." With that, he headed for the door.

Detective White's face looked as if she was ready to pull her weapon and stop Scanlon, but she didn't and shuffled after him. It was clear who was in charge.

Liam put the bed back together and took a nap. The interview went as well as expected, and he was happy that the team looked under the mattress. Despite the FBI's advice, he would go to the bar for lunch after his run.

The bar was essentially empty when he got there. Joe, the bartender, said Steve had not been in, and Liam knew that Josh routinely went to The Man Shop to lift on Mondays, Wednesdays, and Fridays before coming in for lunch. He didn't ask about George.

Josh

He had been tense this morning. Some things were starting to fall apart with the plan. The FBI locking up the warehouse was worrisome as well, even though George said he had cleaned it thoroughly.

He came to The Man Shop early and worked extra this morning, trying to ease his mind with concentrated effort and sweat. He had the weights to himself. That helped his concentration. He got some momentum going and added fifty pounds to his previous maximum lift. He let out a grunt of satisfaction as he posted the new max on the chart that he and his buddies kept on the wall near the racks of big weights. With his mind calmer, he stretched, toweled off, and put on a dry muscle shirt. On Friday morning, he would see what his buddies would try to do about his new maximum lift.

He waved to the manager on the way out, who said, "Way to go, Josh. Have a great day!"

Outside, he was appalled to see three people tearing his car apart! One guy was pulling the spare tire mat from the trunk, the second was spraying something all over the back seat, and the third was sticking some paper under the passenger-side windshield wiper.

He shouted, "What the fuck are you guys doing?" and started to charge across the fifty feet between him and the vehicle. As he ran, he pulled the bone-handled pistol from the belt at the small of his back and aimed at the guy in his trunk. He pulled the trigger once, twice, three times. Nothing happened.

The man at the front of the car shouted, "Stop. FBI!"

When Josh didn't stop, the guy shot him twice in the chest. He sprawled forward, his head coming to a stop five feet short of the right rear tire. The man in the trunk sprang upright, smacking his head on the lid.

He screamed, "Jesus Christ!"

The man who shot Josh was Agent Scanlon. McAllen Police Officer White, who had been spraying the luminol on the back seat, backed out, saw the blood beginning to pool under Josh, and threw up.

Scanlon checked Josh for signs of life and found none. He said, a little breathlessly, "It's too bad we missed him at his apartment this morning. It might not have come to this." After a moment or two, he helped Officer White to her feet and said, "All right, it's CYA time. We found the gun under the mattress. What does the luminol show?"

The back seat showed none of the blue spots that luminol and blood would result in. Scanlon took the luminol can from White's shaking hand and sprayed the spare tire mat, which was lying half in and half out of the trunk. There were no blue spots there, either. Scanlon made a face but remained calm.

Scanlon summarized, "This is my shoot, and it's a clean one. I'm sure that ballistics will show the gun we found was the murder weapon, and it probably still has fingerprints on it. This was our guy. You are a lucky man, Velasco. He tried to shoot you, but the gun didn't fire. Of course, on the run like that, he might not have hit you anyway."

"That's comforting," said Velasco. "I'll be sure to tell my wife."

Scanlon picked up Josh's gun and inspected it. "Full magazine but no firing pin," he reported.

Detective White said, "Eddie makes some of these fancy pistols for display only. Josh must have gotten one of those by mistake. Thank God."

Scanlon said, "Call for a bus and a tow truck, and then we can do the paperwork."

"You can do the paperwork," said White.

"Unfortunately true. No good deed goes unpunished." Scanlon sighed.

The manager of the club had been peeking out the door with his cell phone trained on the scene for the whole time.

Steve showed up at the bar for supper, looking bedraggled.

"Who ran you over with a truck?" asked Liam, dressed this day in a navy-blue polo and khakis.

"The FBI and the police. They showed up at my house this morning and tore it up. My wife took the kids to her sister's and has not come back yet. They took me to the office and grilled me for two hours. I don't think I gave up anything about our trip to the warehouse, but they got me so confused I'm not sure."

"I doubt it's important. Look at the news."

There it was: The shaky cell phone video of the manager showing the whole shooting. This was followed by a reporter's interview with Scanlon made while the tow truck connected to Josh's car and towed it away. The newscaster concluded that the dual murders had at last been solved.

"There you go, Steve. Maybe now you're off the hook with your wife and her sister."

Steve's face lit up. He chugged the rest of his beer and hopped off his stool. "See you tomorrow," he said and took off.

Not likely, thought Liam, but there were still things to do before he could leave.

The next morning, Liam called Agent Scanlon. "Now that you're a TV star, you can give me back my laptop."

"We haven't even bothered to open it. Having the general on your speed dial was all we needed to know. She's been terrorizing the office. In fact, there would be no office here if it weren't for her getting her senator to trot down to the Hoover Building about every other day. All of us here are stationed in San Antonio. We'll be able to go home as soon as the lab guys share the data from the scene and ballistics tests are over. We should get the lab report today. We'll be very busy here today. Call me tomorrow to get the computer back. Thanks for your help, Mr. O'Hara."

The general called a little later. "Liam, I think we stopped a serious plot. The firearms team stopped the van in Virginia. The FBI is on a roll, questioning the driver. Senator Richardson is basking in applause from the Department of Homeland Security, and the Society is now listed as a credible source as opposed to a bunch of old farts flapping their gums. We are all very grateful to you for helping. I know you made a big personal sacrifice to do what you did."

Liam said, "I felt compelled to help Brian and keep him from doing something stupid. The insurrection plot was just icing on that cake. I'll call him before they go to bed over there."

"There's something else I wanted to mention," said the general. "You left Mary's number as an additional emergency contact. Obviously, there is something special going on between you two. I called her this morning to express my gratitude for your visit to Texas and how much it meant to me. That was a mistake. The extent of your personal sacrifice became abundantly clear during that conversation. You are in deep shit, Liam, but then so is she. I think there is a lot of hope. Go and fight for your new lives. Get help from your daughter and Brian. Mary may never forget, but she will forgive. I feel that in my bones."

"Thanks for the encouragement, Eleanor. I'm determined to do my best on that score."

Chapter Thirty-Three

He caught up with Brian and Cathryn at dinner time. They sounded stressed. "What's wrong?" he asked after a minute. "I have some good news for Brian about Texas."

Cathryn said, "We need good news from here. We're hostages!"

"What the hell?"

"Yesterday before dawn, we were awakened by gunfire. Boko Haram had come across the border. They killed the three soldiers guarding the front door, woke the rest of them, and locked them in the wing of the hotel used for meetings. They ran around waving their submachine guns at us and the hotel staff, telling all to stay put and keep working. They did not take our computers or phones. Our PR staff believes that they want us to alert our government and the world to the situation in hope of getting support."

"Are you and your team all right?"

"Yes. The Bokos seem to be waiting for something or someone."

Brian interjected, "Give me the news from Texas."

"Okay, you got what you wanted. Devlin's murderer is dead. He attacked the FBI while they were searching his car for signs of blood, and they shot him. There is no need for further bloodshed."

"Are you sure he was the killer?"

"The FBI is convinced. Tell me what's going on there."

Cathryn resumed the tale. "This morning, four UN peacekeepers came in a Jeep, wearing those light-blue helmets. They were unarmed. Two of them opened folding chairs and sat on the drive at the foot of the hotel steps. They set up inside the low wall that separates the hotel door from the market area between the hotel and the road and keeps the beggars out of the hotel. By the way, this area is loaded with beggars. Some of them bring starving kids with arms as thin as pencils. Our nurse has gone outside the wall several times to try to get some of the baby food we brought into the kids. All that did was bring a dozen more starving kids the next day. The baby food is all gone now, but the mothers still come.

"Back to the story. Two of the Bokos in black headdresses sat facing the UN group, backed by four guys with their guns. They had tea, for Christ's sake, and talked about the weather. After that, they started a serious conversation. Our translator moved out onto the steps to see what he could hear. The Bokos wanted prisoners released in three countries in return for letting us go. The UN guy said that would take time. Soon, the shouting started. The black hats said they would kill one hostage every day until the prisoners were released. The UN pleaded for time.

"One of the guys with guns went into the hotel's meeting complex and dragged a skinny young Niger soldier out onto the steps. It played out like a cheap soap opera: shouting, gun to head, and then a moment of silence. When the UN started their pleas again, the Bokos blew the kid's brains out. Some of his blood landed on our interpreter." She could hardly finish her sentence.

Brian said, "We can get out of here any night we want. They had one kid guarding each door last night, half asleep. I can take care of them without a sound in five minutes. We can all be in our truck five minutes after that."

Liam replied, "And then what is going to happen to the rest of the soldiers, the hotel staff, and probably all of the natives you worked with? Have you been in touch with Sean?"

"Yeah. You have a bunch of soldiers in Cameroon. He thinks maybe they can get a couple of helicopters over here to lift us off the roof. He's going to the top to work the problem."

"Give him a chance, Brian. Give him a chance. He could save a lot of lives. If the shit really hits the fan, you can always do it your way."

"Okay, Liam, but you know I'm not a patient man."

"Patience paid off in Texas. Remember that."

When Liam got back to his hotel after his run at about eight o'clock the morning the day after Josh got killed, he got an update from the general.

"The van from New Mexico was filled with guns, smoke bombs, and radios. Enough for a miniwar. It also had the layouts for the two major electric substations that supply power to DC: one in Virginia and one in Maryland. The firearms people and the FBI are interviewing the driver, but he's just a kid and probably doesn't know much."

"You never know, General. Some of these militia folks are pretty nutty. The news here is that Josh, the guy Devlin thought was trouble, was shot dead yesterday when he charged the FBI agent and local police folks who were searching his car for signs of blood. The FBI guy pranced like a hero on local TV, saying that they had found Josh's old military gun and were doing ballistic tests to prove it was the gun that killed the two men found dead here."

"I guess that wraps it all up then," said the general. "Thanks for your help."

"We'll see. I still have to get my computer back from the FBI guy."

"When will you leave there?"

"As soon as I get my computer."

After his shower, Liam called Agent Scanlon. He was told that the phone number he had been given was no longer in service. He called again and got the same message. He felt his blood begin to boil and acid rise in his throat. *What the hell are these guys up to?*

Breakfast at the hotel did not help. He decided to go back to the beach at Padre Island to try to calm his nerves. The two-hour drive did nothing to help, but the gentle rolling of the waves was good, at least until he called Mary. She did not answer. He drove back with smoke coming out of his ears and acid boiling in his stomach.

Halfway back, he got a call from Detective White. He answered.

"Yeah?"

"I just wanted to tell you that you can come at your convenience to pick up your computer."

"What time tomorrow morning is convenient?"

After an audible deep breath, she said, "Ten works fine."

"I thought Scanlon had it."

"Do you give a damn who gives it back to you?"

"I guess not. I'll be at police headquarters at ten." Then he hung up.

He thought, *Maybe I can get out of here tomorrow, but I still need to call Brian.*

He did not sleep well that night. *Something strange is going on, and I am not happy with that.*

He went for his run earlier than usual the next morning. As he went past the bar, it looked dead. There were no cars in the lot, but why did that surprise him? Was he going completely dotty?

He showered, ate breakfast at the hotel, and arrived at police headquarters at a quarter to ten. The desk sergeant took him to a small conference room with a table and four chairs just off the reception area and offered him coffee. He demurred and sat down, prepared to wait.

Detective White sauntered into the room after just a couple of minutes with Liam's computer in hand. She put it on the table and said, "There are a couple of things I hope you can help us clear up."

"Is that the price for getting my computer back?"

She pushed the laptop across the table until it was under his nose. "I have just a few questions. It won't take long."

"If you insist."

"Can you turn down the hostility?"

"That depends on the questions. Is this being recorded?"

"No, Mr. O'Hara, if that's your name."

"Now who's hostile?"

She sighed. "Okay. Let's get on with it. We believe you were the person who took the pictures of the murder scene and sent them to the general. Then she got them to the Hoover Building. Is that correct?"

Liam thought for a moment. "Yes."

"How did you learn about the warehouse?"

"The guy from the bar whom you interviewed the other day, Steve, told me about it."

"Did he take you there?"

"No."

"How did you get into the building?"

Liam was quiet for a long moment. "Am I being charged with something?"

No, Mr. O'Hara. I'll just assume that the CIA taught you a few tricks for legitimate use. How did you get involved with this mess?"

She opened a small, black notebook and held her pen at the ready.

Liam thought for a full minute on that one. *How far back in my relationship with the general do I want to go?* He decided to keep it as simple as possible.

"The brother of the Irishman who was killed here is working as a security guard for my daughter and her team in Africa. When the general called him to report Devlin's murder, he went bonkers and started making plane reservations to come here and take the law into his own hands. I didn't want my daughter left unprotected. I volunteered to come here to see if I could do anything to help and to keep him there."

"What the hell did you think you would be able to do?"

"I had no idea. Maybe just feed him a bunch of BS to keep him on duty. Enough of this. Where's Scanlon? I tried to call him three times yesterday and got a bullshit message."

It was her time to take a minute to ponder an answer. She sat back in her chair with just the hint of a smirk on her face. "Scanlon's in our jail, along with the bar owner."

Liam jumped from his chair and leaned over the table. "What?"

"Scanlon turned out to be a fanatical America Firster. He was devoted to the plot and kept the bar owner and the network clued in on the FBI's operations. He was the guy who pulled the trigger at the warehouse. Scanlon was smart enough to use his backup weapon when he abducted the Irishman but not smart enough to get rid of it. He was also arrogant enough to think he was smarter than his own lab technicians. When we arrested the bar owner for cleaning the scene, we found multiple calls to Scanlon on his phone."

Liam was still breathing hard. He said, "So Josh died for nothing."

White replied, "Attempting to shoot an FBI agent is still a crime, even if he is a bastard like Scanlon."

Liam said, "It's ironic that Josh was killed by a fanatic supporter of the cause he was working on. Josh was a puzzle, all right."

White filled in a couple of the blanks. "When we searched Josh's apartment, he had already left for the weight room. We found the SIG Sauer under the mattress. Ballistics cleared the SIG for the murder, which pretty much cleared Josh since his new weapon didn't work. So we had no murder weapon and no suspect. We went back for another look at Josh's apartment while Scanlon was doing TV sound bites. We found the disassembled pieces of a weapon in Josh's shoes. In retrospect, Scanlon must have hidden them there during our first search. Maybe he thought the residues in Josh's shoes would show up on the gun. I don't know.

"Then the FBI lab guys came to us with the results of their fancy techniques. They had been amazed to find lots of evidence from Scanlon and the bar owner all over the murder scene. Our ballistics people confirmed the gun we found in Josh's shoes was the murder weapon. The next day, the FBI confirmed that Scanlon's biomarkers were also on it."

She shrugged. "After getting the politics out of the way, we arrested Scanlon. He went to jail justifying his actions 'to keep the foreign commies from sabotaging our election' and bragging about the future of 'the cause' for reclaiming America as it was meant to be."

When he got his breath back, Liam said, "I'll be dipped in shit."

White said, "The FBI is searching their ranks for any more believers and rounding up everybody on the bar owner's contact list. Do you want us to pass all this on to the general, or do you want to do it?"

"I think it would be better if she heard it officially."

"You're leaving our beloved state?"

"ASAP, no offense intended. I have a lot of catching up to do."

"Have a smooth trip."

"Thanks," he said, but he had no idea what he was going to tell Brian about this new information or how he was going to try to fix this up with Mary. He'd be home, but the stress would still be hanging over him like a mushroom cloud.

Chapter Thirty-Four

Liam got back to DC late Friday night. He did not sleep well. He had no nightmares but lots of tossing and turning. A pinch of the Irish did not help. He was trying to figure out what to tell Brian about the truth about the murders in Texas, if anything, but first, he had to talk to Mary.

He was up early on Saturday. He showered for a long time, washing the dust of Texas out of the folds of his body and hopefully turning on his brain. He went to the diner at a time he knew was too early, even for a Saturday, but he could wait no longer. Mary was busy with the last two breakfast customers when he walked in. He caught her eye for a second, but that was the only sign of recognition between them. He went to his usual stool and waited. When the two other patrons left, she walked hesitantly to where he sat.

She said, "What would you like?"

"Some serious conversation."

"That's not on the menu."

"Don't you have some specials today?"

"I'll have to check on that." She turned her back to him.

She turned back and gave a deep sigh. "There may be something called 'heartbreak soup.'"

"I'll take a double order."

"All right, Liam. Let's stop playing around. Why are you here?"

"Because I love you, and I hope you can love me, warts and all."

Mary's eyes filled with tears. She said, "You bastard."

"Yeah, but I think I helped make your life a little better for a while, and you certainly made mine new and more real. I was foolish to make promises to you I couldn't keep. No one knows what tomorrow will bring. Forgive me, please."

She took a napkin from the canister on the counter, wiped her eyes, and said, "This is not the place for this conversation."

She waved toward the front door and took off her apron. Liam leaped off his stool and followed her. Again, they walked to the cathedral, saying nothing, not touching. They sat in the last row, facing the altar, as they had the last time they were there.

Again, a priest was fussing around at the altar.

Mary said, "I confessed my anger, Liam, but the hurt did not go away. I've come here every day since you've been away, praying for peace. I knew we would have to have this moment, but still, I don't know what is right. Have you prayed?"

"You know my faith is not nearly as strong as yours, but I think I've felt God at my side a couple of times in the past weeks. One message was clear. You are the most important thing in my life for the future. Everything else is a distraction, a temptation. Maybe God was testing us, testing the strength of our togetherness during the good times and the bad times. Even the man who Devlin thought was the bad guy had a good side. He worked for a charity that helped refugees every Sunday." He turned to face Mary. "Nobody walks on water, not even that priest. Please forgive me and give us a chance to start over."

"How can I trust you? Brian was more important to you than me. The general was more important than me."

"I can't tell you how to resurrect that trust. I can only hope and pray that you can. The thing I can promise is to never decide anything affecting us without talking to you about it."

"Maybe I had dreamed up a fantasy about us and our future."

"The two of us have paid a lot of dues in our lives so far. We are due some fantasy, some happy ever after."

Mary smiled a little. "There you go with the blarney again."

He reached out to clasp her hand. "You're too smart to fall for Blarney."

"You never know what a girl will do."

"Will this girl do dinner with me tonight?"

"Not even in the White House dining room."

Liam took a deep breath. "Are you going to ten thirty Mass tomorrow?"

"Yes, but Mass is not a social engagement."

"Of course. But I had some hope you were still interested in helping me save my soul."

It was Mary's turn to think for a moment. "Okay. You're a sly devil, Liam Martin. I'll meet you at the back of the church five minutes before Mass." She gestured toward the foyer inside the big, wooden back doors at the center of the church.

"And I trust you with the most important secret of my life," he replied. "See you tomorrow."

*****

Liam was there early on Sunday morning, of course, and Mary showed up promptly, her hair still damp from the shower.

He asked, "Did you run this morning?"

"I did. I'm quite used to running alone these days."

Liam thought, *Easy does it, hoss. This woman is special.*

Liam found himself comfortable praying next to her as he had in the days before Texas. They used to hold hands during the Our Father and kiss on the cheek at the sign of peace. He looked at her when the Our Father began, but she stared straight ahead without even the slightest sideways glance. A minute later, when the priest called for showing a sign of peace among the worshipers, she offered him a fist bump after waving to several others in adjacent pews.

He thought, *Wow, I really hurt her. Is that a mortal sin? Should I avoid communion? On the other hand, I didn't mean to hurt her. I was just focused on helping Brian and not thinking straight. Doesn't a mortal sin have to be intentional?*

He decided to believe in that little prayer just before communion was administered: "Only say the word, and my soul will be healed," and go to communion. He felt like he did when he was a kid at his confirmation fifty years ago.

After Mass, they chatted briefly with Mary's church ladies. Then they had a moment alone. He asked, "What are you doing this afternoon?"

"I'm going to watch my Patriots destroy the Jets."

"Hope it goes that way for you." He then headed home, contemplating methods of filling the hours between noon and dinner.

His cell phone rang during the walk home. "This is Elizabeth Moran."

He answered, "Hello, Elizabeth. Your voice is familiar, but I'm not making the connection to a person."

"I'm the lady who runs the soup kitchen."

"Hello again, Elizabeth. I'm tuned in now. How can I help you?"

"I need some muscle over here late Tuesday morning. Mary thought you might be able to help."

Liam laughed. *Slyness was a two-way street.*

"Sure, Elizabeth. What needs doing?"

"We'll have a van load of food to empty and someone to lift the soup urns. By the way, with all this 'defund the police' stuff going around, our normal police presence is sometimes missing. My ladies will feel better with a man around."

"I'd be happy to help. What time is good?"

"Will eleven work?"

"I'll be there."

That night, Cathryn called. She sounded upset. "We are still hostages. And they have shot two more government soldiers. The chief Boko announced that they are going to start with us tomorrow."

"Have you heard anything from Sean?"

"No good news. He's afraid our cell calls are being monitored. Then he asked me if I knew any Neil Diamond songs. What the hell is that all about?"

"The man has sent you a message in code. Look up Neil Diamond's songs from the peak of his popularity. Check the lyrics. There is a message there. You're smart enough to figure it out."

Brian

They were "up on the roof with the stars out when the day got too tough to tolerate."

But the stairway to the roof was outside the building and used only by maintenance workers. The team was confined to the second floor by the Bokos. They had a man sitting by the elevator on every floor. Brian found that the window at the end of the hall on the second floor would open onto a landing on the roof staircase, but there was no way to open the window.

Brian looked around for a way to break the window quietly. The glass was held in place by moldings screwed into a wall joist. Brian got his combat knife out of his bag and pried at the molding. He could break out all of it except for very short pieces at the sites where the screws attached it to the joist. The window was four feet tall and three feet wide. Brian started to work his way around it. One of the pipe fitters relieved him after half an hour, and in an hour, the molding was off. Brian then slipped the blade of his knife into the crack between the glass and the joist at a corner and pried. The sheet of glass tilted inward several inches, enough for the pipe fitter to insert the head of one of his four-foot-long pipe wrenches into the space. They figured that the leverage produced by a sharp blow to the extended handle of the wrench would break off at least a big chunk of the glass and send it crashing to the floor inside the hall. With luck, the whole window would come crashing in.

Brian announced his plan to the assembled team in the room closest to the window. "Just after dark, I will quietly go to the elevator and disable the guard. One of you big guys will slam a chair or something into the handle of the wrench and knock the glass out of the window. Make sure no one can get hit with the flying glass. Break out any pieces that don't fall with the wrench.

"I believe they will bring the chopper in low over the desert, so it won't be heard until the last minutes. We need to be up there waiting for it."

"Are you sure this is going to work?" asked one of the pipe fitters.

Brian said, "No, but what do we have to lose? One of us is likely to be killed tomorrow."

No one had any answer to that, so they each found a way to fill the hours until sundown.

They were sitting in their room, fiddling with a deck of cards, when Cathryn suddenly asked, "How will you disable the guard?"

"You've no need to know that, lass. And does it really matter?"

In a choked voice, she said, "He could shoot you."

"That is a possibility. Two things in my favor: He'll be bored to tears, and he probably can't shoot very well. I've been down this lane before."

"Oh god! You sound like my father. What am I getting into?"

"Just trying to save your life, love."

As sunset approached, Brian walked down to the elevator lobby at the end of the hall opposite the window they hoped to use as an exit. He had a washcloth from the bathroom in one pocket and the cords from the drapes on their window in the other. He carried a crisp twenty-dollar bill in his left hand and held his hunting knife behind his back with his right.

The guard was sitting in a straight-backed wooden chair in front of the metal elevator doors with his AK-47 across his lap. He was a young man with a black cap, white pajama pants, and a knee-length vest with an ammunition belt across his chest. He straightened up in his chair as Brian approached from his left but said nothing. He moved the AK47 off his lap to his right side.

Brian waved the twenty at the man for the last few steps of his approach. The Boko terrorist reached forward with his right hand to grab it, and Brian smashed a savage punch to the point of his exposed chin. With the heft of the knife handle clasped in hand behind the punch, the man and his chair were knocked over backward. His head struck the metal elevator door. He was immediately unconscious. There's no need to kill this one.

Brian stuffed the washcloth in the man's mouth and tied it firmly in place with one of the drape cords. Then he rolled the man over, tied his hands behind his back with the other cord, tied the shoelaces on opposite feet together, and bound both feet with the terrorist's belt. He took the AK-47.

Brian took just a moment to admire his work. Then he used his knife to pry the call buttons out of the elevator control box and slash the connections. At that point, he heard the window smash onto the floor. Cathryn's team babbled excitedly as they scrambled through the window and up the stairs to the roof. She was waiting for him when he got to the window. "What's with the guard?"

"All tied up like a Christmas present."

"Still alive then?"

"Aye. Get moving."

The group assembled on the roof and waited, muttering quietly among themselves. It was eerily quiet up there. There was little road noise and no wind. More frightening was the absence of any helicopter sounds. They got very restless after ten minutes. Then suddenly, a huge roar rose out of the blackness of the desert, and two, not just one, helicopters approached the roof. The first one hovered for a moment and then settled softly to the roof, the blast from its rotors blowing all sorts of dirt and debris about and shaking the people.

The other copter hovered off to the side about fifty yards. When the Bokos ran into the road at the side of the building to fire at the copter on the roof, they were met with a fusillade of fifty-caliber bullets from the second copter's guns. They fled back toward the hotel's front door. The noise was deafening as the group hurried to climb into the side door of the growling monster on the roof. The air was filled with the stench of jet fuel and gunpowder. The second aircraft moved another hundred yards away so it could pepper the front door with machine gun fire. Their translator, a middle-aged man, lost his grip on the side door of the chopper and fell back to the rooftop.

He looked dazed. Brian hoisted him up through the door.

Cathryn insisted on being the last to board.

Brian flew into a rage. "Don't give me that 'captain of the ship' shit."

She waved him off, pushing him toward the door. He stood for a long moment, trying to decide what to do with this stubborn woman.

Then he handed her the AK-47 and shouted above the roar of the chopper, "If you're going to be the last, you need to be the rear guard!"

He guided her to the shadow of the chopper and had her kneel. He shouted again, "If you see anybody come up that stairway, squeeze the trigger for two seconds. That will fire a dozen bullets at the guy!"

She shouted back, "I'm not going to shoot anybody!"

"Your chances of hitting anybody are almost zero. The barrel of the gun will rise as it fires. The idea is to scare him off while we get you on board." With that, he climbed into the chopper.

Cathryn saw a black-capped head peek over the roof for a second and then duck back down. She froze. A moment later, the head reappeared, a teenager sighting over the barrel of an AK. He started to spray the fuselage of the chopper with bullets. Cathryn screamed, closed her eyes, and pulled the trigger. A cloud of bullets ricocheted off the roof surface and rose higher. There was a shout from the stairway, and the gun disappeared.

Cathryn dropped the AK, stood, and screamed, "Oh my god!"

Brian heaved her up through the chopper door. Cathryn was crying and shaking from head to foot like a flag in a windstorm. He eased her to the floor of the beast. An alert airman slammed the chopper door closed.

She screamed, "I killed him. Like my father, I killed him!"

Brian knew that was true. From his perch in the chopper doorway, he had seen bullets tear the top of the kid's head off, but he was not about to tell her that.

The chopper leaped upward.

Their job done, the two choppers faded north into the dark of the desert. The gunship trailed lest one of the terrorists try to attack with a handheld rocket launcher. That did not happen. The two helicopters turned west and then south to begin their return to their base in Cameroon.

Even with the door closed, the noise inside the metal hull of the copter made it almost impossible for the passengers huddled on the floor to communicate. Cathryn cuddled close to Brian and shouted in his ear, "I hope the hotel staff has the wits not to come to work tomorrow!"

He shouted back, "They have been surviving for years. Besides, I wouldn't be surprised if the Bokos just slipped back over the border during the night just the way they arrived!"

She lay her head on his chest and began to sob, the tension slowly oozing out of her. Brian closed his eyes and savored her warmth. She asked, "Did you see what happened to the person shooting at us?"

"I think your shots scared him back down the stairs. I'm sure they didn't think we had a gun."

"I wouldn't want to think I am a killer like my father was."

Brian wrapped his arms around her and held her close. "He did what he needed to do to rescue you from that hotel room."

"Yeah, but there were other things."

"Whatever they were, they took skill. If any of the shots you fired tonight hit anybody, it was pure luck. God's will—pure and simple."

They rode the rest of the short, noisy trip, clinging together in silence.

Chapter Thirty-Five

The soup kitchen was in a storefront that used to house a restaurant. Its kitchen was in the rear of the building, serviced by an alley from which vans and small trucks could deliver food. The stoves in the kitchen had been modified to make handling and heating fifteen-gallon stainless steel urns of soup easier. The heated urns were placed on carts and wheeled through one of the doors at each end of the room into the serving area.

Food was served from a buffet table draped with a paper cover that ran the full length of the kitchen wall. At one end was a huge coffee urn. The urn of soup was at the other. The other foods available that day depended on what had been contributed by active restaurants and markets and what could be purchased that week. The soup was always hearty, thick with pasta, rice, barley or rice, and plenty of vegetables. Bottles of water filled any empty spaces.

There were a few scarce wooden tables in the open space in front of the buffet table, but most of the food was consumed at the plastic-covered counters that lined both sides of the gray-painted room. The rules of the kitchen were posted on those gray side walls in large, red type.

>   No alcohol
>   No waste
>   No mess

Large, plastic-lined waste barrels were located at the center of each counter. All the serving materials and cutlery were disposable, of course.

The kitchen was located two blocks from an overpass under which homeless people congregated at night, but these were a fraction of the kitchen's clients. Neighborhood men and women made up most of the crowd. During the school year, children would get lunches at school. Mothers often collected some of their soup into vacuum bottles to provide some supper for their offspring. Mothers were not anxious to have their children growing up on soup kitchen lines.

The kitchen opened its doors at 12:30 p.m. There was often a line awaiting this event. Liam got there at eleven and started by hauling crates of vegetables and bread out of a van into the kitchen, where the women chopped things and filled the urns. Next, Liam was called upon to lift the urns onto the stoves. Mary showed up at twelve fifteen and did smile at him, but maybe it was a "Gotcha!" smile.

All went well until about one o'clock. Then one of the later arrivals took issue with the taste of his soup. He was a big guy and very loud. "UGH!" he shouted. He took another sip and shouted again, "This ain't worth eatin'." With that, he threw his tray, soup, and all on the floor and just stood there. He smelled strongly of booze.

Liam came to his side and said quietly, "Would you clean up that mess, please?"

"Who's gonna make me? Not you pissant."

Liam replied, "You can't always tell a book by its cover, big guy."

The whole room got totally quiet.

The guy charged at Liam, who stopped him with a straight arm to his forehead and pushed him back a step. He said, "Why don't we go outside and discuss this like gentlemen?"

The guy swung a wild right at Liam, who easily avoided the punch, caught the man's right hand in his, spun him around so that he was facing the door, and twisted his arm up behind his back.

Mary screamed, "No, Liam."

Liam shouted back, "Relax, everybody. Ole Jerry has this under control. Would somebody open the door, please?"

There was a scramble to do that. Liam marched the guy out and gave him a gentle shove, though he would much rather have kicked him into the street. He closed and locked the door. The guy stormed around outside, shouting profanities and threats. One of the men inside put down his soup and dialed 911. By the time most people had finished eating, two cops in a police cruiser had taken the man away.

Liam collected a bottle of water and a bowl of soup and leaned against a counter. The soup was good. Quiet still reigned in the room. Then a woman started to clap. Liam escaped into the kitchen.

There, he found Mary.

"I'm sorry, Liam."

"For what?"

"I shouted your name."

"Well, there is that."

"There was this look on your face. I thought you were going to kill him right there."

"What made you think that?"

"I don't know. Somehow, deep inside me, I know that you have killed people, those things you won't tell me about, and that incident in New York."

"I offered to tell you my secrets a couple of weeks ago."

"And I was too angry to listen. I have a bit of a temper, ya know. Maybe my imagination was worse than reality."

"We can fix that if you want to go there."

"Did you think of killing that guy?"

"Hell, no. All I wanted to do was throw his drunken ass into the street, but I figured even that would upset the ladies. The face you saw was just righteous anger."

"I'll have to watch out for that in the future."

A light went off in Liam's brain. "Will you sit with me this afternoon? There's a crisis with Cathryn in Africa, and I'm waiting to hear from Sean about whether his rescue operation worked."

"What kind of crisis?"

He told her the whole story. "Come," she said. "We have a lot to pray for."

They sat in the back row of pews in the cathedral as they had in past crisis situations. They held hands but said nothing. Every five minutes, Liam looked at the time on his cell phone, mentally translating it to the time in Niger. When he figured it was long past dark in Africa, he started to sweat and fidget. *Why hadn't Sean called?*

"I need to walk," he said. They got up and started a lap around the nave, forgetting to take the cell phone. As they neared the finish of their circuit, the phone went off, sounding like a bugle in the empty church. Mary sprinted the last twenty feet, beating Liam to it. She pushed the green dot, saw SEAN on the display, and handed the phone to Liam.

Liam wanted to shout, "It's about time!" but instead, he said, "Hello, Sean," holding the phone so that Mary could hear.

"I'm happy to report that Cathryn and her crew just boarded a military transport in Cameroon headed for London. There was a bit of trouble at the last second, but Cathryn took care of it, as you might have. Not a scratch on any of them."

"What did she do?"

"You'll have to wait a few days to hear that story. I have been instructed to inform you that Brian and she were going to spend a couple of days in Ireland with Brian's family on the way home."

Liam said, "Thank you, Sean. Thank you. I owe you big time."

"I'll call it even if you'll just stay out of any more fecken trouble. Maybe your lady friend can help with that."

"I'll do my best," said Mary, eyes locked on Liam's.

"Ah, you're there, are you, Mary? I'm sorry to put such a heavy load on your back, but he's worth it."

"I agree," she said.

Liam said, "The rescue was a superlative effort, Sean. Thank you. You still have it. You're going to have to up your knowledge of current music stars, though. Neil Diamond did not resonate with that generation, but computer magic saved the day."

"You gave them a little guidance, I take it?"

"As much as I could, considering the phones might be compromised."

"The old team functioned one more time."

"Yes, it did. Now tell me what I should know about Brian's history."

"Liam, there's some stuff I've never told my wife, and I bet there's plenty you haven't told this woman you're now friends with. If I were you, I'd just leave Brian's history for the two of them to work out if it gets that serious. Cathryn is no starry-eyed teenager."

Liam was silent for a long moment. Then he said, "History keeps repeating, Sean."

"You can't seem to be able to avoid those situations, but the rest of us seem to be doing fine. Think about that."

Again, there was a long pause. "Good advice. May the wind be always at your back, Sean."

"And Mary's and yours as well, Liam."

The call ended. Mary and Liam wrapped each other in their arms and sat for a long time, each silently praying their thanks to God in their own way.

About the Author

Bill Kenney is a retired engineer, a widower, a father of nine, and a grandfather of twenty-five. He refereed high and college basketball for decades and began his writing career by penning dozens of articles about the rules of basketball and techniques for officiating the game, which were published nationally in magazines dedicated to the subject, such as *Referee*.

Amid all the publicity about superheroes, Bill decided that a thriller featuring a senior citizen protagonist would be a welcome change, hence *Resurrections*.

Printed in the USA
CPSIA information can be obtained
at www.ICGtesting.com
CBHW031812221124
17856CB00010B/140